THE
DEMON'S
KISS

THE DEMON'S KISS

BLOODCASTER CHRONICLES
BOOK ONE

R.L. PEREZ

WILLOW
HAVEN
PRESS

THE DEMON'S KISS

Published by Willow Haven Press 2021

United States of America

Cover Art by Blue Raven Book Covers

ISBN: 978-1-955035-88-0

www.rlperez.com

For Christine, a supporter of my dreams from the very beginning.

CHAPTER 1

CORA

I LEARNED AT A YOUNG AGE TO KILL WITH A BLADE instead of my magic. It protected my identity and hid me from those who sought my blood.

The last time someone spilled my blood, I was twelve. A dark warlock had picked a fight with me.

I lost.

When he struck me, a trickle of deep purple blood oozed from my split lip. The warlock, a haggard man who stank of alcohol, froze with his arm still raised to hit me again. His eyes widened. The color drained from his face.

"It can't be," he whispered.

My heart hardened with fear, and every inch of me screamed to run. To get out before he drained me of every drop of my precious life fluid.

"Blood witch," he gasped, his eyes glittering with

excitement. In his face, I saw what he saw. The possibilities. The powers my blood possessed. The spells he could cast to grant him more abilities.

His brows scrunched together as he no doubt considered his options. He could drain me dry right here. Or he could imprison me and keep me alive to provide an endless supply of my blood.

As he contemplated, I slowly scooted away from him, breathing heavily. My face throbbed, and fresh scrapes stung my palms as I struggled to back out of the alley without him noticing.

But my movements caught his eye. He blinked and lunged again.

I shrieked and raised my hands. A purple glow resonated from my fingertips, blasting against him. He ricocheted backward, slamming into the brick wall.

Panting, I jumped to my feet and sprinted away, but he caught me. He drew a long dagger and held it to my throat. Fury contorted his features, and I knew then what he'd decided.

He would bleed me dry. I wasn't worth the effort.

He swiped his blade. I ducked and barreled into his legs. We wrestled over the hilt of the blade until I rolled, and he slid forward onto the dagger. A sickening, squelching sound was burned into my memory as the blade sank into his chest. He let out a jagged, shuddering breath and then went still.

That was my first kill. I took his blade, changed my name, and never looked back.

Even though it happened eight years ago, I recalled that day like it was yesterday. Sometimes I still heard the warlock's growl or smelled his putrid breath as I slept.

It served as a reminder of why I killed for a living. I would never be helpless again.

Damien groaned in his sleep and swung his arm around my waist, drawing me closer. I sighed and shoved him roughly away before sliding out of bed and slipping my clothes back on.

I didn't cuddle. Damien knew that.

"Wake up," I snapped once I was dressed. "It's after nine."

Damien grunted incoherently and blinked, his inky black eyes focusing on me. I took a moment to relish the way sleep mussed his shaggy dark hair before turning away. I ran my fingers through my short black hair, tucking it behind my ears. In my line of work, short hair was a necessity. I couldn't have a wild mane getting in my way.

"Do you *ever* sleep?" Damien complained before sitting up and stretching. This time, I resisted looking at him. If I saw those muscles flexing, I'd be tempted to jump back into bed with him. And we both knew that was a terrible idea.

Damien and I had a casual sexual relationship. Strictly to fulfill our needs. Nothing more. We'd been down that path before, and we made a horrible couple.

This arrangement was preferable. No rules. No commitment.

I smirked and fastened my belt and holsters. "Not when there's blood to be spilled."

Damien stood and rifled through a pile of clothes on the floor. "So, that's a no?"

I spotted his leather jacket on the floor and tossed it to him. "I've got the Huxton assignment, and then I'll be back. Call if anything changes."

I left the room, walking down the familiar dark hallway of Damien's apartment before checking my bag. Glass potion vials clinked as I sifted through them, looking for my shadow elixir.

There. It glowed deep purple. Like my blood. And my magic.

I clutched the vial in my hand before leaving the apartment. A few blocks away, I stopped at my own apartment, which was so tidy it looked unoccupied, and stashed my bag. At my desk, I glanced over my assignment once more.

Gordon Huxton. Age forty-two. Vampire coven leader.

His demons kept picking fights with Damien's guys, so he needed to be taken out. The vamps would look elsewhere to form a coven, and our demons would be safe.

For now.

That was my job. Clean up the streets, eliminate the threats—all so Damien's coven could live in peace.

The coven was the only family I'd ever known.

After ensuring my dagger was secure, I slipped the elixir into my pocket and left. A tracking spell I'd cast yesterday told me about Huxton's routine activities. I knew right now he'd be retiring, looking to avoid the sunlight. In an hour, he'd be feeding.

That was the time to strike.

I tightened my leather jacket around my body, shivering against the morning chill that swept over me. Hinport was a small hamlet tucked between the worst parts of New Jersey. The winters were bitter and the air constantly smelled of filth.

But still. It was home.

The weight of my blade was a soothing comfort as I strode down the street. My ears prickled with every sound, an instinct that had been drilled into me when I'd first started killing. My blood thrummed with anticipation, eager for the hunt. The chase.

This kill would be easy. They always were. It was almost a shame. I remembered when I'd first worked for

Damien as a contract killer. The exhilaration, the danger, the adrenaline—it had been addicting.

Now it was almost *too* easy.

I weaved down dark, narrow alleys to avoid the main roads. The city was so full of demons that law enforcement was almost nonexistent. But I didn't want to take any chances. My face was too well known around here.

I passed by several unsavory characters lurking in the alley. My hand flexed toward my dagger, and the figures flinched away from me, darting into the shadows. A whiff of wet dog reached my nose. Werewolves. I narrowed my eyes at the dark shapes cowering away from me. One of them whined and ducked his head to me in respect.

Good boy.

My job was beneficial because it marked me as someone powerful and unstoppable. I could defend myself easily. An added bonus was my notorious reputation, which I carefully cultivated.

In this city, I was feared.

The whispers and frightened murmurs that surrounded me sent a bolt of satisfaction through me. I lifted my chin, my hand never straying from the hilt of my dagger.

It's Cora Covington.

The Blade is on the move . . . Who's she after this time?

Out of the way. Don't make eye contact.

My eyes shifted over each person I passed, meeting

their gazes with a challenge. Some shuddered away from me. Others merely dropped their gazes. A mixture of emotions filled the air. Fear was the strongest. I knew its smell like the back of my hand. But I also recognized defiance. Bitterness.

I was used to it. I was a young woman, after all. I'd had to conquer many competitors vying for the position of Damien's Blade.

Let them talk, I thought with a smirk. *Let them hate me.*

The buildings grew smaller as I ventured toward the edge of the city. The towers of the Glen Bridge loomed into view, marking the city border. On the other side of the bridge was a whole different world. A world of mortals and innocence. The city of Ravenbrooke.

No wonder Huxton lived near the border. He wanted access to fresh blood.

My grip on the hilt of my dagger tightened. The bastard was feeding on the mortals of Ravenbrooke. If he kept this up, Hinport would be exposed.

One of the things I loved most about this city was the ability to live out in the open. Demons were free to roam the streets because magic was commonplace. We didn't have to hide.

But if morons like Huxton kept crossing the line, it would draw too much attention. He definitely had to go.

The sharp stench of vinegar filled the air, stinging my nostrils. I slowed my pace, knowing the vampires would be able to smell me instantly. Drawing the vial from my pocket, I uncorked it and swallowed the contents, smacking my lips against the bitter taste.

Black shadows swelled around me, obscuring me from view and masking my scent. Anyone watching would only see a murky mass of darkness floating by.

One benefit of being a Bloodcaster was the infinite number of potions available at my disposal. Just a drop of my blood could transform any elixir into something powerful.

I unsheathed my dagger and grabbed my stake with my other hand. A blade couldn't kill a vampire, but it felt comfortable in my hand just the same. A familiar exciting energy pulsed within me as my body responded to the thrill of the hunt.

I took a breath and surged forward. My shadows swirled around me, but my vision remained clear. The only disadvantage was the loss of my sense of smell. But that didn't matter. All vampires smelled the same.

The streets were quiet and empty. With the morning sun glistening overhead, no vampire would risk getting burned. I kept to the edge of the buildings, using the natural shadows to hide my own. My eyes raked over the buildings, searching for the one I'd canvassed earlier.

There.

A tall, narrow apartment complex stood out among the shabbier buildings. It wasn't anything magnificent—

the bricks were worn and chipped, and some windows had been smashed in—but it was the sturdiest structure on the block.

Of course Huxton would claim this place as his own. He had to be the most powerful on the street.

Avoiding the main entrance, I circled back toward the fire escape. I kept my weapons gripped firmly between my fingers, using my palms to climb up the ladders. The metal bars were like ice against my skin, but the adrenaline coursing through me warded off the chill. I focused my steps, making sure my movements were silent as I counted each floor.

Five . . . Six . . . Seven.

My arms and legs burned, and each sharp gulp of air was like cold knives in my throat. I stopped by the first window of the seventh floor and pressed my ear to the glass, listening. Low voices sounded on the other side. Then, a soft whimper. A cry for help.

My blood chilled. Huxton had abducted a mortal. He'd brought her *here*.

Why couldn't he just use Donors—humans who offered their blood *willingly*—like a normal vampire?

Cursing his stupidity, I wedged my blade underneath the window screen and pried it loose. After several deep breaths, I slammed my hilt against the window. The glass shattered, and I leapt inside.

Alarmed shouts echoed around me, but I didn't give

anyone time to act. Slice. Stab. My blade flashed, and blood spurted. Vampire after vampire fell, but they'd rise again. Only a stake could kill them for good.

But my blade could certainly do some damage.

"Stop!" roared a voice. "Or I'll slit her throat!"

I froze, my shadows roiling fiercely around me. My heart racing, I stared hard at Huxton, who held the mortal girl against him with a knife to her throat. The girl couldn't be older than fifteen. Her blue eyes were wide with terror, her face pasty.

In my mind, I saw myself cowering in fear as the dark warlock advanced toward me. As he struck my face.

A low growl built in my throat. In a flash, I flung my dagger forward. It sank into Huxton's chest, and he howled in pain, stumbling backward. His grip loosened on the girl, and I bounded forward, grabbing her shoulders and spinning her out of the way.

"Stay down," I hissed.

Her eyes roved over my shadows in confusion and fear, but she ducked down obediently.

Huxton roared and lunged for me. I dodged his first strike, landing a punch to his jaw. My blade sliced into his cheek. With my next movement, I slammed my stake into his heart.

He groaned feebly, his eyes round with shock.

"Damien Moretti sends his regards," I said.

And he vanished in a puff of ash.

CHAPTER 2

VINCE

Sweat poured down my neck as I faced my opponent. His eyes narrowed, and he sized me up. Assessing me. My fingers were slick with sweat as I gripped my stick tightly.

A jolt of excitement raced through me. The strategy, the hunt, the thrill of the game.

My eyes flitted about the field, examining my options. My opponent's teammates weren't far. If I was going to make my move, I had to act now.

He edged closer to me.

I remained still. Waiting.

Movement caught my eye. It was Luke. And he was wide open.

I feinted left, and my opponent fell for it, lunging for me. I pivoted to the right, swinging my crosse and launching the ball toward Luke. He caught it, then flung it across the field.

The goalkeeper caught it, and I groaned, trying to squash my disappointment. For the millionth time, my eyes flitted to the scoreboard.

Neck and neck.

We can still do this.

We moved again. My gaze remained fixed on the ball as it hopped from one net to the next. I tightened my hold on my stick as the ball flew to me.

I caught it and zipped forward, dodging opposing teammates, my legs pumping faster and faster.

Move, move, move. My mind chanted the words again and again. Determination pulsed through me. Something crackled in the air and buzzed through my stick as if it were flowing with electricity.

Too late, I realized what was happening. My magic surged to life within me.

A small *pop* burst in my ears, and suddenly, I was on the opposite end of the field next to the other team's goal —about fifty yards from where I'd been standing just seconds ago. The goalkeeper straightened and stared at me with a bewildered expression.

"What the hell, dude?" he shouted.

Confused murmurs rippled through the crowd. Other teammates called out to me.

Alarm pumped through my veins, and for a moment, all I could hear was my pulse roaring in my ears.

Dammit, I did it again.

I swallowed, my throat suddenly turning dry. Then, I lifted my arms. "Sorry!" I shouted, offering a weak smile. "Got confused for a second."

It was a feeble excuse. It didn't explain how I'd vanished and reappeared across the field in a matter of seconds.

But what else could I say?

The referee watched me, his mouth hanging open. He blinked and exchanged a befuddled glance with my coach, who was staring daggers at me. I backed away, returning to my usual spot across the field and hoping they would just resume the game.

They did.

I exhaled a long, steady breath, trying to calm myself. *Don't do that again,* I thought. *Stay cool. You can do this.*

I lingered behind this time. My team surged forward. The ball got passed around until the other team intercepted it.

Swearing under my breath, I followed the ball, trying to keep up. My team took it again, and I inhaled evenly to ready myself.

The ball flew toward me. I caught it and bolted toward the goal, but an opponent jumped in front of me.

"Luke!" I roared.

There he was, a tall, gangly form lifting his crosse high in the air to catch my pass. I flung the ball toward him. He caught it and spun around, tossing the ball so it sailed perfectly into the goal.

A loud whistle marked the end of the last quarter. The game was over.

A euphoric shout poured from my lips, and I raised my arms triumphantly. My teammates leapt up and down, cheering. Luke charged toward me, removing his helmet and grinning from ear to ear. My team formed a circle as we clapped one another on the back. I couldn't stop grinning. Hysterical laughter bubbled up inside me.

We'd done it. We'd won the championship.

I slid off my helmet, my face still covered in sweat. My skin itched from my shoulder, shin, and arm pads, but I didn't care. Luke and I jumped up and down, screaming in each other's faces like little kids until we were red in the face.

The next hour was a blur. Shouts of congratulations. Classmates praising Luke's impressive goal. My coach and fellow teammates huddling together. I swore there were tears in Coach's eyes.

And my magical stunt was long forgotten.

Luke and I finally left the field arm in arm, still chuckling. My face hurt from the constant smiling.

"So, what now?" Luke asked as we strode toward the parking lot.

I sighed, my smile slowly fading. "I don't know," I said honestly. I didn't want to imagine what life would be like without lacrosse. But it was senior year, and the season had just ended. I couldn't pursue this anymore. Not with my magic so wild and uncontrollable. "Maybe I can keep playing . . . for fun." But my voice sounded uncertain in my ears.

Luke snorted, his brown eyes cutting to me. "Not lacrosse. I mean, what about your—you know . . ." He wiggled his eyebrows, his gaze shifting around suspiciously. In an undertone, he said, "Your magic."

I swore and glanced around nervously. "Not here, man."

Luke shrugged his shoulders and grinned again. "It's not like you didn't draw enough attention on the field today, Vince."

"I know, I know." I groaned and ran a hand through my filthy dark brown hair. Luke was the only mortal who knew who I was. Who I *really* was. When he'd found out, I'd nearly had a heart attack. But now, there was something comforting and safe, having a confidant on the outside who knew my secrets and helped me keep them.

Even if I was terrible at it.

No wonder Luke found out. It was a miracle no one else had.

"I still can't believe your dad let you do this with all

that insanity going on with you." Luke laughed, shaking his head. His dreadlocks flopped against his face.

"Dad's not the problem. He's super laid back. It's Hector who will have my head."

"Right." Luke's brow furrowed. "Who is he again, like your HOA committee leader?"

A laugh bubbled in my throat, and I choked on it. Clearing my throat, I said, "No. He's the clan leader. He decides where we *live*."

Luke's face sobered. "Is he gonna kick you out?"

"Well, technically, I'm not eighteen yet, so he can't."

Luke arched one eyebrow. "One more month, man."

"I know." A grim finality filled my body, making my bones quiver. I lived in a Nephilim clan—a neighborhood of angels. My family possessed the strongest light magic in the world.

But I was also part warlock, thanks to my dad.

As Hector impatiently reminded me, I had to choose between Nephilim magic and warlock magic at the Ceremonial Rite in a few months. If I chose the Nephilim, I could remain with the clan as long as I liked.

But I'd have to give up my warlock magic forever.

It felt so unfair. I hadn't even been able to explore my Teleportation powers yet. There was so much I didn't know. So much I wanted to test out.

How could I give up on it without even trying?

"Hey, you're always welcome at my house," Luke said,

noticing my gloomy expression. "We've got a couch with your name on it."

I thought of Luke and his five siblings squashed together in a tiny three-bedroom home. I suppressed a grimace and instead forced a smile. "Thanks, Luke. But I'll be all right."

We reached my small white sedan, and Luke patted me on the shoulder. "I'm free all summer to play, if you want to keep it up." He lifted his crosse with enthusiasm.

I grinned. "I'll definitely take you up on that."

Luke waved and turned away, striding toward his beat-up red pickup truck. I watched him leave, my smile vanishing.

Only a few more weeks left of school plus two months of summer. That was all I had left with my best friend. After that, he'd be leaving for NYU.

And I'd be stuck here.

Because deep down, I knew I couldn't leave the clan. I couldn't leave *Dad*. He was the only family I had. My mom died when I was eight, and I was an only child. Dad had already sworn off his warlock magic by then. So, for ten years, he'd lived powerless in a clan that practiced magic so differently from what he was used to. He was basically a useless mortal now, all because he'd given up his life to be with Mom.

And then she'd died.

A knot formed in my throat, and I swallowed down

the memories before shoving my gear in the trunk of my car. I hesitated before getting into the driver's seat, remembering the crackle of magic pulsing through me.

If I'd been able to train properly, I could just Jump home like any other Jumper would, I thought bitterly.

But no. That was for normal warlocks who lived in normal covens. Not an outcast warlock who lived among the Nephilim. If I so much as *thought* the words "Jump" or "Teleport," I would immediately get filthy looks from everyone in the clan. They were like vile swear words in my neighborhood.

I also had my angel wings, but those were for emergencies only. The power was a temporary gift that only lasted a few minutes at a time. Once I swore into the clan permanently, I'd have full access.

I'd only used my wings a handful of times. The first time I had been five, and it was a complete accident. I'd been trying to play basketball with my dad, and suddenly, I found myself soaring ten feet into the air to reach the basket. My white, feathery wings had sprung out of my shoulder blades as easily as if I'd just been stretching my arms.

The incident had been so terrifying, I hadn't been eager to try it again.

Especially with Hector constantly breathing down my neck. He never explicitly said so, but I knew he thought me using my wings was an insult to the Nephilim clan since I hadn't committed to staying yet.

My mind shifted back to the present as I swung open the car door and froze. Across the lot, standing next to the school courtyard, was a man. He wore jeans and a gray T-shirt, and he was staring intently at me.

My blood turned to ice in my veins, and my heart jolted.

He was *me*. He looked just like me. Same tan skin, same dark brown hair. I even had that exact same outfit in my closet.

My eyes grew wide. I didn't dare blink because I was afraid my mysterious twin would magically vanish. For a long moment, we stared at each other. His gray eyes drilled into mine like he was trying to convey something important.

As I watched him, I realized he held something white in his hands. When I squinted, I recognized it as a lacrosse ball.

A million questions raced through my mind. I stepped toward him.

A *pop* echoed in the lot, and he vanished.

"No!" I cried, reaching forward. Like a moron. My gaze flitted around the lot, my head whipping back and forth. A few stragglers from the game lingered by their cars, oblivious to the strangeness I'd witnessed.

And my clone was gone.

My mouth turned dry. With so much magic in my life, I'd seen some pretty weird things.

But nothing like this.

Trying to ignore the rapid thundering of my heart, I got in my car and drove home. My hands shook as I gripped the steering wheel. My mind raced with questions and doubts, and I didn't even register reaching my gated community until the buzzer blared in my ears.

"State your business," said a crackly voice.

"I'm here for an errand of the highest light magic," I said in a trembling voice. The passcode phrase changed every week. It was just Hector being paranoid about mortals stumbling into our neighborhood.

The gate slowly opened, and I drove through, weaving down streets. I kept a low speed, taking care around the neighbors walking idly with their children. Some of the adults had their pearly white wings spread out before them like it was no big deal. A few random bursts of white light gleamed in different spots along the road as some Nephilim appeared and reappeared.

A mixture of emotions swirled within me. I'd been so bitter about not mastering my Teleportation abilities, but there was so much about Nephilim magic I was clueless about too.

The more powerful Nephilim could Jump just like me. Sometimes, it seemed as if they could stop time itself. Which was ridiculous.

Then again, seeing a version of myself Jumping made me feel like anything was possible.

I finally reached my home, a quaint townhouse at the end of the street. It was no secret Hector stuck my dad with the dingiest home in the neighborhood. He let us stay here without complaint, but he didn't have to be generous about it.

I didn't bother bringing in all my equipment and gear. Still shaking, I leapt out of the car and burst inside to find Dad sitting on our old stained couch while watching TV, his mouth full of nachos. He blinked at me and frowned. "You all right?" he asked thickly before taking another large, crunchy bite.

I ran a hand through my hair and started pacing the length of the small living room. Dad, noticing my distress, turned off the TV and sat forward, his brows knitting together in concern. "Vince," he said, his tone serious.

I cleared my throat and faced him. "Okay. This is going to sound crazy, but . . . is there *any* possibility at all that somewhere out there I have . . . an identical twin?"

Dad burst out laughing, lounging backward on the couch again. "You're right. That *does* sound crazy. Did someone whack you with their stick?"

"Dad," I said sharply. "Answer me."

Dad's expression fell, and his eyes tightened. "No.

Not a chance. I was there the day you were born. Only one baby, I swear."

I cursed under my breath and resumed my pacing. There was no other explanation, then. The person I'd seen in the lot had been *me*. Another . . . version of me, maybe?

"Vince, what's this about?"

I exhaled long and slow before explaining what had happened in the parking lot. I expected Dad to start laughing again, but to my surprise, his expression turned stony, and his face drained of color.

A long silence passed between us. Dad stared absently at the wood floors.

"Dad?" I asked quietly.

"Son of a bitch," he hissed, covering his face with his hands. "Vince, what did you *do*?"

My head reared back. "What? I didn't do anything!"

"That's not true," Dad snapped. Then, he groaned. "Well, technically you haven't done anything *yet*."

Feeling dizzy, I sank onto the couch next to him. "What—what are you talking about?"

Dad glanced around as if expecting someone to be eavesdropping nearby. He scooted closer to me and said in an undertone, "The person you saw who looked like you is called a Mimic. An alternate form of you from a different timeline."

My mouth fell open. "*What?*"

A wrinkle formed in Dad's forehead, and he grimaced. "Yeah. It's heavy stuff."

"I—what—I don't understand," I sputtered. "*How?*"

"It's a side effect of Jumping. It doesn't happen often, but occasionally, when performed the right way, our powers can allow us to . . . manipulate time."

My insides froze, and my heart stopped for a full beat. My tongue turned to lead in my mouth, and I couldn't speak.

"I've never done it," Dad said quickly. "But I've heard of Jumpers who have. Agents for the Council are allegedly sent on special missions to preserve the timeline, but it's very hush hush."

"Then, how do *you* know about it?" I said weakly, finding my voice at last.

Dad fixed a flat look on me. "I have connections on the Council." He shook his head and leaned forward, his eyes blazing with intensity. "Listen to me, Vince. If you saw a Mimic, it means at some point in the future, you will manipulate time. This is *bad*."

"Why is it bad? Manipulating time, I mean . . ." I chuckled weakly and ran a hand down my face. "Can you imagine what we could do with that power? I—we—we could . . ." I trailed off, my eyes glazing over as I pictured my mother's face in my mind. Her bright blue eyes. Her white-blond hair. Her soft smile. A lump formed in my throat. "We could save Mom."

Dad's face turned white as paper. "Vince, *no*. You can't alter events like that. The Council—"

"Screw the Council!" I said, throwing my hands in the air. "They can arrest me, imprison me for the rest of my life, but if I bring Mom back, none of that will matter. She'll be here."

Pain and longing stirred in Dad's eyes, and I knew for a split second he was imagining what it would be like to have her back.

But in the next instant, the emotion left his eyes, and a determined hardness took its place. "I'm serious, Vince. It isn't just a matter of breaking the law. It's a matter of breaking the most sacred vow of the magical community. We do *not* use our powers to alter the way the world works. Doing so will make you some powerful enemies. And they won't just come after you. They'll come after me, your friends, anyone who's associated with you."

I swallowed, thinking of Luke. It wasn't his fault he'd been roped into my world like this. What would happen if magical agents showed up on his doorstep and uprooted his life because of me?

"Just promise me you'll lie low," Dad said. "At least until the Ceremonial Rite."

Damn, I forgot all about that. The Ceremonial Rite was an annual ceremony when all the Nephilim who had turned eighteen would pledge their lives to the clan.

I'd felt uncertain about it before. But now, after what

Dad had just revealed to me, the idea of squashing my warlock magic forever made me feel sick inside.

I couldn't do it.

"I promise," I said quietly.

But despite what Dad said, if there was even a *small* chance I could bring Mom back, then I had to try.

The Nephilim clan be damned.

CHAPTER 3

CORA

I LEANED AGAINST MY CHAIR, MY GAZE SHIFTING TO the men at the table with me. Cigarette smoke swirled in the air, mingling with the stench of alcohol. I watched Damien laugh idly at something Conrad said. Benny and Kip leered at a waitress who walked by.

This was the most boring part of coven meetings.

Then again, I was also the only woman at the table.

The guys learned long ago not to challenge me. The last one who had, Pete Gordon, had wound up in the hospital from a gouged-out eye.

Such a shame.

I sipped my coke, pretending to listen to the men talk about the rack sizes of the women they'd slept with. *Pigs,* I thought, gazing around the bar with disinterest. Though I slouched in my seat and appeared the picture of ease, my mind was still on high alert—which was why

I never drank. A man sat in the corner of the bar. He'd been there for over an hour and ordered nothing. Though his face was cloaked in shadow, I swore he was watching us.

I took another sip, pretending to glance over him as if I were bored. But I kept him in my peripheral.

"Cora had an easy mark today," Damien said, snapping me back to the conversation. "Right, Cor?"

"Yep," I said, raising my eyebrows at him. "Have things settled down with the vamps?"

Damien's teeth flashed with his wide smile. "They're scrambling like cockroaches."

Kip chortled. Benny said, "Those vamps are slimy. Can never trust them. Remember that one from last year? Travis what's-his-name?"

Kip's eyes widened. "I remember him. I heard he was selling secrets to other covens. Didn't you interrogate him, Cora?"

I nodded but said nothing. I remembered the nasty vampire who'd threatened me last year. Like many others, he didn't like having a female assassin in the coven. It didn't take much to break him, though. My methods quickly wiped the smirk off his face.

Silence fell, and I realized the three guys were watching me expectantly.

Kip grunted impatiently. "Well? What did he tell you?"

I stared hard at him. "None of your business." When Kip scoffed, I said casually, "I don't share other people's secrets."

"Doesn't matter anyway," Damien said. "He won't be bothering us anymore." His eyes gleamed, and his smile was predatory.

Kip guffawed loudly. His breath reeked of alcohol, sending a ripple of nausea through me. My skin felt clammy as I remembered the warlock who'd attacked me as a kid, the memories crashing over me like a violent current.

I shoved the weakness aside. "What's my next assignment?" I asked, sitting forward.

Damien waved a hand and dropped his gaze. "We'll get to that later."

I frowned. Damien had never brushed off an assignment like that. This was how the meetings always went. The men bought drinks and shared vile stories as small talk, and then we finally got down to business. Damien gave me my assignment, and we set goals for the coven. Then, the gents went off to perform a blood ritual while I lingered in the bar, looking for anyone who might cause trouble.

Really, it was just my excuse *not* to join the men with their demon rituals. I was the only one of the coven leaders who wasn't a Second Tier demon—meaning a demon who accessed a higher power by sacrificing others.

I had to avoid using my magic. Damien was the only one who knew I was a Bloodcaster. Ordinarily, demon magic was black. If I dared summon my powers in *any* kind of ritual, my purple magic would be a dead giveaway that I wasn't who I claimed to be.

My gaze shifted to the other men at the table, but they'd steered the conversation to the different vampires they'd come across. Their laughter intensified, and when Kip belched loudly in my ear, I decided I was done. I stood from my chair, and Damien looked up at me through half-lidded eyes.

"Call me when you're ready to talk business." I threw down a couple of bills to pay for my drink and stalked off, balling my hands into fists.

What a waste of time.

To my surprise, I'd barely arrived at my apartment when a soft knock sounded at the door. I grabbed my dagger and carefully eased open the door to find Damien on the other side.

I raised an eyebrow. "Not interested tonight. Sorry." I closed the door, but Damien stuck his foot in the way.

"It's not that. Can I come in?"

My brows lowered. "*Now* you want to talk? Look, it's late and—"

"I know I botched the coven meeting." Damien lifted his hands in surrender. "But I can explain. Please?"

With a sigh, I stood back to let him in. Damien shoved his hands in the pockets of his leather jacket and looked around. "I haven't been here in a while. Do you keep a maid or something? It's a little *too* clean."

"What the hell do you want, Damien?" I crossed my arms. I *really* wasn't in the mood for this.

Damien sighed, dropping his arms and running a hand through his dark hair. Something seemed . . . off about him. My eyes narrowed as I scrutinized him.

Then, I realized what it was. I expected his eyes to be bloodshot and his breath to smell of alcohol. But he seemed completely lucid.

Had tonight all been an act? He'd been laughing and jeering just like the other guys. But I didn't smell a drop of beer on him.

"I have an assignment for you, but it's . . . personal." Damien shifted his weight, his eyes flitting to me and back to the floor again.

"Personal," I repeated in a flat voice. *Every* kill had been personal. Because the coven was his life.

"Private," Damien amended. "This can't be shared with the coven."

My heart rate accelerated. "Why not?"

"Because the target is sensitive. If it traces back to us, it could cause trouble."

Now I was intrigued. "Who's the mark?"

Damien drew a small envelope from inside his jacket and handed it to me. I opened it and quickly glanced over a picture and bio of my next target.

My heart lurched, and my jaw dropped. "A *Nephilim?*" I hissed, staring hard at Damien. "Are you insane?" Nephilim possessed the strongest light magic in the world.

And they also didn't live in Hinport. So why did Damien want this one killed?

"Now you know why it's sensitive," Damien said with a shrug.

I glared at him. "*Why?*"

"It's not your job to ask why," he snapped. "It's your job to get it done."

My head reared back. He'd never spoken to me like that before. "Excuse me?"

"Look, Cora, no matter what goes on between us, you can't forget your place. I'm the head of this coven, and you're the assassin. You're not included in these decisions. You just carry them out."

Anger raged within me, and I took a step toward him. In a flash, he raised a dagger to my face. I stilled.

"I've bested you before," he said in a soft voice. "Don't forget that."

"That was years ago," I said through clenched teeth.

"You and I both know I could take you down right here, right now."

His dark eyes bore into mine, unflinching. For a tense moment, we stared each other down, our faces only a breath away. His blade was so close to my skin I could feel the coolness of the metal tickling my cheek.

Damien grinned and dropped his hand. "That's why you're the best, Cor." He slid his knife into his belt and lifted his chin. "You'll get it done, then?"

What game is he playing? "And if I refuse?"

Damien's gaze hardened. "You won't. I have too much on you."

I stared at him, my body going rigid. It wasn't an outright threat, but I could read between the lines. All he'd have to do was share my secret, and I'd be everyone's target.

Unless he'd already told someone.

Damien cocked his head at me, his eyes glinting. Like he *knew* the thoughts that were swirling in my head.

Damn him. The bastard knew exactly what he was doing. He had something over me, something that kept me doing his dirty work for him forever. And he was too difficult to kill. He was a Second Tier demon, after all. He had more power than I did. Even if I *could* use my magic around him, it would be a nasty fight. One that would attract too much attention. I was fairly certain I could kill him if it came down to it, but it would be messy. He wasn't an easy mark like my other kills. Someone would hear us grappling and come running to help.

He had too many allies. Most of whom lived in this same apartment complex.

I was cornered. I had no other choice.

"Yeah," I said shortly, pocketing the paper. "I'll get it done."

And then I'll kill you. I swear on my life, I'll find a way.

CHAPTER 4

VINCE

"Do you remember life before the war?"

I blinked and looked up from the thick textbook on spells I was perusing. Jocelyn, a Nephilim I'd grown up with, was idly tracing her finger on the page of her own textbook, her blue eyes distant. We sat in the library just outside our neighborhood. There was a private section, accessible only through our Nephilim powers, that allowed us to study magic.

Jocelyn believed we were both here to study for the Ceremonial Rite. But I was actually here to research Jumpers and the possibility of time travel.

"Not really," I said shortly, returning to my book. My clearest memory of the Demon War ten years ago was my mother's death. So, naturally, I didn't like to reflect on it.

"Lorna tells me about it all the time," Jocelyn went

on, referring to her cousin. "She says she misses how things were with the clan before. We were encouraged to mingle with other magical covens to strengthen our allies."

That I remembered. Dad told me that was how he'd first met Mom. Dad was a Jumper for the Council and Mom had been an esteemed member of the strongest Nephilim clan. They'd been paired off to seal an alliance between Dad's coven and Mom's clan.

Then, demon covens had attacked. Dad's light coven turned on the Nephilim, abandoning us. Mom and several other leaders had died, and Hector had taken over, isolating us from everyone in a desperate act of self-preservation.

"Would *you* like to be forced to marry someone you didn't know?" I asked in a low voice. My parents had lucked out. They'd been strangers at first, but love had come later.

I didn't want that for me. I wanted to be certain before marrying.

Jocelyn shrugged one shoulder and tucked a lock of red hair behind her ear. "It's not so different now. There are still arranged marriages, just within our clan."

My stomach twisted at her words. I'd tried to avoid thinking about it, but I knew Hector encouraged certain couples to court each other to unify the clan. I was grateful he hadn't approached me, but something told me it wasn't to spare me. It was because he believed my blood was tainted.

"Are you nervous about the Ceremonial Rite?" Jocelyn asked.

Mother of Lilith, this girl won't stop talking, I thought. Jocelyn and I weren't exactly friends, but she'd caught me slipping out of the neighborhood to get to the library, and I had let her tag along to keep up appearances.

Besides, most of the Nephilim my age wanted nothing to do with me. When she asked to join me, I'd been too shocked to refuse.

"No," I said in a stiff voice. *Because I won't be going to the Rite.* But I couldn't tell Jocelyn that. It had been several decades since someone had refused to pledge at the Ceremonial Rite. And those who had were banished from the clan and never heard of again.

It was uncertain what would happen to me when I refused. I didn't want to imagine that those who did were murdered in secret, but I'd never met a banished Nephilim before.

So, where did they go?

Soft footsteps sounded nearby. I glanced up, frowning, but saw no one else in the room with us. Our private study room was as big as a classroom and filled with shelves. It was like a tiny library in itself.

My skin prickled with suspicion. I hadn't heard the door open.

Perhaps I'd imagined the footsteps. I directed my gaze back to the book and read: *Many Teleporters throughout history took dangerous measures to experiment with their powers. The most gruesome of all was Dexter Dougal, who accidentally dismembered himself while trying to Teleport backward in time.*

I winced. That didn't sound promising.

A shelf creaked as if someone had put weight on it. My head flew up, and I scanned the room again. Clearly oblivious, Jocelyn kept her head bent as she studied her book.

"Did you hear something?" I whispered.

Jocelyn looked up, her brow furrowing. "No."

A sharp smell filled the air, tickling my nose. It was pungent and foul, but it mingled with something else. Something almost flowery.

I'd never smelled anything like it.

My skin crawled, and every part of my body screamed to get out. To run.

But I couldn't leave Jocelyn here.

"Hey, do you want to grab a bite to eat?" I asked.

Jocelyn's eyebrows lifted, and she chuckled. "It's ten in the morning. Didn't you eat breakfast?"

"No," I lied, rising to my feet and trying to calm my racing heart. "I'm starving. You coming? My treat."

Jocelyn's eyes brightened, and she shut her book. "I won't say no to that."

Relief spread through me as she stood. But before we could move for the door, a mass of shadows appeared from behind a bookshelf. The inky blackness curled and coiled as if it were alive. A tendril of shadow drifted toward us like an arm reaching out.

My blood ran cold as I stared, wide-eyed, at the strange blob of darkness. It was about as tall as a person and even formed a human-like shape. A large blob on top for a head, a narrower curvy section for a torso, and two thin, black stumps at the bottom that resembled legs.

It was like a *person* made of shadows.

I snatched Jocelyn's arm as she sucked in a breath. Slowly, I dragged her behind me and backed us away from the intruder.

"What is it?" Jocelyn whispered in my ear.

"I don't know. Can you access your wings?"

Jocelyn shook her head, her hair tickling my arm. My body stiffened as I stretched my back and shoulder muscles, trying to unleash my wings.

But nothing happened.

Cursing, I gripped Jocelyn's arm tighter and spun in place to Jump us out of here.

Before I could, an explosion of purple magic burst in my face like colorful powder, momentarily blinding me. Crying out, I raised a hand to clear the dust from my eyes. The strange particles stung my eyes and skin, burning like it was made of acid.

I couldn't Jump if I couldn't see.

I sensed movement in front of me, and I shouted, "Joss, get down!"

Jocelyn cried out as I tugged on her arm, pulling us both to the floor. Two loud thumps sounded behind us, and I impatiently wiped my eyes again. But the purple dust remained, and it thickened into a paste that clung to my eyes.

"Jocelyn," I moaned. "My eyes. Help me!"

"Here." I felt her hands on my face, and a warm glow encompassed me. White magic burned against my eyes, and gradually, the paste cleared, though my vision was still rimmed in purple.

Jocelyn's hands lowered, and we struggled to rise. But a heavy force slammed into me, knocking me backward. Jocelyn's hand was wrenched from my grip. She screamed.

"Jocelyn!" I roared, reaching blindly for her. But the shadows were on top of me, pinning me to the floor. From within the dark mass, the glint of silver flashed.

A knife.

I struggled, but my arms were pinned. And the strangest lilac scent filled my nose. The creature on me breathed heavily, and when I slammed my knee upward, it grunted.

I stiffened. It was *human*. Whoever it was had just made a human sound.

I slammed my head forward to where I presumed the man's face was. My forehead smashed against his, and he groaned. The knife slackened in his grip.

Gritting my teeth, I snatched the shadowy figure and gripped something leathery like a jacket. Holding onto the assailant, I rolled us both over and over until we reached the nearest shelf. I shoved his head into the shelf, but he pinwheeled until his knees were pressing onto my chest. My breath left me, and I struggled to free myself. A fist collided with my jaw again and again until spots danced in front of my eyes. Pain sliced through me, radiating across my entire face.

Jocelyn shouted nearby and slammed a heavy book against the shadowy figure. He slumped over, staggering before righting himself and slashing at Jocelyn with his blade. Jocelyn yelped and danced away from the knife, holding up her book as a shield.

Groaning, I stumbled to my feet and gripped the shelf for support. My head spun, and I struggled to focus on my destination before Jumping again. My hands were slick with sweat, and magic crackled through my body.

Focus, I told myself. *You can do this.*

The air went still as if it held its breath. A faint lemon smell filled my nose, and I clung to it, trying to clear my head. My fingers tightened around the shelf next to me, which thrummed with power. It seemed like every inch of me was pulsing with my magic. I felt alive with electricity.

Still gripping the shelf, I spun in place with a faint *pop*. But instead of Jumping to the door on the other side of the room, I remained in place, still clutching the same bookshelf.

I blinked. *What the hell?*

But as I looked around, I noticed the air felt different. And the room was quiet. I searched for the attacker and saw Jocelyn leaning against the wall with a book clutched to her chest.

I squinted at her. Hadn't she just been fighting with the shadow man?

"Here," said a voice.

I staggered backward in shock, my heart lurching.

The voice belonged to *me*. I stared, open-mouthed as other-Vince—my Mimic—handed a textbook to Jocelyn. He wore the exact same clothes as me.

"Thanks," Jocelyn said, glancing at the cover of the book. I recognized it as the book of Nephilim history Jocelyn had been studying just a few minutes ago.

My tongue turned to sandpaper in my mouth. Sweat trickled down my face as I slowly, quietly, edged backward and out of sight. Hiding behind a bookshelf, I gasped for breath, leaning my head against the shelf as I tried to think.

How long had we been in the library? Half an hour? If

I was handing Jocelyn that book, then we must've just arrived here.

So we had maybe twenty-five minutes at most before the attacker would show up.

Something clicked into place in my mind.

I had just *time traveled*. Granted, it wasn't anything impressive—I'd only traveled back in time half an hour.

But I'd done it.

Completely by accident, of course. As was everything I'd done with magic.

I was either a genius or a complete moron. It was a miracle I hadn't dismembered myself in the process.

Focus, Vince, I told myself. The voices of Jocelyn and my Mimic grew fainter as they moved to the table to study. I wiped sweat from my brow and peered around the corner to find them getting situated in their seats.

Okay, I thought, still feeling dizzy. *The shadow dude can't be far. Maybe I can get the drop on him before he attacks.*

Keeping to the shelves for cover, I slipped out of the study room. The air warbled as I stepped through the magical barrier separating our private room from the rest of the library. I paused for a moment.

The attacker had come through here. Whoever he was, he'd passed through *Nephilim magic* to get to us.

A demon couldn't have done that. So who was it? And were they trying to kidnap us? Or kill us?

I shook my head, trying to ignore the pain throbbing

in my jaw as I made my way out of the library. There was only one entrance. If I just waited by the door, I could catch him as he entered and stop this madness before someone got hurt.

Too late, I thought bitterly, rubbing my jaw.

I paced in front of the library, my gaze darting up and down the sidewalk for any sign of the shadow figure. My legs ached to sprint, to run down the street and grab the attacker before he got closer, but I didn't know which direction he'd come from.

So, I waited. My blood pulsed with urgency, my mind still on high alert from the attack. A small part of me longed to try to manipulate time again, but I didn't dare. Not when I still had the advantage. What if I tried again and failed?

I wasn't sure how much time passed, but with each second that crawled by, a desperate sense of urgency spread through me.

How long had it been? I cursed myself for not grabbing my phone or wearing a watch. Had I missed it? Had the attacker found another way inside?

I darted back into the library and checked the clock. 10:04.

"Dammit," I hissed, racing forward. I sprinted down aisles of bookshelves before leaping through the magical barrier. Jocelyn's scream echoed. My Mimic shouted her name.

How the hell had the attacker gotten past me? Could he go *through walls?*

I crept forward, not wanting to alert the shadow man to my presence. I had the advantage, and I had to keep the element of surprise for as long as I could.

Whoever this guy was, he was powerful. And Jocelyn and I were no match for him, thanks to our useless Nephilim powers.

If this guy had waited until the Ceremonial Rite, we would've been powerful enough to stop him. I was sure of it.

I edged closer to the scuffling sounds ahead of me. Jocelyn cried out, and a heavy smack resonated.

She's just hit him with the book, I thought, wracking my brain as I tried to remember the events. My Mimic was just about to Jump.

Leaving Jocelyn alone with the attacker.

I had to act *now* while the attacker thought there were only two of us to beat.

I rounded the corner and slammed into the shadowy mass, colliding with Jocelyn in the process. We collapsed to the floor in a crumpled heap. Jocelyn moaned weakly, but the shadow figure sprang to his feet, standing there for a moment. Completely frozen.

Across the room, I noticed my Mimic gripping the bookshelf. With a small *pop*, he vanished.

I aimed a kick to the center of the shadow man's

chest. He staggered backward. I stood and landed a punch to his face. Then his chest. Another kick, and he crumpled. His dagger fell from his grasp. I bent over and swiped it from the ground, but before I could use it, another explosion of purple dust filled the room. Swearing, I tried clearing my eyes, but the stinging sensation took over, and I fell to my knees. My grip tightened on the knife as I swung it blindly, prepared to take the man down with me if he tried to grab me.

"Vince. *Vince!*" A hand grabbed my shoulder, and I waved the knife around wildly. Jocelyn yelped and grabbed my wrist before I cut her open. "He's gone," she panted.

A warm glow encompassed my face again, and the purple paste faded. Ragged breaths poured through my lips, my chest heaving from the effort. I felt like I'd just run a marathon. My gaze frantically flitted about the room as I tried to find the shadow man.

But Jocelyn was right. He was gone.

CHAPTER 5

CORA

My whole body throbbed in pain. I kept my shadows around me, though I felt the power of the elixir fading. Soon, my true appearance would be exposed. And my purple blood along with it.

I had to get to safety. *Now.*

But Hinport was too far. I was at least a mile from the bridge. I wouldn't even make it out of Ravenbrooke before my shadows vanished.

Cursing, I staggered up the sidewalk, clutching my ribs. That boy had managed several well-placed kicks.

Along with being in two places at once.

I still couldn't wrap my head around it. But I couldn't focus on that now. I needed help. Fast.

It was the first time my mark had gotten away.

My head pulsed with agony, and I groaned, slumping sideways to lean against a lamppost for a moment.

Sucking in several sharp breaths, I pushed onward until I reached a gas station. Just before going inside, I raised my hands and summoned my magic. A spark of power shot through me, and my shadows vanished. Then, I tore into the store and made for the bathroom, cutting in front of a woman and her daughter to get inside. Ignoring their protests, I bolted the door and went to the mirror to assess the damage.

A trickle of violet blood ran down my nose, and my lip was split open. There was also a minor scratch on my collarbone. But all my other injuries were internal.

A dozen paper towels and ten minutes later, I'd managed to stop all the blood flowing from my wounds and cleaned up so that not a trace of my blood was visible.

This wasn't terrible. I'd definitely had worse injuries. At least my wounds had stopped bleeding.

I'd be in a whole lot of trouble if the bleeding hadn't stopped. As a Bloodcaster, every drop of my blood was precious, and I couldn't risk losing any. In the past, whenever I'd lost too much, it had messed with my head. Sometimes I'd hallucinated. Other times I'd just acted like a crazy drunk. Either way, it was dangerous.

With a deep breath, I limped out of the bathroom and left the gas station, my leg still flaring with pain.

Ordinarily, I walked everywhere because I didn't trust

public transportation. Hinport was a small city, so going on foot or bike wasn't an issue.

But Ravenbrooke was huge, full of suburbs and shops and developments. Tracking the Nephilim to the library hadn't been easy.

I found my bag stashed in the bushes outside a bookstore a mile past the library. Digging through, I finally found what I was looking for: a beacon elixir.

I'd only had to use it once before. And I didn't relish having to use one now.

But I had no other choice. As pissed as Damien would be, he was the only one who could help me. I had no idea what powers that kid had or if he could track me.

I smashed the potion vial on the sidewalk and said in a clear voice, "Damien Moretti."

Purple smoke swirled in front of me, spinning faster and faster until a small orb appeared in the air. Images shifted within the orb so quickly it made me dizzy. Then, Damien's face came into view. He started and squinted at me.

"Cora? What happened?"

Disappointment spread through me as I muttered, "The mark got away. I'm injured and can't make it back on foot."

Damien's eyes flashed, and his jaw tightened. For a moment, he stared at me, his gaze a hard mask of anger.

His nostrils flared as he exhaled. "I'll be there shortly." His voice was clipped.

The orb vanished, and the smoke disappeared. I groaned and leaned my head against the brick wall behind me.

After Damien's threat yesterday, I didn't want to think about what he would do to me now. For years, he'd been the only person in the world I could trust.

Something had happened over the last few days. Something that altered his trust in me. I had to earn it back somehow, or he'd banish me from the coven.

Or worse—share my secret. If he hadn't already.

A small *pop* alerted me to Damien's presence. He appeared on the sidewalk next to the bookstore, his hands shoved into his pockets and his dark eyes surveying the area. His gaze settled on me, and his face hardened before he strode forward. I stood and brushed the grass off my pants before falling into step next to him.

Instead of grabbing my arm and Jumping, he kept walking. I glanced at him—his face was radiating fury. He stared determinedly ahead, and I struggled to keep his pace.

At long last, my leg gave out, and I hissed, "Dammit, Damien, slow down!"

"Was he Second Tier?" he snarled.

Anger and indignation rose in my chest as Damien stared at me, his eyes feral.

"I—no," I said. Damien knew full well that only demons could Ascend to the Second Tier.

"Did his clan come to his aid?"

I wanted to argue that there had been two of them—well, *three*, if you included his double—but my protest died in my throat. "No," I said through clenched teeth.

Damien drew closer to me. I could practically feel the fury emanating from his stiff form. "Then how the *hell* did this kid escape your clutches, Cora? You're the Blade! The dreaded Cora Covington! You haven't missed a mark in what, two years?"

"I know!" I snapped, crossing my arms and dropping my gaze. "I—I don't know what happened."

Damien cocked his head, and something unreadable stirred in his eyes. He looked me over as if seeing me for the first time. "You're injured." He sounded surprised.

"You think?" I snapped.

Damien frowned, his gaze roving over me, slower this time. "What did this kid do to you, Cora?"

I waved a hand pathetically. "I—I can't explain it."

"Try."

I sighed. "He was . . . somehow in two places at once. One second he was across the room after I'd beaten him. Then, he was tackling me. Someone else was with him, a Nephilim girl. I was outnumbered."

"Being outnumbered never stopped you before."

"I was caught off guard, okay?" I shouted, dropping my hands on my thighs. "I've never seen someone do that before." I glanced at him. "Have you?"

Damien's gaze shifted, and his eyes grew distant. His jaw ticked back and forth in contemplation.

"Come on." He grabbed my arm, his grip firm but not painful, and we spun on the spot. After a small *pop*, we appeared in the shadowy alley of Hinport, right outside his office.

I blinked. "Why are we here? I've got healing elixirs at my place."

Damien just jerked his head forward, indicating I follow. With a groan, I limped to the entrance, and he held the door open for me.

Damien's office building was small, but it helped him remain discreet. A few other coven leaders were in their offices nearby. Their low, muffled voices echoed through the thin walls.

Damien held open the door to his own office, the biggest one in the building, and stood back to let me in. I sank into the armchair in front of his desk, my skin crawling with apprehension. Was he about to fire me or something?

Damien closed the door and sat in his desk chair, swiveling back and forth to assess me for a long moment.

"What?" I finally snapped. "Whatever you want to

say, just say it. I failed. I screwed up. You think I don't know that?"

Damien raised a hand, his focus far away again. Something stirred in his eyes. Something like . . . hunger. The wild look in his eye made me stiffen and hold perfectly still as if I were facing a dangerous predator.

"Describe to me again what the boy did," he said in a soft voice.

I bit back a nasty retort and went over the details again without leaving anything out. I explained the sound I recognized as Jumping, but this was different. I saw Damien Jump all the time, but he'd never been in two places at once.

Somehow, this stupid kid *had*. Even though Damien was Second Tier and older and more experienced, this kid had managed something he couldn't do.

Now I understood the hungry look in Damien's eyes.

After I finished talking, Damien sat back in his chair, twiddling his fingers together. His eyes narrowed in concentration, and I recognized the spark of inspiration that flashed in his gaze.

He sat forward and placed his palms on his desk. "This may work out in our favor. Cora, I want you to go undercover. Get in this kid's life. Gain his trust. *Find out how he did it.* Do whatever you must to coerce him, but try to avoid arousing his suspicions. You used your shadow elixir on him, right?"

Stunned, I couldn't speak for a moment. "I—uh—yes, but—"

"Good. He won't recognize you. The file said he was a high school student. Pose as another student and get close to him. Be subtle and *don't kill anyone* until I say so."

Damien turned to several files on his desk and sifted through them as if our conversation was over. I sat there, frozen in the chair, my hands stiff and glued to the cushions. A hard lump formed in my throat.

Finally, Damien glanced up at me as if just realizing I was still there. "What is it?"

Anger flared to life inside me, but I squashed it down. "I just—I don't understand. You want me to . . ."

"Go undercover. Yes, I already said so. What's the problem?"

Why was he being such an asshole? Leaning forward, I said sharply, "The problem is, I'm a killer. Not a con artist, Damien. You know that's not my forte. How am I supposed to get this kid to trust me and share his secrets with me?"

Damien lifted one shoulder. "You're creative. You'll think of something."

Another shocked silence rippled over me. How could he do this to me? "Damien," I said, trying again. "We've trusted each other for years. What the hell is going on with you?"

Damien slammed his hands on the desk, and I

jumped. His eyes flashed with anger again. "What's going on is there are several other more experienced demons vying for my position right now. And I cannot afford to have them undermine me by pointing out *your* failures, Cora. So, consider this a demotion. You screwed up, so now you have to do the dirty work to regain my trust."

"Or what?" I snarled.

"Or I'll hire Benny in your place and leave you to fend for yourself. I doubt another demon coven will be anxious to hire a dark witch who won't use her magic." His eyes glinted with triumph. "Or maybe they *would* . . . if they knew just what kind of witch you were."

"You wouldn't dare—"

"I *would*, Cor. And I already have. Benny knows."

My blood turned to ice in my veins. Benny? The *were-wolf?* No, it couldn't be true.

"He needed to know what he was signing up for when I asked him if he wanted your job."

My mouth opened and closed as I struggled to breathe. My words came out as a strangled gasp. "You— already asked him?"

"You're slipping, Cor. I'm not the only one to have noticed."

"I have *not* been—" I started angrily.

"Why do you think the other covens have been acting up? They can sense my weaknesses. They think my coven is crumbling and they want a piece of it for themselves.

But if you can access this kid's powers and show *me* how to do it . . ." He trailed off, and a slow grin spread across his face. "Then, I'll be unstoppable. Those covens won't be able to touch me. And, of course, you'll have your job back."

I stared at him, my blood boiling. *What the actual hell?*

Damien had been my best friend for three years. And yet he was willing to throw me out because I slipped up once.

Something else was going on here. I hadn't screwed up a job in years . . . well, until now. How could he blame the coven's unrest on *my* failures when I hadn't done anything wrong?

It felt like he was using this misstep as an excuse to blame me. To manipulate and blackmail me.

It had to do with this Nephilim, I was sure of it. There was something different about this assignment. Something he wasn't telling me.

My hands balled into fists. I could kill him right here, right now. Then, all I'd have to do was track down Benny and I'd be free.

But free to do what? Damien was right. No other demon coven would have me. Even if I'd made a name for myself, they'd insist on swearing me in with a blood ritual. And I couldn't do that.

My only hope was this bargain with Damien. A

bargain that didn't suit me at all. I had nothing to gain—but everything to lose if I failed.

A knock sounded on the door behind me.

"Come in," Damien said lazily without looking up.

It was Kip. "We've got company."

"That's fine. Cora was just leaving." Damien offered a cold smile, his eyes still shining. That hungry look still gleamed in his expression.

This was a completely different Damien. I didn't know this man at all.

Rage and panic quivered through me as I hopped to my feet and strode out of his office, grateful that my leg didn't give out as I felt the men watch me leave.

I wasn't the one who'd changed. Damien was. I'd performed my job perfectly over the years. But Damien was the one who slowly shoved me out. He no longer trusted me.

And deep down, I knew that even if I fulfilled this task for him, it wouldn't be enough.

It would never be enough.

CHAPTER 6

VINCE

I SAT NEXT TO JOCELYN IN THE MEETINGHOUSE, FACING the panel of our clan leaders. Hector sat in the front, his short black hair gleaming under the fluorescent lights. Behind him sat five other officials who represented our clan, one of whom was Peter Wilkes—Jocelyn's father. Though they all had relatively young faces, I knew some —like Hector—were hundreds of years old. Their Nephilim magic kept them looking young.

I shifted in my chair, painfully aware of how much of a child I was compared to these veterans. Jocelyn exchanged a worried glance with me, and I knew she shared my fear.

Did they believe us? Would they take this threat seriously? Or would they dismiss our worries as idle, childish fears?

And a strange, selfish concern: would they know I'd lied about my powers?

Jocelyn hadn't known I'd time traveled. When we relayed what had happened in the library yesterday, I omitted it. I wasn't sure why, but some innate instinct warned me not to tell.

Instead, I'd squashed it down, trying not to dwell on it. Because if I did, my brain would explode with possibilities.

Hector cleared his throat loudly after conferring with the other officials. He clasped his long fingers together on the table and surveyed us carefully with his brown eyes.

"We have further questions for you," Hector said, his deep voice echoing in the vast room.

I suppressed a groan. *More* questions? Jocelyn and I had already been here for an hour as we relayed every single detail of the attack yesterday.

"We believe your story and the dangers involved," Hector went on. "Now we must consider *why* this person —or thing—attacked you."

I sat up straighter in my chair, hope blossoming in my chest.

"Have either of you done anything to anger another magical being recently?" Hector asked.

"No," Jocelyn and I both said at once.

"Have either of you used a powerful amount of magic in the presence of other magical beings?"

Jocelyn replied immediately, "No."

But I hesitated.

Hector noticed. His eyebrows lifted as his shrewd eyes fixed on me. "Mr. Delgado?"

I swallowed. "I just—uh, I'm not sure."

"Can you elaborate?"

I rubbed the back of my neck, suddenly finding it hard to breathe. "My—my powers . . . I can't always control them. Sometimes—sometimes I use magic by accident. And I'm not sure if any of the witnesses were magical beings or not." My face burned as I spoke the last words in a rush.

Hector straightened and exchanged a stern glance with the official closest to him. "How often has this happened?"

My mouth felt dry. "Uh . . . a few times. Not many." That was a lie, but I didn't like the grim set of Hector's eyebrows as he stared me down.

"Foolish boy," Hector spat. "I shouldn't be surprised. You've always been incompetent."

My face burned, and sweat trickled down my brow. Hector turned and murmured something to the other officials. I made out the word "disappointment."

Something raged inside me, threatening to burst. Part indignation, part shame . . . I couldn't stop it. My insides felt like they would explode if I didn't do *something* to eliminate this awful embarrassment that crept into my skin.

"I have a theory," I blurted out.

The murmuring stopped abruptly, and Hector fixed a cold gaze on me. "Do you?" The words sounded more like a threat than a question.

I nodded, my pulse roaring in my ears. "I just—I was trying to imagine who would want to attack me or Jocelyn. I mean, we're underage. We don't even have full access to our abilities yet. Why would anyone want us dead?

"Then, I thought of another alternative," I said eagerly, the words tumbling out of my mouth before I could stop them. "What if the attacker wanted to *abduct* us instead of kill us? That would make more sense to me because, well, we're still children. When looking at it that way, I think the attacker was most likely after Jocelyn. She's the daughter of a high-ranking official of the clan. Someone capable of making powerful decisions. If abducted, she—"

"That's enough," Hector said sharply. Behind him, Peter Wilkes's face drained of color, his wide, horrified eyes fixed on his daughter. I heard Jocelyn's sharp intake of breath, but I couldn't dare look at her. My face flushed. I sank low into my seat, realizing I'd gone too far.

"Your fearmongering isn't welcome here," Hector said, his tone icy. "Do not cause unnecessary panic when you have no *proof*. Remember your place, Mr. Delgado. You have no authority here. This panel is far more experienced in these matters than you are."

"But—" I argued.

"Why don't you put your *brilliant* mind to more important things—like mastering your abilities? Clearly, you need some work in that department." Hector's mouth curled into a satisfied smirk.

I only stared at him, my face on fire. I opened my mouth, but no words came out.

"We will contact you if we have any further information," Hector said, rising from his chair. "In the meantime, we advise you to carry on with your normal routine. You two are dismissed."

I blanched, jumping to my feet. "*What?* But the attacker's still out there!"

"Yes, *one* attacker. If we hide you both away, they likely won't try again. But, if we proceed as normal, we may be able to catch whoever assaulted you."

"You want to use us as *bait?*"

"You will be heavily guarded, I assure you," Hector said in a tired voice. "Like I said, we aren't amateurs. We can handle the threat."

I took a step forward. "You can't—"

"*Dismissed,* Mr. Delgado," Hector said in a booming voice.

I flinched, then balled my hands into fists. After several angry breaths, I turned on my heel and left the meetinghouse. My loping strides carried me half a block before I heard someone shouting my name.

I stopped and glanced over my shoulder to find Jocelyn hurrying after me, her long red hair whipping behind her.

My heart dropped to my stomach, but I forced a smile and turned to face her. Her eyes were tight with worry when she reached me. "I—I just . . . Did you mean what you said back there?" she panted, crossing her arms.

"Jocelyn—"

"I'm not mad," she said quickly. "But I need to know if you said that because you really believe I'm in danger or if you were trying to deflect their attention."

Shame crept into my cheeks, and I suddenly felt hot again. "Yes, I meant it," I admitted. "I'm the son of a dead Nephilim and a powerless warlock. Why would anyone want to hurt me? But you, you have this potential. Even without your adult magic, you're powerful. And you're the only child of a Nephilim official." I shrugged one shoulder. "But it's just a theory, and Hector dismissed it, so it's probably nothing."

Jocelyn bit her lip and shot a nervous look behind her toward the meetinghouse.

"You could stay home," I suggested. "If you're worried."

Jocelyn sighed and shook her head. "My dad would never let me disregard a direct order from Hector."

My mouth twisted in a grimace. "Right."

An awkward silence passed between us. I shifted my weight from one foot to the next as I briefly entertained the idea of disobeying Hector and staying home myself. But if Jocelyn *was* the target, I couldn't just let her go out in the open on her own. I was a poor fighter, but I still had to try.

"I'm sorry," Jocelyn said quietly. "If it *is* me they're after, I'm sorry I dragged you into this."

"No, no!" I said quickly, shaking my head. "Jocelyn, don't say that. If you hadn't involved me, they might've taken you. Maybe . . . maybe it's better if we fight this together. Better chance of success."

Jocelyn offered a small smile. "I, uh, guess I'll see you in Trig."

I nodded. "Yeah. See you."

She strode down the road toward her house while I stood frozen on the sidewalk. *Trig,* I thought dizzily. Going to class seemed so stupid compared to what Jocelyn and I had faced.

But if she was going to school, then so would I.

I brushed off Dad's anxious questions when I got back to the house and hastily packed my backpack. I paused, my hand hovering over the textbook I'd checked out from the library. With a jolt, I realized I'd forgotten about my magic—my strange new Teleportation ability.

My jaw ticked back and forth as I contemplated. Then, I shook my head, exhaling slowly.

Now wasn't the time to experiment with dangerous powers. I was in enough trouble already.

I bid my dad farewell and hopped in the car. After hesitating a moment, I drove to Jocelyn's house and caught her before she got into her car.

I lowered the window and asked, "Want a ride?"

Jocelyn blinked in surprise and then smiled before sliding into the passenger seat. We were both silent while I drove to school, my knuckles turning white as I gripped the steering wheel.

"It'll be fine, Vince," Jocelyn said quietly, but her voice trembled.

I nodded and said nothing.

When I parked at school, I slammed my car door and looked up to gaze at the courtyard. I found the spot where I'd seen my Mimic, and my throat tightened with apprehension.

Had he been trying to warn me? Did he know what would happen to me and Jocelyn?

I shook the confusing jumble of thoughts from my mind and walked to the office with Jocelyn to check in.

We both used the "family emergency" excuse and got passes to give to our teachers.

My mind was elsewhere as I sat through my classes. I lost focus as my teachers droned on and on about concepts that passed right over me.

The Ceremonial Rite is in just a few months, I thought. *I already can't control my Teleportation powers. Now, suddenly, I find out I might be able to time travel. Then, Jocelyn and I are attacked, but we don't know who did it or why.*

It was all too much for me.

But the more I thought about it, the more I wondered if maybe I *had* been the target. Hector was right—my magic was powerful, and it was taking over. What if someone saw me as a threat and wanted to take me out before the Ceremonial Rite—before my powers matured?

Get over yourself, Vince, I chided myself. *You're not that important, and you're not that powerful.*

"Hey."

I blinked, realizing I'd automatically gone to my locker after class without thinking about it. Turning, I found Luke leaning against the locker next to mine, his eyebrows raised. "You all right?"

I cleared my throat. "Yeah. Sorry. Crazy stuff's been going on."

Luke grinned with mischief. "Tell me all about it. I love to hear about your angelic family drama."

I rolled my eyes and glanced up and down the bustling hallway. "Later," I said quietly.

"I'm gonna grab a coke. You want one?"

I shook my head. "I'll meet you in the cafeteria."

"You got it."

Luke ambled off while I took my time sorting through my textbooks, trying to bring my mind back to the present. But it kept rolling through the events of the past few days, trying to make sense of everything.

"Get a grip," I muttered angrily before slamming the locker door.

I turned and ran straight into someone. We both yelped and staggered backward. A stack of papers floated to the floor, and I hastily bent over to pick them up.

"I'm sorry," I said with an exasperated laugh. "I'm a mess today." I glanced up and found the brightest blue eyes I'd ever seen. They were sharp and intuitive and made me feel as if they could read my very soul.

I realized my mouth was hanging open, and I shut it. My gaze roved over the girl in front of me. She was tall—almost as tall as me. Her black hair was cropped short around her face, and her bangs hung low, almost covering her eyes. The cold, sharp angles of her face made her look uninviting . . . until she smiled. The change lit up her features, sending a wave of relief spiraling through me.

"No problem," she said in a firm voice. "I'm new here,

so maybe you can help me. I'm looking for the front office."

I handed the stack of papers to the girl and nodded. "Right. Uh, you can come with me. The office is this way."

"Thanks."

"I'm Vince, by the way. Vince Delgado" I stuck out my hand, and the girl took it. Her hands were pale and calloused.

"Cora Covington."

CHAPTER 7

CORA

I SHOULDN'T HAVE GIVEN HIM MY NAME.

But I was inexperienced in the art of conning. Lies didn't come easily to me.

There was nothing more honest than killing. A kill reveals a person's darkest secrets. But living—betrayal, torture, trickery—that was a true art of deception.

And one that I was no good at.

Damien, however, was a master at it. And, naïve as I was, I hadn't believed he would con *me*.

But the more I thought about our last conversation, the more I realized that was exactly what he'd done. He'd spent years manipulating me, acting like he cared for me, earning my trust, only to blackmail me to do his dirty work for him.

And now I was trapped.

I let Vince lead me to the front office, though I knew

exactly where it was. I kept my eyes trained on his shoulders, wondering if there were scars underneath his shirt where his wings would come out. His lithe, casual swagger made me envious. I never walked like that. I always walked with purpose. Ever alert. Ready for an attack.

"Here we are," Vince said with a nervous chuckle, rubbing the back of his neck. As his gray eyes shifted to me and then to the door of the office, I realized he wasn't casual or confident at all.

He just carried himself that way.

"Thanks," I said, flashing another smile. My cheeks hurt from smiling. I wasn't used to it.

Vince turned to leave, and I knew my window of opportunity was closing. I had to drop a hint somehow.

I cleared my throat. "Do you wear cologne?"

Vince froze and raised an eyebrow at me. "Uh, no. Why?"

I laughed, but it sounded too airy and forced. "Oh, sorry. It's just—you smell like mint. Mingled with . . ." I paused, pretending to think. "Woodsmoke?" My eyes shifted to his, and I lifted my eyebrows suggestively.

Vince's whole body went rigid. I watched a dozen emotions cross his expression as he registered my words.

He knew casters had a specific smell. All magic had an ashy scent to it. Light magic smelled sweet. Dark magic smelled sharp.

But he hadn't smelled anything on me.

So how could I smell *his* magic? I knew the question was eating away at him.

His Adam's apple bobbed as he swallowed hard. He swiped a lock of umber hair out of his eyes. A nervous smile lifted his features. Though I could sense the tension in his body and the fear emanating from him, the smile came to his face easily. His eyes crinkled, and they seemed to glitter with joy.

I envied that too.

"That's weird," he said, shoving his hands in his pockets. "Maybe someone in the office made cookies or something. I'll, uh, see you around, Cora."

He sniffed once before turning away from me. I realized what he was doing—trying to get a better whiff of me.

But, being a Bloodcaster, my scent was different from light and dark magic. And Vince didn't know what to make of it.

For a moment, I watched him walk away. His body carried that same easy stride like he didn't have a care in the world.

What a poor, ignorant fool.

After Vince disappeared from view, I dumped my stack of papers in the trash and circled around the office to grab the bag I'd stashed in the bushes. A gaggle of giggling girls walked by me, their laughter shrill and high-pitched. I rolled my eyes, ducking down to avoid being spotted as they passed.

Lilith, I hate high school.

I dropped out when I was fifteen and got my GED online. I'd been attacked too many times by demons posing as students.

Oh, how the tables had turned.

I slipped a few potion vials in my pocket and went to the cafeteria. While standing in line to buy a limp slice of pizza, I took the opportunity to survey the area. I spotted Vince at once—he was too tall to ignore as he sat next to a skinny kid with dark skin and dreadlocks. Vince was muttering fervently, his eyes constantly shifting around.

Whatever the two were talking about was serious.

I wondered if he was telling his friend about my failure to kill him. Shame washed over me, and my cheeks burned. I turned away, gritting my teeth.

You're the best at what you do, Cora, I told myself. *They call you the Blade, for Lilith's sake.*

But that didn't stifle my rising nausea. Despite my skills, I was still trapped. Damien controlled me like a puppet, and no matter how many people I killed or high schools I infiltrated, I would always be stuck under his thumb.

Unless I could find a way to kill him.

If I had the time, I knew I could concoct a potion or

write a spell that would get the job done without turning the entire coven against me. But, unfortunately, I was saddled with this stupid high school job.

Perhaps that was exactly why Damien gave me the assignment. To keep me too preoccupied to attack him.

The conniving bastard.

I got my slice of pizza and pretended to gaze around the cafeteria with a forlorn expression on my face. I bit my lip. I looked around with my eyebrows lifted in false hope that an unknown friend would welcome me over.

Then, my gaze settled on Vince. I'd already known he was watching me. He saw me as soon as I stepped out of the line.

Conflict creased his brows, and his gaze darted to his friend before shifting to me again. He lifted his arm and waved me over.

Perfect.

I let a relieved smile spread across my face as I strode forward, sitting across from Vince. I felt his eyes on me as I settled in my seat and waved politely to his friend.

"I'm Cora," I said.

"Luke." He nodded at me, his eyes roving over my body. "You, uh, seem a little *mature* for high school." His eyes glinted as if he knew something I didn't.

Damn. Vince *had* been talking about me—but not as the assassin.

As the girl who could smell magic.

I cleared my throat and tucked my hair behind my ear. "It's the short hair. It makes me look older."

This wasn't untrue. When I'd first started killing, I cut my hair short to keep it out of the way. An added benefit was that it made me look more mature. I'd gotten too many snide remarks about how young I was.

Vince elbowed Luke. "*I* like your hair," Vince said to me.

"Thanks." I took a bite of my pizza and tried not to gag.

"So, Cora, where are you from?" Luke asked, his tone a bit too chipper.

"New York."

Luke's eyebrows shot up. "Really? What brings you here?" I heard the obvious surprise in his voice, but I was ready for it.

"My dad lost his job. Wanted a change of pace. There's more . . . stability in small towns."

"What does your dad do?"

I dropped my gaze and rubbed my nose. "Uh, he works for the city."

An awkward silence fell between us. Luke and Vince shared a confused glance.

"What does that mean?" Vince asked.

I refused to meet his gaze and shrugged one shoulder. "I don't really know what he does, to be honest. Something in an office with a desk. He answers phones." I forced a laugh and took another bite of pizza.

More silence surrounded me. It felt uncomfortable, but it was exactly what I wanted. *Let them wonder what my dad actually does.*

I swallowed and asked, "What about you guys? What do your parents do?"

Luke jumped in. "My dad's a soccer coach at Wisteria Elementary, and my mom's a teacher there too."

I smiled politely and looked at Vince, who shifted in his chair. "My dad's a consultant," he said.

"What does that mean?" I asked, mimicking Vince's suspicious tone from earlier.

Luke snorted and disguised it as a cough.

Vince sighed. "He consults city officials on how to do their job. Lobbies on their behalf. Manages PR. That kind of thing."

I raised my eyebrows and leveled a gaze at him. "Really."

"Yeah."

We stared each other down, and for a moment, I couldn't look away. His eyes held me there, pinning me in place. A thrill rushed through me as I accepted the challenge.

Which of us would break first?

Well, certainly not me.

As expected, Vince dropped his gaze. I tried not to look too smug about it.

"Have you guys lived here your whole lives?" I asked.

Luke said, "Yes," at the same time Vince said, "No."

I glanced between them, my eyes settling on Vince again. "Really? Where are you from?"

He lifted his chin. "New York, actually."

I already knew this, but I straightened, my expression brightening. "Really? What part?"

"Albany."

"I'm from New York City," I said. "Did you go there much?"

Vince's mouth twisted slightly, and he cleared his throat. "Uh, once."

The Demon War had taken place in New York City. Vince's mom had died there. I knew that from his file.

I felt Luke's eyes on me. Did he know?

Time to drop another hint.

"My parents took me away for a few years to live with my aunt. There was some weird stuff going on and they didn't feel safe there."

The air grew still as Vince and Luke stared at me.

"When was this?" Vince asked in a quiet voice.

I screwed up my face in concentration, pretending to think hard. "Uh, ten years ago, I think?"

Vince stiffened, and his jaw went rigid. A low thrumming pulsed from his body, and the minty scent swelled around me.

Luke coughed and nudged Vince, who flinched before relaxing slightly.

My eyes widened. *What the hell was that?*

But I knew what it was. His magic.

What would've happened if Luke hadn't nudged him?

My eyes settled on Luke. So, he *did* know.

I looked at Vince again, my gaze hard and determined. *Look at me,* I ordered. His eyes were fixed on his plate as he hunched over to avoid my gaze.

Then, for the briefest second, his eyes met mine. My mouth curved upward in a knowing smile. *Gotcha.*

Vince glanced away, then back at me again. He shifted in his chair.

Luke took over again. "We play lacrosse," he said eagerly. "Do you like sports, Cora?"

I carried on a conversation with Luke about our hobbies. I claimed to enjoy poetry and jogging while Luke prattled on about the different books he'd read recently. But my eyes kept shifting back to Vince. He had a conflicted look on his face, and his eyes were hard and distant. I wondered if he was thinking of his mom or of me and the secrets I kept.

I needed to give him time to stew over everything. Conning him would be a slow process. Another reason I hated this mission.

Killing was easy. Killing was *quick*. A knife to the throat, then done.

But this was exhausting.

I made an excuse about going to my locker before class. Instead, I hid in the bushes where my bag was waiting for me. I knelt on the ground, obscured from view by the prickly brush around me, and sifted through my potion vials, muttering to myself.

I had Vince right where I wanted him. Which meant that I needed to spend all my spare time plotting how to eliminate Damien without putting a target on my own back.

But Benny was a problem. If he knew who I was, then he would suspect me first when Damien died.

How could I pin this on someone else?

My thoughts returned to Vince, and my insides froze, my blood pulsing with excitement.

Of course. I could kill two birds with one stone.

What if I could convince Vince that Damien wanted him dead? It was the truth, after all. If Vince relayed the information to his clan, surely they would wage war on Damien. Damien would be killed, and the Nephilim would be blamed. It would start a war between the clan and my coven, but at least I would be safe.

Something within me deflated. Vince held no sway in his clan. My research told me he wasn't respected. His mother was Nephilim, but she was dead. His father was a warlock who'd sworn fealty to the clan, abandoning his magic forever.

Vince was nothing.

I shook my head, scribbling down notes for another potion to make with my blood. I could do it. I just had to work carefully. If Vince trusted me enough to let me into his clan and introduce me to other Nephilim, I could plant seeds in their minds.

This could work.

The bell rang, loud and shrill, and I shoved my things into the bag before stowing it in the bushes again. I carried a textbook against my chest like every other kid and made my way to class.

CHAPTER 8

VINCE

"She has magic. I'm sure of it." I kept my voice low so others nearby wouldn't overhear.

"She definitely seems odd," Luke agreed before taking a swig of coke.

I shook my head, grimacing. The way she'd spoken of the Demon War in New York City . . . It was like she hadn't even realized it happened.

Or she was trying to brush it off because she didn't know if *I* had magic.

Maybe, in reality, it tortured her like it tortured me.

"What kind of magic do you think she has?" Luke asked, his voice eager. "Good magic or bad magic?"

I snorted. "It isn't that simple."

"Why not?"

"Because . . . well, there's light magic and dark magic. Each has a specific scent, but I can't smell either on her."

I sighed. "Granted, I'm not very skilled at it." Only Demonhunters could smell specific magical beings and identify particular scents. The most well-trained Nephilim could identify some. But I'd never shown an interest in Nephilim studies, so, naturally, I was a bit out of practice.

"You could just *ask* her."

"What if she's a demon?" I raised my eyebrows.

Luke frowned. "Can demons come out during the day?"

I rolled my eyes. "Some can. They aren't all vampires, you know."

Luke's expression brightened at the word "vampires," and I interrupted before he could ask questions. "No, I don't know any. You know, if you actually *met* a vampire, you wouldn't be so eager."

"Are you kidding? Even demons bring some excitement to my poor, boring life."

My mouth twisted. What I wouldn't give for a normal, boring life. Without magic, Mom would still be alive. My dad wouldn't be an outcast. I could play lacrosse without worrying about accidentally Jumping across the field.

I kept hoping to see Cora in one of my classes. I was eager to scrutinize her and see if she gave any clues about her magic. But the more I thought about it, the more I realized I wouldn't even know what clues to look for. I'd never met a demon before.

She wasn't a vampire because she could come out during the daytime. And I'd read that werewolves often had yellow-rimmed eyes, so that was unlikely. She could be a dark witch. That was my best bet.

Or . . . a light witch?

I didn't like the way hope blossomed within me at the thought. I barely knew this girl.

Still . . . it would be nice to befriend another light caster like me. I lived among the Nephilim, but it was only half of who I was.

If Cora practiced the same magic as me, it would make me feel less like I was living a half-life. I could enjoy aspects of both sides instead of feeling like I was constantly missing something.

Just when I'd given up hope of seeing her again today, I entered my last class—Chemistry—and found her sitting at a table near the back, hunched over as she read a book. My heart lurched in my throat, and I approached her slowly, my pulse pounding in my ears.

She didn't look up as I drew nearer. Her eyes were glued to the pages of her book, and she absently chewed on one of her fingernails as she read. Squinting, I found the title at the top of the page: *Persuasion* by Jane Austen.

I raised my eyebrows. "So, you like classics?"

Cora jumped, her eyes widening as she looked up at me. She dropped her hand and hastily closed her book with a nervous laugh. "Uh, yeah. *Persuasion* is my favorite."

I took the seat next to her, and half her mouth curved upward in a smile. She dropped her gaze, tucking her hair behind her ears.

"You probably don't read Jane Austen, do you?" she asked.

I shrugged one shoulder. "I like *Pride and Prejudice*."

Cora stared at me for a long moment. Something unreadable flashed in her eyes. "Really?" Her voice lifted in such genuine surprise that I laughed.

"Yes. Really."

"Did you lose a bet or something?"

I grinned. "No. It was my mom's favorite."

Cora's eyes crinkled with her smile. "She must be very proud of you for reading it. Not many teenage boys would."

My smile faded. "She passed away when I was a kid."

Cora's eyes widened, and her mouth became very small. Her eyes closed in exasperation. "I—Oh, Vince, I'm so sorry."

I frowned, shaking my head. "Don't worry about it. You didn't know."

Cora grimaced. "How did it happen? If you don't mind me asking."

I looked at her, searching her bright blue eyes that gazed at me with such innocence and curiosity.

Should I tell her? I wondered.

No. It would be too blunt to say, *My mom was killed in a battle of demons.* If Cora *was* a demon, that would scare her off.

Then again, would that be a bad thing? I didn't want to associate with a demon at all.

I cleared my throat. "She was murdered on the streets of New York City." Technically, this was the truth. But instead of the usual sinking sensation in my stomach, it made my heart quiver with anticipation.

I might be able to bring her back.

The thought was so clear that I ached with longing.

Cora's eyes grew wide, and she pressed a hand to her chest. "Lil—I mean, uh, that's *terrible.*" Her brows creased. "Is that why you left New York?"

I stared at her. Had she almost said "Lilith"? Only those with magic swore in Lilith's name.

Hector hated it. Which was why I often did it.

"Yeah," I said shortly, shifting in my chair to face the front as Mr. Hudson entered the room.

I felt Cora's eyes on me during the lecture about chemical bonding. Every time I glanced her way, she dropped her gaze, pretending to write copious notes.

I couldn't read her. Did she pity me? Or was she just curious about what *really* happened to my mom?

She had to be an idiot not to know about the Demon War. Maybe she *did* know and was just trying to figure out if that was really how my mom died.

I cut a glance at her and found her watching me. Her lips turned downward in a slight frown, and her eyes were contemplative. Calculating. There was such a sharp intuitiveness to her eyes that I hadn't seen before.

When she caught me looking, she blinked and dropped her gaze again. But the image of her concentration and slight confusion remained imprinted on my mind.

Something about me puzzled her.

I inhaled slowly, deeply, trying to get a better whiff of her magic. I smelled something faint and flowery. But that could've been her shampoo. There was another brief whiff of something electric.

Could that be her magic?

I'd read that demons smelled foul. But Cora definitely didn't.

She glanced at me again, then looked away. She bit her lip as she scribbled something in her notes.

Did she wonder the same questions about *me*? If she was a demon, perhaps she was like me and had never come across a Nephilim before. A light caster, sure, but a Nephilim? We kept to ourselves after the Demon War.

Maybe she couldn't place *my* scent, either.

For some reason, the thought made me relieved. It made me feel like less of a failure.

Well, maybe I could give her a tiny hint. Something to ease her mind.

Slowly, I stretched my arm backward, pretending to yawn. Before dropping my arm, I slid my hand under the back of my shirt and scratched the scars on my shoulder blades. The markings where my wings were.

I felt Cora's eyes on me, and my gaze flicked to her. Her eyes trailed the length of my bicep before widening as she stared at my shoulders. Wonder filled her expression, and she swallowed.

Oh yeah. This girl totally knew.

I dropped my arm and returned my gaze to Mr. Hudson. But I couldn't focus on the lecture at all.

When the bell rang, Cora packed her bag slowly, her eyes far away as she collected her things. I took my time as well, wondering if she wanted to get away from me or linger to ask questions.

We both knew something weird was going on with each other. The question was, who would break first?

When her bag was packed, Cora looked at me. I looked at her. Our gazes held during a long moment of silence, and I felt like so much more passed between us in that look.

As the students around us filed out of the room, Cora whispered, "You're different."

I nodded. "You're different too."

"I am." Fear shone in her eyes. "*Too* different."

My brows furrowed. "What does that mean?"

Cora's breath hitched, and alarm crossed her features. "It means . . . it isn't safe for me to tell you more."

Before I could respond, she snatched her bag and bolted from her seat, disappearing from the room in a flash.

CHAPTER 9

CORA

*D*AMN *YOU, C*ORA, I THOUGHT ANGRILY AS I GRABBED my bag from the bushes before striding purposefully toward the parking lot. *You shouldn't have told him that.*

Too different? I was an idiot. I might as well have told him, *Hey, I'm a blood witch!*

This job was giving me a headache. I constantly had to watch myself and my actions.

And I couldn't deny that Vince intrigued me. He was a jock who read Jane Austen. He was tortured over his mom's death, but not broody. He was sly and subtle enough to drop a hint he was Nephilim without giving anything away.

Yes, that move had been good. I'd almost been too distracted by the way the muscles bunched in his arm to notice what he was doing.

But what *really* bothered me was that he was almost as good as I was. Hadn't I been dropping hints all day too?

I gritted my teeth, my fingers tightening around the strap of my bag. *I can do this,* I told myself. *I'm Cora Covington. The Blade of Hinport. Fearless assassin. I can con a high school student. This will be a piece of cake.*

But no matter how many times I said it to myself, I kept envisioning Vince's piercing gray eyes and the way his gaze kept sliding to me, his face filled with the same blatant curiosity I felt.

Who are you? we'd both wondered.

All I knew was what I'd read in his file. Half warlock. Half Nephilim. A high school senior.

But who *was* he? I knew Nephilim had their own way of living. He couldn't be both. So which would he choose? Was he more Nephilim or warlock? And if he didn't live with his clan, where did he go?

And none of this explained how he'd been in two places at once. Maybe it was a Nephilim power I didn't know about. The idea sent a spark of relief through me. It meant I wouldn't have any helpful information for Damien.

My head spun with questions as I walked away from campus, striding down the sidewalk toward town. Yesterday, I'd bought a room at a small inn around the corner, paying in cash so it couldn't be traced to me. I'd also given a false name so I could claim a parent had reserved the room. That way, if I was followed, I could easily say we hadn't found a place to live yet and I was staying with my parents at the inn. I'd already forged documents for Bill and Nancy Covington, my fake parents, in order to register myself as a student at Vince's school.

My hand automatically reached for my dagger, which wasn't there. Vince had taken it during the fight, and I couldn't exactly ask for it back. Maybe I'd find an opportunity to retrieve it.

It was my favorite dagger.

The sun beat down on me, undeterred by the small shops and buildings surrounding me. I found myself missing the narrow alleys and generous shadows of Hinport, thanks to the towering apartment complexes in the area.

This place was all suburbs and glistening white sidewalks. It made me sick.

I reached the inn and waved to the man stationed at the desk. I didn't want to attract too much attention, and the people of Ravenbrooke seemed overly friendly. Best to blend in.

When I got to my room, I bolted the door and stuck a chair under the doorknob for good measure. I whipped out the potion-making materials from my bag: a hot plate, a small pot, a mallet for grinding, and various dry ingredients.

After sifting through my spell notes, I combined the billing's root, cardamom, and henbane into the small pot and mashed the ingredients together while waiting for the hot plate to warm. When the mixture formed a grayish powder, I dug through my bag until I found my sheathed knife. It was small enough to fit inside my thigh holster, which I would have to start wearing. I couldn't go anywhere unarmed.

I dragged the tiny blade against my palm and squeezed my fingers into a fist, letting the droplets of violet blood splash onto the powder. I mixed the ingredients until it formed a paste. Then, I uttered the spell.

"Magic above, and powers that be,
Hear my call and answer my plea.
Strengthen these magical ingredients.
Acknowledge my blood and its elements.
Grant me the ability to See beyond,
And with the Nephilim forge a bond."

My hands glowed purple and white, the colors shimmering together and momentarily blinding me. The pot rattled slightly, and the paste swirled of its own accord. Energy crackled and thrummed around me. I held my hand over the ingredients, allowing more blood to drip freely. The paste liquefied even more, darkening in color.

Slowly, the magic faded, and energy drained from me.

I sagged backward against the wall, panting. For a moment, I sat there, sucking in deep breaths and trying to clear my head. When the dizziness subsided, I sat forward and scraped the magical paste into an empty potion vial before corking it and returning it to my bag.

I hadn't used the gift of Seeing in a long time. I was a little excited. Using my blood for extra powers always gave me a thrill.

I'd just unplugged my hot plate when a loud knock sounded at the door. My eyes darted up, and I instinctively clutched my knife, which was still bloody. It looked like it was coated in blackberry jam.

Lilith, my blood is so weird. I thought this all the time.

I hastily wiped the knife on a tissue before removing the chair and unlocking and opening the door.

It was Damien. He offered a crooked smile that had once made my heart skitter.

Now, it made me nauseous.

"I'm busy," I said flatly before shutting the door.

He stuck his foot in before it fully shut. "I just want to check in."

I fixed a flat look at him. "Things are going *swell*, Damien. Thanks for stopping by." I tried closing the door again, but he shoved his leg farther in.

"Let me in, Cora."

"No."

Damien smirked and crossed his arms. "All right.

Would you like to have this conversation in the hallway? How are things going with conning the *Nephilim warlock* into trusting you before you *kill* him?" His voice grew louder with each word.

Gritting my teeth, I snatched his arm and dragged him into my room before bolting the door again.

My nostrils flared as I faced him. "Like I said, things are going swell."

Damien raised his eyebrows. "Really? How well? Have you figured out how he uses his powers?"

I scoffed. "I've known him for a day, Damien. Trust takes time. He won't just tell *anyone* his darkest secrets."

Damien's eyes glinted. "Ah, so you've learned he's keeping dark secrets?"

I rolled my eyes, but an uncomfortable feeling slithered through me. Had I just unknowingly hinted at what I'd figured out from Vince?

I quickly shoved that thought away. Why did it matter? This was my job.

But as I looked at Damien's smug smile, I couldn't help the anger and resentment that rose within me. Yes, a small part of me *did* want to thwart Damien's plans. Just to see the look of defeat on his face.

No, I told myself. I needed to play the good and obedient assassin if I wanted to kill him later. If he suspected me of duping him now, he would never let down his guard.

Lifting my chin, I said, "Yes. He's hiding something. But I'm not sure what. Give me a few more days."

"What will you do to gain his trust?"

My eyes narrowed. "I don't share my methods."

Damien snorted. "Cora, you've shared *everything* with me."

I balled my hands into fists. "Get out. We're done here."

Damien lifted his hands. "That's it? No goodbye kiss?" He inched closer, his eyes gleaming.

I shoved him backward. "*Get out*, Damien. I'm not interested."

Damien chuckled. "That's fine. You'll come begging for it. You always do." He winked before spinning on the spot and vanishing with a soft *pop*.

Still seething, I chucked my knife onto the floor and growled in frustration.

I didn't have many regrets in my life, but Damien was now definitely one of them. I regretted falling for him, sharing his bed, and revealing my secret to him.

Deep down, I knew he'd hold it over me for the rest of my life—until I was no longer useful to him.

Determination pulsed through me as I plopped down on the floor and opened my book of spells, turning the pages until I found the one I was searching for: *Poisoned Balm*.

A slow smile spread across my face. I'd only used this

once before. Generally, I didn't prefer putting my mouth anywhere near my victims. But, in this case, it might be perfect. Once I spread it on my lips, it would prove fatal to whoever kissed me.

I'd certainly give Damien his goodbye kiss. And it would be the last kiss he ever tasted.

CHAPTER 10

VINCE

I STOOD OUTSIDE THE FINE ARTS BUILDING, WAITING for Jocelyn to finish band practice so I could take her home. Most of the other students had already left. The late afternoon sun beat down on my face as I leaned against the brick wall.

I stared hard at the courtyard down the sidewalk. My eyes were glued to the same spot I'd seen my Mimic just the other day. I wracked my brain, trying to recall any details. Had my Mimic been significantly older? Or had he been the same age—meaning I would figure out how to time travel sooner rather than later?

I tried not to let that notion excite me. But as the hope within me grew, so did the idea that I could go back in time and save my mom.

But if my Mimic had been older—even by just a few

years—then it would drive me mad to wait that long before figuring out the secret to time travel.

And it also meant that I wouldn't join the Nephilim clan. I'd be banished.

Somehow, the idea didn't make me feel as disappointed as I thought. My only concern was for my dad. What would happen to him? Would he be thrown out too? The Nephilim clan employed him, so he would be jobless *and* homeless. How would we live?

I shook those torturous thoughts from my mind and again recalled the image of my Mimic. As far as I could tell, it had been like looking in a mirror. My hair hadn't seemed longer *or* shorter—it had still fallen on the Mimic's forehead but remained neatly trimmed in the back. No facial hair or five-o'clock shadow. I hadn't seemed much taller, either.

Granted, I'd only gotten a glimpse. If I'd been closer, I might've been able to notice more details.

I straightened before glancing around. The parking lot and courtyard were empty. Anyone who stayed this late would be in the Fine Arts hall practicing.

Swallowing, I flexed my fingers, trying to awaken my powers. Something flared to life within me, but I wasn't sure what it was—my Nephilim powers or my Teleportation powers.

I exhaled and closed my eyes, trying to focus on my objective.

Go back an hour. Just one hour. You can do it.

I spun on the spot.

With a small *pop*, I arrived in the courtyard—at the exact spot I'd been staring at.

A brief elation filled me before I whirled around and realized nothing had changed. The courtyard was still empty.

I'd merely Jumped. Which I already knew how to do.

Frustration boiled within me, but I shoved it down, determined to figure this out. I took several more deep breaths, screwing up my face in concentration before spinning again.

Pop. Back to the Fine Arts building.

Pop. Back to the courtyard.

Pop. Fine Arts building again.

A growl of fury built in my throat, and I slapped my hands against the hot bricks of the building next to me.

What was I missing?

In all my years of using magic, I'd never been able to manipulate it the way I wanted to. It just *happened*. Like it had a mind of its own.

Gradually, my breathing returned to normal as I recalled the details of the fight against the shadow man.

What exactly had I done?

I closed my eyes as I remembered. I'd been injured, so I'd grabbed the bookshelf for support. Fear and pain radiated through me. I'd been out of breath. Full of adrenaline.

Maybe I needed to simulate those feelings again. Make my body believe I was in danger.

It was easier said than done. I focused intently on the event—fearing for my life, trying to protect Jocelyn, struggling against the attacker—but no matter what I did, I couldn't convince myself I was in danger. There was nothing to be afraid of here. I was alone. I was safe.

And I was also horribly incompetent.

I shifted, turning to halfheartedly Jump one last time, when the door to the building burst open, and I froze. My foot hovered awkwardly in the air.

Jocelyn's face was bright and her cheeks pink, no doubt from playing the flute for so long. She arched an eyebrow when she saw me. "What're you doing?"

I dropped my foot and cleared my throat, feeling my face burn. "Uh, nothing. You ready?"

"Yeah. Thanks for waiting. Sorry if it was a bother."

I shrugged one shoulder, falling into step beside her as we headed toward the parking lot. "No bother." Truth be told, it made me nervous leaving her at the school unprotected.

Not that I provided much protection. Still, it felt better than fretting about her while I was useless at home.

We were both silent as we got in my car. When I

drove out of the parking lot, my thoughts turned to Cora and whatever secrets she was keeping.

It isn't safe to tell you any more, she'd said.

"Have you ever met a demon before?" I blurted before I could stop myself.

Jocelyn didn't answer for a long moment. "Yeah, I have."

I waited for her to go on, but she didn't. I cleared my throat. "What do they smell like? Do they all smell the same?"

She shook her head. "They all smell foul to me, but each one has their own distinct scent. Vampires smell like spice and vinegar. Werewolves smell like wet dog and something acidic. Dark witches and warlocks are trickier. They still have the same sharp scent, almost like rubbing alcohol, but it's mingled with something else."

"Something . . . flowery?" I prodded.

Jocelyn shot me a bewildered look. "No," she said, chuckling. "Something . . . smoky. Like charred wood. Or fireworks."

I frowned. Cora hadn't smelled like that at all. I'd smelled the familiar smoky scent that all magic had, but nothing sharp or acidic. Nothing that screamed *demon*.

"Why do you ask?" Jocelyn asked, her voice laced with suspicion.

I shrugged one shoulder, keeping my gaze fixed on

the road as I drove. "No reason. I've just never met a demon before, so I was curious."

"Yeah, well, you aren't likely to find demons here. Most of them live in Hinport."

I stilled. "Hinport?"

"The city across the bridge."

"I know where Hinport is," I said quickly. "But why do the demons live there?"

"They run the place. It's where the dark covens do business. From what my dad says, they keep to their turf, and we keep to ours. It's better that way."

Her dad. *Right.* Of course she was more knowledge-able about demons than I was. Her dad was a high-ranking Nephilim. I had no doubt he often met with members of the Council, the magical body of govern-ment made up of both light and dark casters. Maybe she'd gone with him to one of these meetings and that was how she met demons for herself.

All these thoughts made me feel pitifully insignifi-cant. I had two brands of magic in me, sure. But what did that mean if I stayed locked in my cozy little town for my entire life?

"Trust me, you don't want to encounter a demon," Jocelyn said with a shudder. "They're eerie. And statisti-cally speaking, more than half of them feast on human flesh."

A coil of nausea swelled in my stomach. I already

knew this, but the reminder still filled my body with icy horror.

Jocelyn was right. I wanted nothing to do with demons.

And I was infinitely more relieved that Cora wasn't one. But just to be sure, I decided I should introduce Cora and Jocelyn to each other and see what happened. Maybe Jocelyn would notice something I hadn't.

When I got home, Dad was sitting at the small dining room table, his dress shirt rolled up to his elbows and his black hair falling forward into his face. Lines creased his forehead and eyes, and he placed his fingers on his temples.

I opened my mouth to greet him but then heard the warbly sound of a voice on speakerphone.

"That's the fifth extension we've given to you, José." I recognized the voice on the phone as Hector's.

"I know." Dad sighed, closing his eyes. "I swear it'll be the last."

Hector was silent. I could almost hear his doubt seeping through the phone. "This is contingent on your son's pledge at the Ceremonial Rite."

Dad's eyes flicked to me before focusing on the phone. "I understand."

"Good. I'll see you tomorrow."

Dad hung up and buried his face in his hands.

I gripped my backpack so tightly my fingernails dug

into my palm. For a long moment, I stared at my dad. He seemed as helpless as a child who just wanted to be comforted. A hard lump formed in my throat.

I dropped my backpack to the floor loudly and coughed. "Everything okay?"

Dad dropped his hands and looked at me with a weary smile. "Yeah."

"Hector's asking for dues again?"

Dad nodded, his mouth spreading into a thin line. "I don't know where our money keeps going. Every time I get paid, I see it all there and how it'll pan out. But then this bill comes, and the money's just . . ." Dad waved a hand. "Gone."

Guilt wriggled through me. I shifted my weight from one foot to the other. "If this is because of lacrosse—"

"It's not," Dad said quickly, offering another smile. "I promise."

Slowly, I approached the table and sat down across from him. "About the Ceremonial Rite . . ."

Dad raised a hand to stop me. "You don't have to decide anything right now, Vince."

"I know. But . . . Dad, what'll happen to you? If I refuse?"

Dad's eyes tightened, and something hardened in his expression. "It's not me I'm worried about. It's *you*."

Anxiety lanced through me. "What do you mean?"

"Vince, there's a reason we never encounter dark

angels. They're called Reapers, and they're highly dangerous. They embrace dark magic and are much more
susceptible to it than Nephilim are."

I swallowed. My mouth suddenly felt dry. "But . . . I
won't be a demon. I'd be a light warlock like you were."

Dad shook his head. "No, swearing off Nephilim will
be like swearing off light magic. It's different."

A sour taste filled my mouth.

Noticing my expression, Dad leaned forward, his dark
eyes intent. "I'm not trying to scare you, Vince. I just
want you to consider everything before you choose.
Don't worry about what happens to me. Choose what
feels right to you. But please be careful. Don't fill your
head with these fantasies of what it would be like outside
the clan."

Dad held my gaze for a long moment before rising
from the table to disappear into the kitchen. I sat in my
chair, slumped backward, my body numb with shock as I
processed what Dad had told me.

No one in the clan talked about Reapers. They were
an abomination. A disgrace to the name of angels.

I'd always been curious about *why*, but I'd never
pictured this. Demons.

If I refused to pledge at the Ceremonial Rite, would I
become a demon? The thought sent ripples of unease wriggling through me like snakes.

My gaze fell to the mountain of bills on the table that

Dad had been working through, and I remembered Hector's words: *This is contingent on your son's pledge at the Ceremonial Rite.*

It wasn't just the possibility of becoming a demon that gave me pause. It was the idea that our already difficult lives would get even worse after we were kicked out. Dad was barely making ends meet here—and he *had* a stable job.

What would happen if we were kicked out? We'd be homeless. Dad would have to look for another job that probably wouldn't pay as well.

All because I wanted to keep my warlock powers.

My heart twisted. I couldn't do it. Even if it gave me the chance to save my mom's life, I couldn't sacrifice one parent's well-being for another.

My lips pressed together so tightly my chin trembled. My decision was made.

I would pledge at the Rite.

CHAPTER 11

CORA

THE NEXT DAY WAS NOTHING BUT RAINFALL. WALKING to school with the rain billowing around my pitiful umbrella was miserable. I had a spell to repel water, but I didn't want to risk anyone seeing me use my magic.

So I clutched the handle of my umbrella, shivering as the wind and rain whipped around me. The umbrella didn't do much good since the droplets were coming at me from every direction.

At long last, I made it to the cafeteria, sopping wet. My hair clung to my forehead, and I knew my bangs looked ridiculous.

But I was early. There were only a few teenagers here. No doubt most of them put off coming to school in hopes the rain would let up.

I knew the New Jersey weather well. It wouldn't let up anytime soon.

Dropping my bag down on an empty table, I ran my fingers through my hair. Flecks of water sprinkled onto the floor. I swept my bangs off to the side and gazed around, hoping to find something warm to drink. Coffee would've been great.

But no. A small table in the back had cups of steaming hot chocolate that some of the kids were sipping.

I guess that'll have to do, I thought grumpily, stomping toward the table. My wet socks squished in my boots.

Note to self. Wear rain boots next time. I was so accustomed to using magic freely in Hinport, where demons were commonplace and everyone expected the mystical and unusual. Sure, I couldn't use my magic in public for fear of being exposed as a Bloodcaster. But I could drink a potion granting me special powers, and no one would bat an eye if they saw a bubble around me that kept the rain off.

The back of my neck prickled as I drank my hot chocolate. I felt a pair of eyes on me.

This wasn't unusual. I was tall, and Vince's friend had been right—I looked a little too old for high school.

But my instincts told me it wasn't a stranger watching me. Someone was hoping I'd turn around.

I waited an extra moment and grabbed a second cup of hot chocolate. Drawing my potion vial out of my pocket, I poured a few drops of my Seeing elixir into the second cup. I'd already drank my portion this morning.

Now it was Vince's turn.

With a deep breath, I turned around. Sure enough, there he was, drenched from head to toe. His wet hair—so dark it almost looked black—was plastered against his forehead. His light blue shirt clung to his chest in all the right ways. He shook the water from his hair and ran a hand through it, and I found my eyes drawn to the pull of his biceps.

Enough, Cora, I snapped at myself. I caught Vince's eyes and smiled before striding toward him.

"Hot chocolate?" I asked, handing him the cup with my elixir in it.

Vince raised his eyebrows. "For me? Thanks." He took a long sip and moaned with pleasure. "Delicious."

I tried to stifle the coil of heat rising in my belly and took a sip of my own drink. My eyes roved over him. "No umbrella, huh?"

Vince shrugged one shoulder. "Wouldn't do much good."

I couldn't argue with that.

He sat across the table from me as we sipped our drinks in silence. I kept my gaze lowered, but I felt his eyes on me. I let him fret for several moments, refusing to be the one to give in first.

"How old are you?" he finally asked.

Not what I was expecting.

I cleared my throat. "Just turned nineteen." In truth, I'd just turned twenty. I figured keeping my age as close as possible to my own would be best.

Vince arched an eyebrow.

Before he could respond, I said quickly, "I flunked third grade." This was technically true. But in my head, it didn't matter because I ended up dropping out of school anyway. "What about you?"

"Eighteen next month."

I nodded politely and fixed my eyes on the table. "I suppose now you'll ask me if I'm enjoying the weather?"

Vince laughed. The sound was nervous, but his eyes crinkled. "That bad, huh?"

I smiled. "Well, we *did* just meet yesterday. It's not like I expect you to share your deepest, darkest secrets with me."

I looked away again, but I sensed him stiffen. *Good.*

Silence passed between us. Vince shifted in his seat.

"About what you said yesterday," he said quietly, leaning forward. "What did you mean about it not being safe?"

I blinked and stared hard into my cup of hot chocolate. "I didn't mean anything."

"I don't believe you." His gray eyes hardened like steel.

"I just meant there are things you don't know about

me," I said slowly. "Things that other people might find . . . dangerous."

"Other people?"

"People not like us," I amended.

Vince's eyes narrowed. "And what does that mean?"

I watched him over the rim of my cup as I took another long sip. His eyes glinted as if he'd caught me.

Oh, how wrong he was.

"Turn around," I said.

Vince blinked. "What?"

"Turn around." I made a circle with my finger and leveled a stare at him, challenging him with my eyes. "Humor me."

The corners of his mouth twitched, and his eyes sparkled with amusement. "Okay." Slowly, he shifted in his chair until his back was to me.

As I expected, there were long ridges along his shoulder blades, standing out beneath his wet shirt.

I set my cup down and reached forward, running my pointer finger along the left ridge.

Vince's whole body went rigid. A shiver rippled over him, but I couldn't tell if it was from pleasure or revulsion. I dropped my hand.

He spun in his seat to face me, his eyes darkening. "Why did you do that?"

"Just . . . confirming a hunch," I said, my voice barely above a whisper.

Vince cocked his head at me. His eyes were guarded now—an iron fortress closing himself off from me. "That hardly seems fair. You're at an advantage. You seem to know more about me than I know about you."

You have no idea. I wiggled my eyebrows suggestively. "I'm an open book, Vince. Ask me anything."

Vince sat back in his chair and crossed his arms, looking over me carefully. "All right. What are you?"

I snorted. "You'll have to be more specific than that, or I'm going to be a smartass and say *a girl.*"

Vince laughed. "All right, fine. I'll make a guess." His eyes darted around the room to make sure he wouldn't be heard before he muttered, "A witch?"

I nodded.

Triumph flashed in his eyes, followed by something unreadable. Something that looked a lot like fear. "Dark . . . or light?"

I watched him for a long moment as conflict stirred in his eyes. Why was he so nervous about my answer?

Before I could respond, a voice said, "Vince!"

We both turned and found a girl walking toward us, her long red hair darkened with rain and clinging to her shirt. Her blue eyes were fixed on Vince, and she smiled. "Thanks for waiting."

I raised my eyebrows at Vince. *Waiting?*

Vince straightened, his eyes shifting to me before

returning to the girl. "No problem. Uh, Jocelyn, this is Cora."

I nodded. "Nice to meet you."

"You too." Jocelyn's eyes tightened ever so slightly. She looked at Vince again. "I've got to run to my locker. Come with me?"

"Sure." Vince rose from his seat and then turned to me. Unease mingled with longing in his eyes. His fingers curled into a fist and then relaxed. "I'll, uh, see you later, Cora."

"See you." I watched them both leave. Vince glanced over his shoulder at me before they stepped out into the rain.

I stared at the door long after they'd gone. Something uncomfortable wormed its way into my stomach, but I couldn't tell what it was.

I was caught off guard. That was all. I didn't know Jocelyn, and I was irritated with myself for being surprised by this. I had to find out more about her.

Yes, that was it.

I forced my thoughts away from Vince as I drank my hot chocolate, trying to ignore the knotted feeling in my gut that wouldn't go away.

The rain finally let up by the end of the day. I lingered under the covered area of the courtyard, dreading my long walk back to the inn. So, I took my time. I sat on a bench and wrote in my journal, jotting down more ideas for spells and potions. I pulled out *Persuasion* and read some more.

It wasn't just a ruse for Vince. I *did* enjoy the classics. I just rarely had time to read them.

The best con was the one that kept close to the truth.

Most of the students had already left by the time the rain faded to a drizzle. I packed my bag and made for the parking lot—and then stopped, my eyes drawn to the building down the sidewalk.

A lone figure leaned against the brick wall, his gaze hard and his eyes distant. He wore a burgundy jacket. His clothes were sopping wet again, but he seemed oblivious to this.

A lump formed in my throat. This was a good opportunity. How could I pass it up?

Inexplicably, anxiety filled my chest, making me hesitate. I hadn't planned for this. I'd planned to go back to my room and cook up more potions. Maybe research more about this girl in Vince's life.

But here he was. Alone. It was the perfect opportunity for me to get him to open up.

I took in a deep breath and strode purposefully toward him. His eyes met mine almost instantly, as if he'd been waiting for me to spot him. Waiting for me to join him.

Had he?

"You were quiet in Chemistry," I said, setting my bag down beside his.

"So were you." Vince lifted his chin.

"I didn't want to interrupt your brooding," I said with a smirk.

He rolled his eyes. "I was *not* brooding."

"Oh, of course not. You were just doing this." I leaned against the brick wall, mimicking his stance by crossing my arms. My eyebrows lowered as I stared moodily at the same spot he'd been looking at. My jaw hardened, and my lips stuck out in a pouty frown.

Vince dropped his arms and scoffed, but his eyes shone with amusement. "That is *not* what I look like."

I lowered my eyebrows even more, glaring fiercely in the distance. I ticked my jaw forward and flared my nostrils.

Vince laughed and shoved my shoulder lightly. "You look like a stoner."

I laughed too. "Yeah, because I'm copying *you*. What does that say about you?"

Vince said nothing, but his expression was softer, and his eyes still crinkled with his fading smile.

"But seriously, what are you brooding about?" I asked, relaxing my posture.

Vince glanced at me briefly before dropping his gaze. "Nothing."

"Liar."

Vince shook his head, then eyed me suspiciously. "I'll make a deal with you. I'll answer your question, if you answer the one I asked this morning."

"What question was that?" But I knew. He wanted to know if I was a dark witch. A demon.

"Are you dark or light?"

I hesitated for a long moment. I told myself I only paused to make him squirm, but truthfully, something inside me swirled with anxiety. Would he close himself off if he knew?

But no. This was my plan. He *had* to know. Surely, if I opened up to him, he would eventually open up to me.

I lifted my chin. "Dark."

Vince stared at me. Then, his expression smoothed into an unreadable mask, and he looked away. "I see."

"Does that bother you?"

Vince rubbed the back of his neck. "I—I don't know, to be honest. I've never met a demon before." He flinched, like he hadn't meant to say that.

"Really?" I straightened. "Well, we aren't all bad, you know. Not all of us crave human flesh." I laughed wryly, but Vince's expression remained grim.

"So, you're part of a demon coven then?"

My smile faded. "Yeah. Only witches and warlocks."

Except for Benny—the lone werewolf—this was true, and it was how I preferred it. Nothing against vampires and werewolves. I just didn't fancy being around creatures who feasted on humans.

Vince frowned and nodded, his expression distant. "And your dad . . .?"

"He works for the Council." That had been my cover story, and it worked, now that I knew Vince didn't know any demons. He couldn't exactly check my story if he wasn't associating with anyone outside of his clan.

"I figured."

Only because I let you think that, I thought smugly. "Your turn."

His gaze flicked to me. Something changed in his eyes. All humor from earlier had vanished. His gaze seemed colder. More solemn. "My turn?"

"What were you thinking about?"

Vince exhaled and dropped his gaze. His jaw ticked back and forth as he no doubt contemplated whether to share this information with me.

I lifted my hands. "It's okay if you don't want to tell me. I'm still a stranger, and, well, now you know I'm a vicious *demon*, so . . ."

"I never said that," he said.

"You didn't have to. It's written all over your face."

A tense silence passed between us. I forced a dejected expression on my face and wouldn't meet his gaze, but the truth was, I was challenging him. Would he defy the ideals that had been ingrained in him since birth and open up to me? Or would he shut me out and prove my point?

At long last, he said quietly, "I was testing out my powers."

My mind sparked with interest. "Nephilim powers?"

"No. My warlock powers."

My eyebrows lifted. "I thought you were Nephilim."

"I'm both. My father was a Jumper."

"Was?"

"He gave up his powers to live with the clan. It's a rule. When you come of age, you have to pledge fealty to the clan and swear off all other brands of magic."

"And what if you don't?"

His face hardened. "You're banished."

His eyes were so grim and his expression so full of tension that I burst out laughing. I couldn't help it.

He glared at me. "Why is that funny?"

"I'm sorry. It's really not. It's just, you say that as if you'll be *executed* or something. But . . . you'll only have to leave. Just find a light coven to join! It's not hard."

"It isn't that simple."

"Why not?"

"Because—"

A low growl interrupted our conversation. I held up a hand to silence Vince, but he'd already stiffened, his eyes widening in alarm. Slowly, we both turned toward the sound.

A large creature lingered in the shadows next to the building behind us. The faint smell of wet dog tickled my nose.

Dammit. A werewolf.

I grabbed Vince's arm. "Get behind me."

"Why? What is that thing?"

"A wolf. Now *get behind me.*"

I stared at the wolf, whose yellow eyes gleamed in the shadows. *I'll be damned if this thing kills Vince,* I thought. *That's* my *job.*

My eyes flicked over the empty courtyard. Only a few cars remained in the parking lot, but they no doubt belonged to the students staying for practice.

Vince and I were alone out here.

"He won't," I whispered to Vince, stretching out my arms to block him from the wolf's view. "He won't attack in broad daylight."

"Are you sure?"

I wasn't sure, but I said nothing.

The wolf growled again. His teeth glinted against a mass of dark fur.

I didn't move. I kept my arms outstretched, my gaze still glued to the wolf. My mind scrambled to come up with a solution if the wolf *did* advance. I had no silver, so if I wanted to kill it, I would have to banish it.

Which would require me to use my magic and reveal who I really was.

I was all for opening up to Vince, but not about *that*.

"What are you doing?" Vince asked in bewilderment. I glanced at him and found him eyeing my outstretched arms like I was crazy. He must've just realized I was trying to shield him.

"Are you a Demonhunter?" I snapped.

"No, but I'm not completely helpless."

Yeah, right. "Just stay behind me."

Vince started to argue, but then the wolf moved. Thrashing and twitching, the wolf shuddered violently before he shifted to his human form.

Or rather, *her* human form.

I hadn't met many female wolves. Most werewolves refused to bite women because they tasted blander than men. Any females who *did* Turn were often beaten or enslaved by the alpha.

It was disgusting.

I found my arms relaxing by my sides as the woman approached us. Her eyes still gleamed yellow. Her skin was brown, darker than Vince's, and her black hair cascaded around her in wild curls.

"What do you want?" I said sharply. Though my hands were by my side, my body was stiff and ready for battle. All I had was the small knife in my boot, but I knew I could take her down.

Not without silver, a nagging voice said in my head.

But I shoved the thought away. Maybe if I bested her, she'd give up and flee.

The woman cocked her head at me, her eyes glinting with hunger. "I want *you.* Bloodcaster."

CHAPTER 12

VINCE

I STARED AT THE STRANGE WOMAN, MY BROW furrowing. What was a *Bloodcaster*?

But Cora stiffened in front of me. Whatever it was, she knew.

"There's no Bloodcaster here," Cora said, her voice soft and dangerous. Her right hand flexed toward the ground.

The wolf woman chuckled, shaking her head. "Don't lie to me. I could smell you from a mile away."

Cora cursed under her breath. "Then, what are you waiting for? Go ahead and take me."

My eyes widened as she raised her hands in surrender. What the hell was she doing?

The woman's eyes narrowed. "I wanted to give you a chance to come quietly. Your friend there doesn't look like he'd be up for a fight."

My cheeks burned, and I glared at the woman. "Try me," I growled. A faint tickling sensation prickled along my shoulder blades.

For a long, tense moment, the three of us stared at each other. The woman's gleaming eyes flitted from me to Cora. Cora didn't move a muscle. Her body was arched forward, her fingers still flexed downward.

"So, you will *not* come quietly?" the woman asked softly.

"Not a chance in hell," Cora said.

In a flash, the woman shifted to her wolf form and leapt for Cora. Cora ducked down, dragging me with her, and the wolf soared over us. Cora reached into her boot and drew a small knife. My blood ran cold. Why did she have that?

"Get out of here, Vince!" Cora shoved me out of the way while she lunged for the wolf, burying her knife into the wolf's fur. The wolf roared, snapping her teeth at Cora, who expertly rolled out of the way to avoid getting bitten. I scrambled to my feet, my arms shaking as I watched the two demons battle.

Yes, *demons*. Cora had admitted it herself. She was a demon.

So why did this wolf want her?

The wolf pounced, pinning Cora to the ground. Cora snatched the wolf's fur and tugged, ripping several chunks free. The wolf howled before leaning in, her snout only inches away from Cora's face.

I had to do something. I couldn't just stand there like a coward.

But my body was frozen with terror. I couldn't move. Couldn't think.

What the hell is wrong with me?

Cora shoved the wolf, rolling them both until Cora was on top. She tugged her knife free and embedded it into the wolf's flesh again. And again.

The wolf's shrill bark burned in my ears. All I could see were her razor-sharp teeth. Her hungry yellow eyes. The murderous gleam in her gaze.

It's not a wolf, I told myself, eyes shut tight. *It's a lacrosse opponent. You just have to get the ball past her. Dodge her.*

In my mind, I was on the field again. The opposing team surrounded me. In the distance were my own team-mates, too far for me to toss the ball to. I had to make my way to them on my own.

My eyes opened, but I still saw the field. Smelled sweat and grass all around me. I could practically feel the comforting grip of the stick in my hand.

Power crackled through me, and I dived forward. The wolf glanced up as I charged. She lifted her mouth to intercept me, but I feinted right, catching her off guard. Her head swiveled around as she searched for me, but I attacked from the other side, wrestling her away from Cora. The wolf and I rolled, and my arms burned from the concrete that tore at my skin. My shoulders started thrumming. Energy pulsed through me.

The wolf's claws tore through my shirt, and white-hot pain erupted in my chest. I cried out, and a blast of white magic exploded from my hands, sending the wolf flying backward.

My Nephilim powers had been awakened. But they wouldn't last long.

I jumped to my feet, ignoring the throbbing in my chest, and strode toward the wolf.

"Vince, *stop!*" Cora cried, rushing forward.

Ignoring her, I stretched my arms, and my giant white wings sprang from my shoulder blades. Feathers sprouted, blocking the sun and casting a shadow on the wolf. A heavy weight settled behind me, threatening to drag me down. I wasn't used to the mass of the wings behind me. But I had to use them.

The wolf froze, and her ears flattened behind her. She stared at me with fear and apprehension.

In another flash of white light, I surged forward, wrapping my arms around the wolf. Gritting my teeth, I flexed my back and shoulder muscles, searching for the feel of my wings behind me. After a few attempts, I found them, and my wings stretched wide. They trembled so violently I felt feathers tickling my arms.

Come on, I thought. Sweat formed on my brow as I strained from the pull of my wings and the weight of the wolf in my arms. She snapped at my jaw, but I clenched her more firmly against my chest before taking off into the sky.

My wings beat wildly behind me as I flew. Wind whipped against my face, stinging my eyes. My shoulders burned with each thrust of my wings. Pain blossomed all over my body.

When I was a hundred feet above the school, I dropped the wolf.

She screamed, a shrill whine that echoed in the parking lot as she fell. She landed with a loud crash in front of Cora, who slammed her knife into the wolf's snout.

The wolf went still.

And I plummeted like a rock. I tried stretching my wings, but they drooped behind me, and I was too weak to work the muscles.

I was falling to my death. My stomach dropped, and weightlessness overcame me.

A burst of purple light burned against my eyes, and my body suddenly froze, suspended in the air. A foreign magic gently guided me down until I stood on the concrete.

Blinking against the eerie violet glow, I found Cora

with her hands stretched toward me. Her fingertips glowed *purple.*

My jaw dropped. Purple magic? But . . . dark magic was *black.* Light magic was blue.

What *was* she?

Cora dropped her hands, panting. A sheen of sweat coated her forehead, and her blue eyes blazed. She stared at me, lifting her chin as if daring me to ask her.

I could only gape at her.

The wolf shifted behind us.

Cora groaned. "Just *die,* you bitch!" She lifted her hands again, this time toward the wolf, and uttered a spell.

"Vile demon of unholy crimes,
I banish you 'til the end of time!"

An ethereal purple glow resonated from her hands, surrounding the wolf. The creature screamed as the light intensified until I had to close my eyes. The ground thrummed, and the wolf vanished, leaving behind a sickly dog smell.

Cora's magic faded, and we stood there, gasping for breath. I stared at the spot on the ground where the wolf had been, but only a few drops of blood remained.

My wings flattened until they shrank inside me, buried beneath my skin. Once their weight was gone, I felt the pressure release from my body. My back and shoulders still ached and the cuts on my chest pulsed with pain, but I felt like I could breathe again.

I turned to Cora. "She was after *you*." The words were an accusation.

Cora's lips pressed together in a thin line. She opened her mouth to respond, but the door to the Fine Arts building burst open. Several students filed out, muttering excitedly.

"I swore I heard something," one of them said loudly.

Cora tugged on my arm, leading me to the shadowy area behind the building where the wolf had first emerged. "Yes," she hissed. "The wolf *was* after me."

"Why?" Anger pulsed through me, but I had no idea why. It wasn't *Cora's* fault that a werewolf attacked us.

Unless . . . it *was* her fault.

"Why did she want you?" I grabbed Cora's shoulders.

"For my blood," Cora said through clenched teeth.

I shook my head, not comprehending her meaning.

With a sigh, Cora rolled up the bottom of her shirt to reveal a long gash over her belly.

But instead of oozing crimson blood, a dark purple liquid surrounded the injury. The same color as Cora's magic.

My mouth fell open. *Her blood is purple?* "I—I don't understand."

"I'm a Bloodcaster," she whispered. "Otherwise

known as a blood witch. I'm not light or dark. That's why I can banish demons."

Now that I thought about it, that *had* been weird. Everything I'd read said only light witches could cast banishing spells. "That werewolf said she *smelled* you."

Cora rolled her eyes. "Wolves have an impeccable sense of smell. And, if you know what to look for, my scent is easy to track. Not so easy if you don't know about Bloodcasters to begin with. Most people believe we're just a myth."

"Why did that wolf want your blood?"

"A Bloodcaster's blood is rare and powerful. It grants certain . . . abilities."

"What kind of abilities?"

Cora's nostrils flared. "All kinds. Look, I can't answer all your questions right now. We're both injured, and—"

"Vince?"

I turned and found Jocelyn standing there with her backpack. Her gaze flicked from me to Cora, and shock flared in her eyes. I realized my hands were still on Cora's shoulders, and I quickly dropped them.

"What—what are you guys doing?" Jocelyn asked, stepping forward. Her voice was laced with suspicion.

Cora raised her eyebrows at me, and I knew what she was trying to say. *Do we tell her?*

I swallowed. A large crowd had gathered outside and was looking around for the disturbance they'd heard.

Sooner or later, they'd notice Cora and me—and our injuries.

I stepped forward, snatching Jocelyn's arm. "I'll tell you on the way home. Let's get out of here."

Jocelyn cast a bewildered look at Cora before following me to the parking lot. I didn't glance back once.

CHAPTER 13

CORA

I DREAMED OF VINCE THAT NIGHT. HIS WHITE WINGS were outstretched behind him, massive and magnificent. His entire face glowed. His gray eyes were like sharpened steel ready to slice right through me.

I'd always envisioned Nephilim to be frail, wispy angels—almost like fairies.

But in my vision, Vince was no angel of mercy. He was an angel of vengeance.

His eyes blazed, and his face burned with fury and might. Just the sight of him made me tremble.

Then, with a soft *pop*, he appeared right in front of me, close enough for me to smell his mint and woodsmoke scent.

"Come with me," he murmured, his voice burning like the sound of a thousand whispers. He took my hand. His fingers were warm and soft.

I jerked awake, gasping for breath. I pressed a hand to my chest, trying to calm my racing heart. In my mind, I still saw Vince and his wings. Just the thought sent my heart skittering again.

Get a grip, Cora.

I'd known this would happen. The elixir I'd taken would momentarily give me visions of the future. Visions of Vince.

But I didn't like how unsettled I was after the vision. My brain felt like mush. I rolled over to my left side, pressing my face against the soft pillow and trying to relax and go back to sleep.

The one consolation to my disorienting dream was that Vince was probably dreaming of me too.

Vince arrived at school with Jocelyn. I sat in the courtyard, obscured by shadows as I watched for his arrival. He greeted Luke in the parking lot, and the three of them walked together.

I tried not to let the sight of Jocelyn next to him bother me.

But if they were riding together, surely that meant they were dating, right? I had no idea the rules of relationships these days.

I squinted, staring hard at the three of them as they

drew closer. Jocelyn and Vince weren't holding hands. At least that was something.

Why did that make me feel relieved?

I was up against the wall, hidden from view. I'd expected the three of them to pass me by.

But once they reached the courtyard, Vince's steely gaze settled on me immediately. Like his eyes were drawn to me.

My heart lurched. I felt locked onto his stare, and I couldn't look away.

It wasn't a soft, affectionate stare. His eyes were hard, and his expression taut. The look he gave me was almost accusatory.

I didn't blame him.

"I'll catch up with you guys in a sec," Vince muttered. Luke nodded at me, wiggling his eyebrows. Jocelyn lingered a moment longer, her eyes hopeful as if Vince might change his mind.

Oh yeah. She was smitten.

Vince strode toward me, and Luke and Jocelyn continued walking. I put my book in my bag and stood to greet him. He crossed his arms, his expression closing. Revealing nothing.

"Hi," I said lamely after a solid minute of silence.

"Hi."

More silence. Why'd he come up to me if he wasn't going to speak?

I took a breath. "You all right? Your injury—"

"I'm fine," he said sharply. I noted how he didn't ask after *my* injury, though I'd patched it up easily.

"Why are you here?" he demanded.

I frowned. "What do you mean?"

"I mean, why are you *here*? In Ravenbrooke? If your blood is so valuable, shouldn't you be holed up in some bunker for protection?"

I smirked. "That's hardly a way to live one's life, wouldn't you agree?"

"Not when your *life* affects the lives of the people around you." His eyes flashed.

Guilt swelled within me. "Look, I'm sorry. I didn't know they would find me here. And most demons wouldn't dare attack during the daytime. That rarely happens."

"But it *does* happen, doesn't it?"

I didn't answer.

"How could you do this, Cora? How could you threaten the lives of everyone in this school by being here?"

"I could ask you the same thing," I snapped, leaning closer. Fury boiled through me. I'd had enough of his accusations. "You know what I've heard? Your powers are uncontrollable. You do strange things at school, things people remember and whisper about. Maybe *you* should be locked in a bunker for the rest of *your* life."

Vince's nostrils flared and his jaw hardened. "That's not the same thing."

"Really." I crossed my arms and glared at him. "So, your clan is perfectly fine with you Jumping for all the world to see?"

Vince's mouth snapped shut, and he clenched his teeth. He made no response.

"I thought so. Save your self-righteous judgment and leave me the hell alone."

I strode away from him, but he caught my arm. Something roared within me, and I'd snatched my knife from my boot before I realized it.

Vince's eyes widened, and he released my arm, backing up a step. "Easy."

"Don't touch me again," I hissed before putting my knife back. I meant to turn away, but something in his eyes held me there. It wasn't fear or bewilderment.

It was respect. His mouth curved upward slightly, and his eyes glinted. He was impressed.

I lifted my chin. "I've learned to defend myself. I had to. My whole life, I've been hunted."

"I can't imagine what that's been like," he said softly.

Something between us had changed in the split second when I'd drawn my blade. His eyes were softer, and though there was a grimness to his face, there was also understanding. Something that cooled the fury within me.

"So, what are you doing here?" he asked again. This time the question was gentler. He seemed to ask out of concern.

I swallowed. My mouth felt dry. I stared at him for a long moment before I whispered the truth. "Trying to make a new life for myself."

While I wasn't looking to make a new life in Ravenbrooke, I *was* hoping to detach myself from Damien's clutches. I'd lived under his thumb for far too long.

Vince nodded. "I envy that."

"Don't." I laughed. "Someone tries to kill me every day. It sucks."

Vince laughed too, his eyes crinkling in that endearing way that made my chest feel light.

"What about you?" I asked, leaning comfortably against the brick wall. "Why are *you* here?"

Vince's face sobered. He knew I wasn't just looking for the obvious answer. "I have . . . nowhere else to go," he said softly. "The clan is my mother's family. It's all I have left of her."

I cocked my head at him. "That's not true. There's *you*. You're the greatest legacy she could leave behind."

Vince's eyes warmed. "Thank you. But it's not just me I worry about. It's my dad. He gave up everything to live among her people. Now, if he leaves, he'll be powerless."

"Not powerless. Just a mortal."

"To warlocks, that's the same thing."

"Would that really be so bad?" I asked, gazing wistfully toward the parking lot. If I didn't have magic, I wouldn't constantly be hunted. I could live freely. My skill with the blade meant I could always defend myself.

"Dad's lived around magic his whole life. I can't imagine cutting him off from all of that. It would turn his world upside down."

"Change is hard," I said quietly. "But we can't always avoid it."

"What would *you* do?" Vince asked, his tone sharpening. "If you could choose a life where you could live freely—but it meant your parents had to suffer for it—would you do it?"

I opened my mouth to tell him my parents were dead and then froze. The words had been on the tip of my tongue. It felt easy. Natural. To just confide in him like this.

Shock rippled over me, and I straightened. I wasn't talking with a friend right now. I was manipulating my mark.

How had I forgotten that?

"Yes," I said stiffly. "I would do it. My parents lived their lives and made their choices. If I spend my whole life making choices based on *their* lives, I'd never live my own life."

Vince's brows creased, but he said nothing. I could tell he disagreed with me.

Lightly, I said, "I had a dream about you last night."

Vince stiffened, his eyes snapping to me. "You did?"

I nodded and dropped my gaze, pretending to be bashful. "You had your wings out. And you were magnificent." I couldn't hide the awe in my voice.

Vince's mouth opened and closed. His cheeks reddened. He cleared his throat. "Actually, I dreamed of you too."

I blinked, my eyebrows lifting. "Really?" I wasn't surprised . . . but I *was* deeply curious. "What was it like?"

"You were in New York City. In the middle of a gruesome battle."

My stomach dropped. Numbness swept over me. My heart twisted, and I struggled to keep my voice even. "Was I winning?"

"You weren't fighting. You were just . . . watching."

I stared at him. What did that mean? In what world would I just stand by and *watch* other people fight?

Vince read the confusion in my face and chuckled. "It's just a dream, Cora."

That's what you think. It had been risky sharing the elixir with him. But it was the only way to ensure our visions were synced. If I'd just drunk it myself, I would've had visions of everything. Nothing concrete.

"Right," I said, shaking my head and smiling. "It's just odd, that's all."

"That we're dreaming about each other?" Vince's voice was low and a bit husky. It made my stomach clench.

"Yes," I murmured, though that wasn't what I'd meant at all. His eyes looked smoky in the shadows. His gaze pinned me in place, unrelenting.

He's a mark, Cora, a small voice said in my head. *Don't forget that.*

Something snapped within me, and I broke eye contact. "I have to get to my locker." I grabbed my bag and turned away. "Catch you later, Vince."

Ignoring his startled protests, I strode away from him, struggling to regain my composure.

CHAPTER 14

VINCE

"Hey."

I looked up, my face brightening with a smile before I'd registered who it was.

Jocelyn stood in front of me, clutching her flute case. Her other hand gripped the strap of her backpack.

I didn't realize I'd been expecting Cora until my stomach sank with disappointment. I tried not to let it show.

"Hey," I said. "How was practice?"

"Brutal. I'm ready for the weekend." She peered up at me, squinting against the afternoon sun. "Sorry you have to keep waiting for me."

I shrugged. "I don't mind."

"Really?"

I glanced at her. Her blue eyes shone with hope and

admiration. "I'm still worried about the attacker," I admitted. "I want to keep you safe."

I wasn't sure why I said it. But I was wary of the heat in her gaze. I hoped this explanation would set the record straight.

The light in her eyes didn't fade, though. I cleared my throat and looked away as we strode toward the parking lot.

"So, you and Cora were kind of tense this morning." Jocelyn's voice sounded too forced.

"Yeah. We, uh, had a disagreement yesterday." *That was an understatement.* I frowned. "Hey, did you . . . notice anything weird about Cora?"

"Weird like what?"

I shook my head, not wanting to reveal too much. "Nothing. I don't know."

"She did smell different."

I said nothing. My heart lodged itself in my throat.

"Like . . . flowery. It reminded me of a light witch I met years ago."

"You think she's a witch?" I said too quickly.

Jocelyn looked at me. "I have no idea. *You're* the one who's gotten cozy with her. You tell me." Her tone was biting.

I pressed my lips together. "Joss—"

"I'm sorry," she said quickly. "That was unfair."

An awkward silence fell between us. We finally

reached my car and got in. I glanced at Jocelyn before starting the car, but she wouldn't look at me.

I drove to her house and parked in the driveway, but she didn't move. She sighed heavily, her gaze fixed on the garage door in front of us.

"Vince," she said quietly. "Are you going to leave the clan?"

The question startled me so much my head whipped in her direction. "What?"

"We only have a few months left. And I know you've been undecided about it."

I gaped at her. Sadness and uncertainty stirred in her eyes. I didn't know what to say.

"You can tell me," she added. "I won't say anything to my dad."

"I didn't think you would."

The corners of her mouth lifted in the smallest of smiles.

"I don't know," I said honestly. "It's a tough decision."

"What's tough about it? This is your family. You have a home here."

I shook my head. "It doesn't feel like a home." The words were out before I realized what I was saying.

Jocelyn's head reared back. "How can you say that? This clan practically raised you!"

"No, they *tolerated* me," I snapped. "They don't give a damn about me or my dad. We're barely getting by. Dad gave up *everything* to live here, and now he's swimming in debt and working a job that demands too much of him." My nostrils flared, and I dropped my gaze. "The only reason I'm undecided is because he might be worse off if we left."

I didn't look at her, but I felt her stunned gaze on me. She swallowed. "So . . . if it was *just* you . . ."

"I'd be out of here in a heartbeat."

"Vince." Jocelyn's tone was shocked. Defensive. Bewildered.

I groaned, realizing I was taking this out on her. It wasn't *her* fault. "I'm sorry. I don't mean to lash out at you." I rubbed my face with my hands. "It's just—if my mom were alive, she'd be ashamed of how we've been treated."

"Oh, come on," Jocelyn said with a hint of incredulity. "Your life can't be *that* terrible."

I stared at her, this girl I'd known for years—but hadn't *really* known. We were neighbors, sure. But not friends. She knew as little about my life as I knew about hers.

But one thing I *did* know—as the daughter of a high-ranking clan official, she certainly wasn't poor.

She had no idea what it was like.

"Have you really not noticed Hector's snide comments to me?" I said. "How the other Nephilim avoid hanging out with me? How the clan looks down on my dad because he has no magic? Spend one day with us —spend just an hour with my dad at work—and you would understand." The words sounded harsh to my ears, but my blood was boiling from her offhanded remark, the way she casually dismissed my complaints as if *I* weren't seeing things clearly. These people—my *family*—treated my dad like garbage. Treated *me* like garbage just because I was part warlock.

Jocelyn's cheeks flushed, her eyes flashing with indignation. I hadn't meant my comment to sound like an accusation.

But that's what it was.

Jocelyn's mouth pressed into a thin line. She swung open the door. "See you later, Vince," she said stiffly before slamming it shut.

My hands were slick with sweat as I swung my crosse, lobbing the ball toward Luke across the field. He dived to catch it, then righted himself as he swung his stick toward the goal. The ball soared neatly inside.

Luke whooped and grinned at me. "Nicely played. I almost didn't catch that one."

I forced a smile. Playing one-on-one was nothing like playing the real game. Hardly any strategy.

It was Saturday morning, and the chilly air whispered

against my skin. In the distance, families enjoyed picnics and kids ran around in pure bliss.

It really was a perfect day. I just wasn't feeling it.

Luke's smile faded as he sensed my apathy. Dropping his stick, he strode toward me. "Clan stuff again?" he asked.

"Sort of." So much had been on my mind. The Ceremonial Rite. The attack on Cora. Jocelyn's anger.

And with each passing day, something nagged the back of my mind: Jocelyn and I had resumed our routine, just like Hector had ordered. It had been a week since the incident at the library.

But the attacker had vanished.

Why? Hector had been certain they would try again. That the assailant would be caught.

Hector had also assured us we would be well protected. But I hadn't seen any clan members at school. Where had they been when the werewolf attacked?

Something wasn't right.

"So, tell me," Luke said, his tone brightening. "If you had to pick—Jocelyn or Cora?"

I raised an eyebrow. "Pick for *what*?"

Luke wiggled his eyebrows suggestively.

I grimaced in disgust. "Come on, dude."

"Seriously!"

I sighed, then made a face again. "Cora. Hands down.

Joss is like a sister to me. Or . . . like a cousin I don't see very often."

"Does *she* know that?"

After our argument, Jocelyn probably wasn't too fond of me. Instead of answering, I said, "What about *you?*"

Luke rubbed his chin in contemplation, his eyes glinting. "Cora's sexy, but she's intimidating. I'd pick Joss."

My eyebrows lifted. "Really?"

"Really. I dig redheads." He grinned wolfishly.

I shoved his arm. "You're such an ass."

Luke laughed. His eyes fixed on something over my shoulder. "Hey, speak of the devil."

I cringed inwardly, expecting to turn and find Jocelyn standing there. But as I glanced over my shoulder, surprise and—oddly, excitement—wriggled through me.

It was Cora.

She sat reading at a picnic table, one leg crossed over another. She slouched comfortably, as if she'd been there for hours.

But I knew she hadn't. I would've noticed.

"You don't think she heard . . ." Luke said nervously.

I chuckled. "Nah, she's too far away." *I hope.* She *did* say her blood gave her certain abilities, but I wasn't exactly sure what that meant.

Luke clapped me on the shoulder. "I'll, uh, leave you two alone."

My face burned, and I shoved him again. "Come on,

man, you can stick around. She doesn't bite." I almost laughed and thought, *No, but she does stab . . .*

"Vince." Luke's face was suddenly serious. "She's here for *you*."

I was about to object, but when I glanced at Cora again, her gaze was on me. She lifted a hand and waved. I grinned and waved back.

Luke snorted and raised his eyebrows. "Don't let her cast a spell on you."

I lightheartedly slapped him on the back, and he walked toward the parking lot. Suddenly nervous, I cleared my throat and crossed the field to where Cora sat with her book on her lap.

"You following me?" I asked, sitting down beside her.

Cora wrinkled her nose. "You stink."

I laughed and leaned closer. "What was that? Couldn't hear you."

Cora laughed and elbowed me in the gut. She eyed my crosse. "You play . . . cricket? Rugby?"

I raised an eyebrow. "Very funny."

Cora grimaced apologetically. "I don't know sports."

"It's lacrosse."

"Right. That was my next guess."

I grinned. "You should play sometime."

Cora chuckled without humor. "Yeah, right."

"Seriously. I'll teach you."

Cora shook her head. "Books are more my thing."

"Then, why are you here?"

Her icy blue eyes met mine, glinting like diamonds. "I enjoy reading outdoors."

I gazed around the park. The grass was a stark green against the pale blue sky. Not a cloud was in sight. "Yeah, I can understand that."

Cora smirked. "You should try it sometime."

"What . . . reading?"

"Seriously. I'll teach you." A slow grin spread across her face.

I burst out laughing, and Cora's eyes danced with amusement. Her features were usually so sharp. So cold. But when she smiled, she looked young and carefree. Not like the hunted witch I knew her to be.

It was weird to think that just yesterday morning, she'd threatened me with a knife.

As my smile faded, I glanced around to ensure no one could overhear us. Then, I leaned close and asked, "So, now that we aren't bleeding or under attack or anything . . . can you tell me what's so special about your blood?"

Cora's lips pinched with her smile, but her eyes tightened. She dropped her gaze to her book, but I knew she wasn't really looking at it. She ran a finger along the edge of the cover. "I'll answer your question if you answer mine first."

"What question?"

"Right before the werewolf attacked us, you said you were testing out your warlock powers." She leveled a gaze at me, her eyes contemplative. "What exactly were you trying to do?"

My heart rate quickened. How did she know to ask that question? "I was Jumping," I said quickly.

Cora shook her head. "It was more than just that. I saw the look on your face."

I chewed on the inside of my lip, considering how to respond. I hadn't told anyone about my new power except Dad. "How do you know? I'm pretty terrible with my powers, if you haven't noticed. You said it yourself that I Jump uncontrollably during lacrosse games. Maybe I was trying to master it."

Cora straightened. "Were you?"

I looked at her. Her gaze challenged mine. And for some ridiculous reason, I found I couldn't lie to her face. "No," I admitted. "I was . . . testing out a new power."

Cora's eyebrows lifted, her eyes sparkling with interest. "Really? What kind of power?"

I hesitated. "I don't feel like I should tell you. It's dangerous." I remembered my dad's warning. *We do not use our powers to alter the way the world works. Doing so will make you some powerful enemies. And they won't just come after you.*

Cora's mouth spread into a thin line. A gust of wind tousled her black hair so it swirled around her face, contrasting against the brightness of her eyes. "When my blood is used in potions, it grants the caster new abilities."

I stared at her. "What kind of abilities?"

Her eyes locked onto mine, and a grimness settled on her face. "*All* kinds of abilities. Seeing, Jumping, Pushing, clairvoyance, camouflage. Anything from a simple charm to repel rain to Teleporting across the continent."

My eyes widened, and my blood ran cold. "You—you can *Jump*? Like me?"

Cora shook her head. "The potions are temporary. It's only good for one or two occurrences, if it's potent enough."

Disappointment sank in my stomach, though I wasn't sure why. As I searched within myself, I realized I was hoping she *could* Jump all the time like me. Then, she could teach me how to do it right. "Does—does it work for everyone? Or just you?"

"If the potions are done right, it works for everyone. It's why I'm constantly being hunted. If I were enslaved, I would provide an endless supply of the most powerful blood in the world."

An image of Cora chained and starving in someone's basement flashed through my eyes, and I shuddered. "Is there any way to change it?"

Her brow furrowed. "Change who I am?"

I felt silly, but I nodded.

Cora smiled wryly. "I wish. But it's about as likely as you being able to change being a Jumper."

I winced.

"What is it?"

"Funny you should mention that . . ."

Cora's eyes widened with realization. She laughed. "Oh, right. I guess you *could* change that with your clan. Have you decided?"

I shook my head.

Cora set her book down on the table and drew her legs to her chest, propping her chin on her knees. "Have you talked to your dad about it? If he knew you were planning on giving up everything for him . . ."

"That's not the only thing. If—if I leave the clan, I'll become a Reaper."

She cocked her head. "A Reaper? Like, the Grim Reaper?"

"I don't know. All I know is Reapers are more susceptible to dark magic. They can't access light magic like other light casters can."

"Are you saying you wouldn't be a light warlock anymore?"

"I'm saying I might not be a warlock *at all*. No one's met a Reaper before. They just . . . vanish. For all I know, the separation from Nephilim magic is so painful that it kills them." My gaze flicked to her before dropping again. "Have you ever met a Reaper?"

"No."

My heart dropped. If Reapers used dark magic, why wouldn't other demons know about them? Unless my fears were right and Reapers *did* die after leaving their clan . . .

"I can ask around for you. If you like."

I looked at her. Her eyes softened, and she offered a small smile. "Thank you," I said quietly.

Our gazes held for a long moment as if pulled by some magnetic force. Something tangible churned between us, linking us together and blocking out our surroundings. There was no park. There was no picnic table. Just the two of us and the strange heat between us. Cora's lips parted, and my eyes were drawn to them. I found myself wondering what they would feel like. Would they be soft like velvet? Smooth like flower petals? If I ran my thumb along her lower lip, what would it feel like?

What would it taste like?

I leaned in. The smell of lilacs filled my nose.

Cora's eyelashes fluttered. She sucked in a breath. "It's your turn," she whispered.

"For what?" My voice caught in my throat.

"Tell me about your new power."

I drew away from her. Embarrassment burned in my face. Of course she hadn't been thinking about me like that. She'd opened up to me and shared her secrets. Now it was my turn.

We were having a friendly conversation. Nothing more.

Besides, like she said—I smelled awful.

I swallowed as a lump formed in my throat. I rubbed the back of my neck and stared at the field where Luke and I had been playing. "Right. Sorry." I took a breath, trying to steady my nerves. "I, um . . . Lilith, this is gonna sound crazy."

"You can tell me."

I licked my lips and nodded. "I may have found a way to . . . time travel."

CHAPTER 15

CORA

I STIFFENED. MY BREATH HITCHED. "*WHAT?*"

Vince grimaced. "I know it sounds insane. I was just trying to Jump like normal, and . . . I found myself transported to like half an hour earlier in the exact same spot."

"So there were two of you? In the same place?"

Vince nodded.

My entire body went still. Even my heart seemed to pause for a full beat. *This is it. This is what I'm here for.* My throat felt dry as I whispered, "How did you do it?"

"I don't know."

Anger and disappointment swirled in my chest. "How do you not know?" I tried to keep my voice level, but it still sounded like an accusation.

Vince shrugged one shoulder. "I told you. I'm terrible

with my powers. Half the time when I use them it's by accident."

"That wasn't how it seemed with the werewolf. You used your wings like it was no big deal. It was *amazing*."

Vince's lips curved in a bashful half-smile. "That was a fluke."

I dropped my legs and leaned toward him. "Okay. Walk me through it. Tell me exactly what happened. Maybe I can help you figure it out."

Vince raised an eyebrow, his expression doubtful, but he sighed. "All right. Um, I was under attack, and I—"

I held up a hand. "Slow down. You were under *attack*?" I tried to sound shocked and appalled, but my heart skittered in my chest. This was an opportunity for me to find out how much he knew.

"Yeah. Some demon surrounded by shadows. I think. Anyway, he attacked me and Jocelyn. I was injured, and I was trying to Jump to her to help, and . . . I time traveled instead."

I shook my head. "More details. Were you sitting? Standing? What exactly were you thinking about? I'm assuming you tried spinning in place like for a normal Jump?" I'd Jumped a few times myself. I knew exactly how it felt.

Vince nodded. "My body was numb with pain. I couldn't see straight. I had to hold on to the bookshelf for support."

I frowned. "You were holding the shelf when you Jumped?"

"Yeah, why?"

"I just—everything I've heard is that if you're holding something when you Jump, it travels with you. Did you take the shelf with you?"

"No, I . . ." He trailed off, his eyes growing distant. "I didn't Jump." His voice was barely above a whisper. "I stayed in the same place. By the shelf."

I blinked, my head spinning with this information. *He held an object that didn't travel with him. But he didn't Jump at all—because he was holding the object?* But if that were the case, then anytime someone tried to Jump while holding an object, it wouldn't work. They would just time travel instead.

Something else was missing.

"Show me," I said.

Vince's gaze snapped to me. "What?"

I gestured to the grass on the ground. "Show me what you did. Right here."

Vince chuckled nervously and glanced around the park. "I'm not just going to use my powers out in the open, Cora."

"Come on. There's no one around."

Vince pointed over my shoulder. I followed his gaze and found a family having a picnic about fifty yards away.

I rolled my eyes. "They won't see anything. Even if they *were* looking this way, by the time they realize you're doing anything weird, you'll have disappeared. Come on, Vince. Let me help you."

Vince's jaw ticked back and forth as he contemplated. Conflict warred in his eyes.

"Worst-case scenario, you'll spin in place and look like a moron."

Vince snorted, covering his mouth with his hand. I grinned too.

"All right, you win." Vince's cheeks were pink as if he was nervous. But he rose to his feet and rubbed his hands together.

"Grab onto the picnic table," I suggested.

Vince shot me a bewildered look, but he obeyed. He curled the fingers of his left hand around the edge of the table. After several deep breaths, he spun in place.

Nothing happened.

"Try again," I urged.

Vince's face was even redder now. He spun again. Still, nothing happened.

Struggling to keep my frustration at bay, I said, "What exactly were you thinking about when you did it last time?"

Vince shook his head, his brows creasing. "I—I don't know!" he sputtered. "I was injured. I was focused on trying to save Jocelyn before she got hurt. I—I was *terrified*."

"Adrenaline," I said, nodding. "Can you replicate the feeling?"

"Can I *replicate* adrenaline?" he asked in a flat voice.

I looked at him with a deadpan expression. "Can you get your heart racing? Make your body feel like you're experiencing that fear, that rush?"

"Rush," he said quietly.

"Yeah."

Vince's eyes were unfocused as he stared at something I couldn't see. He blinked, and his gaze shifted to me. "Like during a lacrosse game?"

My mouth opened and closed. "I . . . guess?"

"That's how I used my Nephilim powers against the wolf," he said, his eyes alight with excitement. "I imagined myself in the middle of a lacrosse game. No fear. Just the thrill of the game. The itch to maneuver and strategize. To *win*."

I watched him for a long moment. A slow smile had spread across his face, and I knew he had transported himself there now. For one odd moment, I found myself wishing I could see him play.

I bet he was incredible.

"That makes sense," I said. "I feel the same way when . . . when I'm sparring."

I'd almost said, *When I'm hunting down my next victim.*

Stupid Cora. I had to remember why I was here.

Vince was a mark. Not a friend.

I smoothed my expression and looked at him, trying not to see the pinch of his eyebrows or the glint of his steely eyes. The slight curve downward of his mouth as he concentrated. The taut muscles in his arms. The bronze tone of his skin. The windswept dark brown hair that looked tousled and distractingly sexy.

I dropped my gaze, my heart lodging itself in my throat. This was *not* good.

"I'll try one more time," Vince said. I could hear the grin in his voice even without looking at him.

"Okay." I crossed my arms and stared at his feet planted in the grass. I suppressed a grimace and forced my gaze upward. No matter how unsettling it was to look at Vince, no matter what I was starting to feel for him, I had to remember the mission.

To find out how he used this power. I wouldn't get that information by staring at his feet the whole time.

Clenching my teeth, I watched Vince, whose eyes were closed. His brows pulled together in determination, but his jaw relaxed, and half his mouth quirked upward. His expression was calm. Confident.

He gripped the edge of the picnic table once more. Something crackled in the air, and I stiffened. The wind itself seemed to stop. A whiff of ash tickled my nose, mingling with something new. I inhaled deeply. It smelled like citrus.

Vince spun in place, still gripping the table.

Then, he vanished.

CHAPTER 16

VINCE

I SMELLED LEMONS. VAGUELY, I REMEMBERED THE SAME smell when I'd time traveled the first time. I'd thought the scent had to do with the attacker.

But now I knew it was a mark of this kind of magic.

My hands were slick with sweat as I gripped the picnic table. Shapes blurred past me like I was driving on the freeway. The edge of the table thrummed against my skin.

I had to let go soon.

My eyes flitted around, trying to make out details as I traveled. But it was like the park was on fast forward and I was the only one remaining still. It almost made me feel nauseous trying to keep up.

I let go, and the world slammed into the present. Gravity hit me hard, and I collapsed. My palms and knees met the cold grass, still moist from morning dew. A shiver swept over me, and I lurched to my feet. Darkness surrounded me. The sun hadn't risen yet. The park was eerily empty. A thick fog hovered in the air, enveloping me like a lurking shadow.

I swallowed, my eyes wide as I glanced around. I rubbed my arms, and my sweaty shirt was suddenly cold against my skin. Had I traveled backward . . . or forward in time? I tried not to get too excited about the prospect of seeing the future.

I squinted as I looked around, trying to take in any details that might give me a clue. Then, I focused on the mist that tickled my skin.

It had been foggy early this morning. I remembered that when I'd gotten in my car to meet Luke.

It *was* possible it would be foggy again tomorrow or the next day. But going back in time was the most likely scenario.

With a deep breath, I strode forward, determination pulsing through me. But as I trudged through the misty grass, my resolve faded.

What was I doing? What *could* I do? I'd been so desperate to succeed this time. So eager to test it out and see what I was capable of. How I could change things like I had with the shadowy attacker.

But here, in the early hours of morning, what could I possibly do? My car wasn't here yet. I'd have to walk home, and it would take hours.

Besides, nothing noteworthy had happened last night. If I'd traveled backward two days, maybe I could've intervened with the werewolf attack. I wracked my brain, trying to think about the days past.

No, I realized as my memories clicked into place. No other days had been foggy. Each morning had been clear when I'd driven to school.

Stupid Vince, I chided. I should've thought this through. Maybe taking Cora with me would've helped.

I shook my head. No. This was my mess. I could get out of it.

I gripped the picnic table again and was about to spin in place when I froze.

The smell of lemons still lingered in the air, growing fainter with each passing minute. If I'd gone backward in time—again—then how was I supposed to go forward? Would I have to wait it out like I had in the library?

My mind raced as I thought through my options. Thinking of lacrosse seemed to spur my magic to action. The rush, the adrenaline, the thrill of it all. How could I manipulate that?

I closed my eyes, trying to ignore the biting cold against my skin. *Lacrosse,* I thought, my brow furrowing as I tried to focus. *You're playing lacrosse.*

For a moment, all I felt was the chill. But then, my mind slid easily into the mold I'd made for lacrosse. Like the sport was a puzzle piece that helped everything else fit into place. I was on the field again, holding my crosse. Luke stood opposite me, tossing the ball my way. Another opponent stood in my way. I lunged, ready to catch it.

Forward, whispered a voice that vibrated through me. *Forward.*

A small part of my consciousness stayed in the park, focusing on the feel of the picnic table in my grasp. I hunched over, leaning toward the ground. I spun again.

This time, I kept my eyes closed. Though I was aware of myself in the park, my mind returned to the imaginary lacrosse field. There I stood, crosse in hand. The familiar adrenaline swept over me. I swung the crosse and zipped between the opponents, catching the ball. When I turned to face one of my teammates, I stiffened.

I'd been expecting to see Luke. But it was *Cora.* Her blue eyes met mine, locking onto me. She held no crosse. She wore the same black shirt and sweater I'd seen her in before I'd Jumped. Her expression slackened in shock.

"Vince," she whispered. Her voice was like a caress against my ears. Even though I knew she wasn't real, that this was all in my head, the sound sent a shiver of pleasure rippling through me.

My shock made me let go of the picnic table. The vision of the lacrosse field vanished. A force barreled into me, knocking me on my rear. The grass felt soft under my legs. The sun shone brightly overhead.

I was back in the park. In the middle of the day.

And in front of me, her back to me, was Cora. She ran her hands through her hair. Then, she straightened and whirled to face me, her eyes wild with fear.

"*Vince!*" She rushed to my side, eyeing me up and down. "Are you hurt? What happened?"

I shook my head, but vertigo disoriented me, keeping me on the ground. I groaned and leaned backward so my head rested on the grass. Even though I remained still, everything spun around me.

Cora swept a lock of hair out of my eyes, her finger-tips smooth against my skin. "Vince." Her voice sounded just as tantalizing as it had been in my imagination.

I cleared my throat. "How—how long was I gone?"

"Five minutes."

A shocked laugh burst from my lips. It sounded more like a wheeze. "I . . . I did it."

Cora went very still, her hand still hovering near my face. "You . . ."

"I time traveled."

She paused. "When?"

"Early this morning. Before sunrise."

"And you—you came back? How?"

I closed my eyes. "I . . . can't explain it. I pictured myself on the lacrosse field again. I envisioned what I wanted to do. Where I wanted to go." *Who I wanted to see.* I almost said the words, but they caught in my throat as I realized how desperately I *had* wanted to see Cora on that lacrosse field. A knot formed in my stomach. My voice tight, I went on, "Then . . . then a voice whispered, *forward*. I kept my mind on the game. When I saw you, I let go."

"You saw . . . me?" Cora whispered.

I opened my eyes to look at her. She was still leaning over me, her face taut with concern, but something else stirred in her eyes. Something that made my stomach coil with desire. "Yes," I said. "When I saw you, I knew."

"Knew what?"

My mouth opened, but I forgot what I was going to say. My tongue felt like sandpaper, and I couldn't speak even if I wanted to.

Cora leaned in. The smell of lilacs overwhelmed me. She pressed her palm against my cheek. Her fingers were warm and soft. Her other hand touched my shoulder. Locks of black hair fell forward, and before I could stop myself, I reached toward her, tucking her hair behind her ears. My fingers lingered on her skin, trailing the length of her jaw. Her breath hitched, and she swallowed. I was acutely aware of my filthy, matted hair and the sweat that had dried, forming a salty layer over my skin. My shirt and shorts were dirty and sweaty.

But Cora didn't seem to mind. Her blue eyes shimmered like diamonds as she leaned in. Her breath tickled my lips. I could almost taste her. My heart drummed against my chest, flustered and eager all at once.

Just as my mouth brushed against hers, Cora stiffened and drew back. She sucked in a sharp breath, closing her eyes. Her lips pressed together, and her brows creased. She withdrew her hands, and a strange coolness swept over me from the absence of her warmth.

"I'm sorry," she said in a choked voice. She rose to her feet and spun away from me, covering her face with her hands.

I stood. Still dizzy, I gripped the table for balance. "Cora—"

"I shouldn't have—I'm sorry," Cora repeated, turning to me, then away again. She fumbled for her bag, her hands shaking as she pulled the strap over her shoulder. "I—I'll see you later, Vince."

She didn't meet my gaze as she strode away from me. All I could do was gape after her, wondering what had—or hadn't—happened between us.

CHAPTER 17

CORA

My stride was forceful and angry as I stomped down the road toward the inn. *You're a fool, Cora Covington,* I told myself.

Was I really nothing more than a flighty girl who always needed to bone someone? First, I fell for Damien, which obviously turned out swell, and now Vince? My *target?*

My fingers itched to grasp my dagger, but then I cursed when I remembered Vince had it. *Of course* he did.

The smart thing to do would be to back off. To give the assignment to someone else.

But I couldn't do that. For one thing, it would mean failure. Damien would out me as a Bloodcaster—and put a target on my back. For another thing, I couldn't stand the idea of someone *else* being tasked with killing Vince.

I didn't really know why. But something in my gut ached and throbbed at the thought.

I *had* to see this through. Even if the idea of killing Vince made my chest tighten so painfully I couldn't breathe.

When I got to my room, I bolted the door and dug through my bag of weapons, trying to decide which one would be most suitable for killing Vince Delgado. I squashed every weak thought and feeling from my mind, focusing only on my task.

Extract information. Kill Vince. Take down Damien.

I was the Blade of Hinport. This was my calling.

I drew a small revolver that I only used for emergencies. As a rule, I hated guns because they were loud and drew too much attention.

But they were effective. Fast. If I stabbed Vince, he might still have the strength to Jump to safety before he bled out.

But a gunshot wound, if aimed precisely, would kill him instantly. And if I had a Teleportation Elixir ready to go, then *I* could Jump away from the scene before anyone came looking.

A small smile flickered across my face. Yes, it was perfect.

Then, my gaze fell on the Poisoned Balm I'd made a few days ago. Uncertainty swelled within me. An echo of the heat I'd felt with Vince threatened to rise in my chest, but I gritted my teeth and shoved it down. I snatched the balm, my hand trembling. Resolve pulsed through me as I dipped my finger into the balm and dabbed it on my lips. A stinging sensation tickled my skin, and for a moment, my mouth felt like it was on fire. But after a while, my lips went numb and I no longer felt it. I knew I was safe—the blood I'd used to make the balm was my own, so if I accidentally ingested it, my blood would negate the effects.

As a contingency plan, I vowed to wear the balm constantly. If I dared to have another moment with Vince, it would kill him.

And if Damien should come knocking, asking to share my bed? Well, that would be an added bonus.

Once I had a plan—and the frustrating and confusing heated emotions had finally abated—I regretted parting with Vince. The weekend was the perfect opportunity to get closer to him, to get more information. And I'd already learned so much.

I'd learned how Vince time traveled.

Per Damien's orders, I could kill Vince now. But I still had further uses for Angel Boy.

I pulled out my laptop and browsed various social media sites. It didn't take me long to track down Vince's cell phone number. The idiot had it posted for the world to see.

After purchasing a burner phone, I used it to text Vince: *Hey, it's Cora. Hope you don't mind, but Luke gave me your number. I just wanted to apologize for wigging out at the park.* I drummed my fingers against the keypad for a moment, debating adding something else. A smiley face? Should I thank him for spending time with me?

When I realized I was playing the lovesick fool again, I chucked my phone into my bag—maybe a little too forcefully.

It didn't take Vince long to text me back. I hated how my heart lurched in my chest when the phone chimed with his response. I snatched it and read his text.

Don't sweat it. I had a good time. Thanks for helping me.

Half my mouth tugged upward in a reluctant smile. Clearing my throat, I thought hard before responding.

Can I make it up to you? Bring you lunch? What's your favorite fast food?

My pulse quickened as I waited for his response, internally begging him to take the bait.

When I saw his response, my heart sank.

Dad's drowning in paperwork, so my house is a mess. I'd love to get out. Meet you at Kelso's?

I frowned and took a minute to look up Kelso's on my laptop. It was a local diner. Figures this stupid town would have a quaint little diner.

As much as I wanted to get closer to Vince's clan, I couldn't be too pushy, or he'd get suspicious. Begrudgingly, I texted, *Sure, meet you there in a bit.*

When I dropped my phone back in my bag, something warm spread through my chest. It mingled strangely with the knots in my stomach and the frantic skittering of my pulse.

After a moment, I realized what it was: I was about to go on a date with Vince. And I was *excited.*

This was *not* good.

I spent the next ten minutes jotting down notes about topics to discuss on our date—purely with my mission in mind. Questions about his family and his clan, expressing a desire to visit his house (subtly, of course), and other ideas. I also researched Jocelyn on social media and found some juicy information I could use to my advantage.

Just before leaving, I glanced at myself in the mirror. I was wearing the same outfit I'd worn at the park. Should I change?

Idiot, I thought to myself. I smoothed back my hair, fixed my bangs, and grabbed my bag before tearing out the door.

Vince was already there when I arrived. A sliver of satisfaction swelled within me at the thought of making him wait. *Make him fret.*

I casually walked in and pretended to look around for

him. He waved at me from a booth, his eyes energetic and his smile infectious. I found myself returning it and inwardly cringed at how eager I was.

"So, what's the best meal here?" I asked as I sat down across from him.

Vince crossed his arms over the table and leaned closer to me. "Definitely the triple bacon cheeseburger. Hands down."

I laughed. "Heart attack, here I come."

"Oh, please. You don't go to a fast food place because you're concerned for your heart."

I smirked. "Fair enough."

When the waitress arrived, Vince ordered two triple bacon cheeseburgers and a coke. I ordered a small coffee, and Vince raised an eyebrow.

"I'm a coffee-holic," I said with a shrug.

Vince grinned and ran a hand through his hair. It was wet and clean, and he smelled of mint and soap. I swallowed down the hot lump that rose in my throat as his scent filled my nose.

A comfortable silence passed between us. A million thoughts crossed my mind, but I held them at bay, knowing this would take time. I couldn't ambush him with everything all at once. Little by little.

"Thanks for reaching out," Vince said, leaning back against his seat. "I felt weird the way we left things."

The way we left things. And how exactly was that? I

cleared my throat and dropped my gaze. "Me too. Sorry . . . again."

"Can I ask . . . Why *did* you wig out like that?"

I peered up at him. He offered a half-smile, and his eyes were timid. But I sensed a burning curiosity in his tone.

I took a deep breath. *The truth is the best con,* I reminded myself. "I, uh, just got out of a nasty relationship. I felt . . . a moment between you and me. It freaked me out, is all. I wasn't ready for . . ." I trailed off, unable to label whatever it was that had passed between us.

Vince grimaced. "Cora, I'm sorry, I didn't mean—"

I raised my hands to stop him. "Don't worry about it. It was my fault too. I—we—" I broke off with a nervous smile. "Let's just pretend it didn't happen."

Vince nodded, though his expression tightened slightly. *Good. Let him fret some more.* "Sure," he said. "No problem."

After the waitress brought our drinks, I said, "You said your dad was drowning in paperwork. What kind of paperwork?" I kept my tone light and stirred some cream in my coffee.

"He's a consultant for the clan. He manages financial transactions and offers legal advice."

My eyebrows lifted. "So, is he a lawyer or an accountant?"

Vince laughed. "Unofficially both. He went to law

school for a bit, then became a CPA, but his license expired. Now he kind of just does consulting work on an unofficial basis."

I smiled. "Whatever pays the bills, right?"

Vince winced, and I knew I'd hit my mark.

"What is it?" I asked. "Did I say something wrong?"

Vince drummed his fingertips on the table, his eyes hardening as he stared into the distance. "Dad doesn't get paid very well. And the fees for living in the clan are pretty steep."

My eyes widened. "There are *fees* for living there?"

"It's for protection." His tone was defensive.

I scoffed. "Where was this *protection* when we got attacked by a werewolf?"

Vince's jaw hardened, and his lips pressed together in a thin line. He knew I was right.

"All magical covens offer protection," I went on. "And you can join them for *free*."

Vince remained silent, but his gaze was pensive.

Time to go in for the kill.

"Seriously, Vince, a coven can take care of you. Especially—" I clamped my mouth shut and dropped my gaze.

"Especially what?" Vince asked.

I shook my head. "Forget it."

"Cora."

With a sigh, I met his gaze. "Especially with

your . . . *new powers*," I said, my voice barely above a whisper.

"What's that got to do with anything?" Vince's eyes were wide with fear.

"Power attracts enemies. Your clan might be equipped to handle your average demon attack, but they're not used to having a warlock living among them. What if someone comes after you? Do you really think your clan will protect you?"

Vince's expression turned stony, and his mouth twisted. The color drained from his face.

Bingo.

The waitress arrived with our burgers, but Vince paid her no notice. I thanked the woman before looking at Vince again. His face now took on a greenish tint.

"Vince?" I asked tentatively.

He swallowed, his brows creasing. "You—you really think someone might come after me?"

"I know a few demons who would."

"But—but how can they hope to take my power? It's not like they can suck it out of me!" His voice bordered on hysteria.

I shot him a dark look. "You'd be surprised what you can do with the right potion."

Vince sat back in his seat, still looking faint.

"Or it could be another Jumper like you," I said

offhandedly. "A dark warlock looking to expand his powers and do what you can."

Vince's gaze slid to me, and I remained perfectly still, keeping my expression smooth.

I waved a hand. "But this is all hypothetical. For now, you're safe, right?" I took a huge bite of my burger and moaned with satisfaction. "You're right, this *is* good," I said, my mouth full.

"Cora—" Vince said hoarsely.

"Look, I'm sorry." I leaned forward to press my hand against his. "I really didn't mean to scare you. But I know demons are an unknown territory for you. I wanted you to be aware of the risks so you can prepare yourself."

"How would you do it?" Vince asked, his tone desperate. "If someone were coming after you, how would you prepare yourself?"

I held his gaze. "I'd kill him before he got the chance."

CHAPTER 18

VINCE

I HARDLY TOUCHED MY FOOD. ALL I COULD THINK about was what Cora said: *I know a few demons who would.*

She was right. My clan *couldn't* protect me.

Especially if it was me the attacker was after. Not Jocelyn.

If Hector knew it was me, I wasn't entirely sure he would do anything about it. He might hand me to the attacker on a silver platter.

But if he believed Jocelyn's life was at stake—and he had hard evidence of the attacker's intent—then maybe he *would* do something.

"What might a demon do with the daughter of a high-ranking Nephilim official?" I blurted after Cora and I had finished our food. "Hypothetically, I mean."

She blinked at me and took a sip of her coffee. After a

lengthy pause, she said slowly, "Lots of things. Ransom, coercion, torture for information . . ."

I shuddered at the thought of someone torturing Jocelyn. "It would be beneficial for a demon, right? Almost as beneficial as coming after me for my powers?"

Her brows knitted together. "I guess. Why do you ask?"

I sighed. She couldn't help me if she didn't know. My voice lowered to a whisper as I hastily filled her in on my suspicions that Jocelyn was being targeted by demons.

"But now you think *you're* the target?" Cora asked, her blue eyes sharpening like ice.

"Possibly," I hedged. "But I can't know for sure. And, like you said, it's also highly probable Jocelyn could be the target. That's what I need to convince Hector."

"Hector?"

"Hector Moses, the clan leader."

Cora snorted. "His last name is Moses?"

I rolled my eyes. "I know. An angel named Moses. I get it. Listen, I may need your help for this."

Cora straightened, her eyes alight. "What can I do?"

"Can you come with me to meet with the clan officials?"

Something unreadable sparked in Cora's eyes. She frowned. "Why would they listen to me?"

"You're familiar with demon ways. You know how to protect yourself against them."

"Yeah, but they won't believe anything I say. They'll think I'm just a demon trying to trick them."

"Maybe. But . . . you don't smell like a normal demon." I grinned. "After all, you fooled *me*."

Cora chewed on her lower lip as she considered this. Then she smiled. "All right. I'll help."

Relief spread through me, and I relaxed in my seat. "Thank you. But first, there's something else I need your help with."

"What's that?"

"Forging evidence."

It was surprisingly easy. Part of me felt uncomfortable that Cora could effortlessly forge files and documents about Jocelyn, but the other part wasn't surprised. She'd had a tough life. A dark past. I couldn't blame her for what she'd learned to do to survive.

We stood in the tiny room at the inn Cora stayed at with her parents. Luckily, they were out. The room was neat and organized, though various weapons were strewn on the desk. Cora quickly shoved them aside and tossed them into a bag before getting to work.

"There." Cora stood back and let me survey her work. I leafed through a file with Jocelyn's report cards, up-close photos of her at school, as well as the terms of the hit.

"Wanted dead or alive?" I whispered, glancing at Cora.

Cora shrugged. "Interrogation, remember?"

I shuddered. Though I knew the documents were falsified, it still felt all too real to me.

And it could've been. I still didn't have proof it was me the attacker had been after.

I squashed my discomfort. This had to be done. It could save Jocelyn's life. Our entire coven was in danger. I had to warn the officials somehow and make them listen. Putting a target on Jocelyn was the only way to do that. The only way that made sense.

Because no one would care if I was targeted. They all thought I had one foot out the door already.

"Are you ready?" I asked Cora.

Her eyes glinted with steely resolve. "Absolutely."

We walked back to the diner where my car was parked. Cars whooshed past us, creating a steady stream of noise to break our awkward silence. My mind was reeling as I considered what to say to Hector. My head throbbed from how often I ground my teeth together.

Cora shifted restlessly next to me as we walked. She crossed her arms. Dropped them again. Rubbed her hands together. Scratched her nose.

Finally, I asked, "Are you nervous or something?"

Her gaze flicked to me. "No. It's just—this is a lot slower than I normally walk."

I raised an eyebrow. "Are you calling me slow?"

"Not at all."

We stared at each other with equally somber expressions. The corners of my lips twitched.

Cora broke first. Her face split into a wide grin, and she burst out laughing. "Yes, Vince. You walk slowly. And it drives me *nuts*."

"Well, we can't all be sprinters like you."

"*You're* the one who plays lacrosse!"

I shoved her arm, and she laughed again. My chest felt lighter as I smiled, reminding me that laughter often eased the tension in my head.

"Can I ask you something?" Cora tucked a strand of hair behind her ear.

"Sure."

"Why Jocelyn?"

Unease spread through me. "What do you mean?"

"Why make this about her and not you? Wouldn't your clan care if *you* were the one being targeted?"

My smile vanished, and the hardness in my chest returned. "No. They wouldn't care."

"Why not?"

"Because my blood is tainted."

Cora's head reared back. "*What?*"

I sighed. "They haven't said as much. But I know they

frown upon my warlock magic. They believe there's nothing more important or holy than Nephilim magic, and blah, blah, blah . . ."

"Sounds a bit . . . racist."

I barked out a laugh. "Yeah. Which is funny because my dad is Latino, so . . ."

Cora snorted, then covered her mouth. "Sorry. I shouldn't laugh."

"It *is* kind of funny."

"So, if they hate you so much, why don't they kick you out?"

"Oh, they want to. But when Nephilim turn eighteen, they pledge themselves to Nephilim magic at an event called the Ceremonial Rite. Once that pledge is made, they're bound to that magic forever—but they've also sealed their life within the clan. After that, they won't be able to kick me out."

Cora was silent for a long moment, but I felt her watching me as we walked. After a while, she said softly, "Is that really what you want? To live this frustrating and degrading life . . . forever?"

I exhaled long and slow. "If it kept my dad safe? Yes."

Cora paused before asking, "What about your mom?"

"What about her?"

"Did she disapprove of your warlock powers?"

The warmth of my mother's smile and laughter, her amazement when I Jumped for the first time, flooded my mind. A soft smile spread across my face. "No. She thought it was incredible. But things were different then."

"How so?"

I bit my lip. "What do you know of the Demon War?"

"New York City. Ten years ago, right?"

"Yeah. Right around the time you left."

Cora's eyes tightened and she grimaced. "Is that how she died?"

I nodded.

"What happened? Were you there?"

"No. I was too young to fight. But Dad was there. He told me that twenty years ago, the demon god Asmodeus was summoned, and a huge battle took place. Ever since then, there's this . . . convergence of dark magic at the battle site every year. It grew stronger and stronger until after ten years, it exploded. The demon covens took advantage of it and struck the light covens hard.

"Mom was the clan leader at the time. She was respected. Feared, even. She led the clan into battle.

"But something happened. A powerful force of demons overtook them, even though the Nephilim had the upper hand. They—they executed my mother on the spot."

Cora sucked in a breath. "I—I'm so sorry, Vince."

A warm lump rose in my throat. My eyes stung, and I

blinked, gazing up at the sun. "Dad told me when they were married, it was celebrated. Back then, the Nephilim sought to forge alliances with other magical beings."

"Like an arranged marriage?"

"Kind of."

"But . . . I mean, did your parents love each other?"

"Not at first. But they were fond of each other. And Dad had no family, so he needed somewhere to go. To keep him safe. The more time they spent together, the more they fell in love. I saw it on their faces every day." I was smiling again, remembering the way Dad gathered Mom in his arms and pressed a soft kiss to her forehead. She would run her fingers through his long black hair, ruffling it until it looked ridiculously untidy. We'd all laugh.

"My parents are dead," Cora whispered.

At first, I thought I hadn't heard her correctly. When I looked at her, her mouth was a hard line, and her eyes blazed. "They're . . . *dead*?" I breathed.

She nodded stiffly.

"But you said—"

"I lied." She shot me a wry smile. "I knew it would be suspicious if I just *showed up* without parents. But the truth is, I never knew them. I was born into foster care. Abandoned at birth. Now that I'm old enough to know better, my parents were probably killed for their blood."

"They were both Bloodcasters?"

"All my research shows you have to have Bloodcaster genes on both sides. It's why we're so rare."

Something dissolved in my chest, making me feel hollow and empty. "So, you grew up on your own?"

"Pretty much. I hopped from foster family to foster family. And yes, one of them was in New York just before the Demon War. But demons always caught up with me. They tracked me down. Eventually, I had to learn how to defend myself. So, I ran away and trained to —" She stopped short and stiffened, her body taut and alert.

"What is it?" I glanced around as if to find an attacker approaching us. But we were alone on the sidewalk. The diner was only a block away.

Cora swallowed and crossed her arms. "I trained to become a killer."

I nodded. "Right."

Cora's eyes shot to me. "You knew?"

I laughed. "I figured as much. The way you drew your knife and threatened me. The way you handled that werewolf."

She stared at me, her brows pinching together. "It . . . it doesn't bother you?"

I frowned as I considered this, remembering how uncomfortable I'd felt with the idea that Cora was a demon. As I re-examined those feelings, I realized I'd only felt like I *should* be uncomfortable with it. Once I'd found out who Cora truly was, it hadn't bothered me at all.

I offered a small smile. "No. It doesn't." Our gazes locked, and though a million questions churned between us—who had Cora killed? Was she still a killer now?—we remained silent. A quiet bond formed between us. A bond of likeness and understanding.

We remained quiet as we got in my car and I drove us to my neighborhood. My mind raced again, but I felt calmer than before. More assured.

When we passed through the gate at the entrance, Cora sucked in a sharp breath. "Merciful Lilith, it's Cookie Cutter Central."

I laughed, glancing around at the rows of identical polished houses that lined the street. "Yeah. Welcome to my world."

Cora gave me a look that was half sympathy, half disgust.

I drove down the road, ignoring the curious looks from the Nephilim walking on the sidewalk. They stared at Cora, immediately identifying her as a stranger. She sat up taller in her seat, her chin lifting in defiance. Pride swelled within me.

At the end of the road, I parked in the vast parking lot in front of the meetinghouse. Cora stared at the magnificent pillars lining the porch. "What is this, the Country Club?"

I chortled. "Spare your judgment."

We got out, and I crinkled Jocelyn's file nervously in my hands. Cora touched my arm, and I stopped. Her eyes were soft as she looked at me.

"You can do this," she said.

I took a breath and nodded. "Thanks for being here."

She smiled, but it didn't reach her eyes. Though she exuded confidence and strength, I could tell she was nervous too. "Are you sure they're in there?"

"Yes. They meet every Saturday to settle town affairs. My dad's in there too."

Cora looked at me. "Are you okay with that?"

I nodded. "It has to be done. I can explain the truth to my dad later."

"What *is* the truth?" Cora asked.

I hesitated. "I don't know. But we don't have time to find out." If I truly *was* being targeted, then my attacker had two months before my Teleportation powers were gone forever.

That was way too much time. I needed the clan to intervene *now*.

A small voice inside me whispered, *You'll still have your powers if you don't pledge at the Ceremonial Rite.*

But a larger part of me knew I'd already made up my mind. I would do anything to help my dad. And once I graduated, I could get a job and help him make ends meet.

It was better than living on the streets.

My insides were a jumbled mess of nerves and anxiety. To calm myself, I recited our plan: *Present the evidence to Hector. Convince him that demons are after Jocelyn—after the clan. If he sees proof, if he thinks the attacker* isn't *after me, he'll take it seriously. He'll take precautions to keep our clan safe.*

I took a deep breath. Though my insides trembled, my exhale was smooth and steady. "All right. Let's go."

We strode inside the building.

CHAPTER 19

CORA

I KNEW IT HAD BEEN STUPID OF ME TO OPEN UP ABOUT my parents and my life as a killer.

But Vince had opened up to *me*. And I was sick of playing this game with him. Telling him about myself felt right.

Besides, in a few minutes, it would all be over anyway. He'd know why I was here. And he would despise me.

The thought made me feel frustratingly gloomy. So, instead, I focused on the tiny moment when my chest had turned to mush: when he'd genuinely asked me for help.

No one had ever done that before.

Damien and the demons from my past had only ever issued orders. Commands. Foul insults.

Vince was the first one to come to me as a friend. A friend who didn't judge me for my past or my blood.

It was gloriously refreshing.

Together, we strode into the meetinghouse like we owned the place. Down the elegant carpeted hallway, past several locked doors, to an open conference room that looked more like a ballroom.

What the hell is this place, the White House? I resisted the urge to snort.

Seated at a large table were a dozen middle-aged men, backs stiff and expressions stern. I felt the cool gazes of each one of them as we interrupted their meeting.

"What is this?" a tall, dark-haired man asked in a booming voice, rising to his feet. Hector Moses, I presumed. His gaze was steely as he looked from me to Vince. His eyes settled on me and narrowed with suspicion. "Why have you brought a stranger to our clan?"

"She smells different," another man said, his dark eyes sharp and lethal. "What *are* you, girl?"

I bristled, my fingers itching to grab the knife in my boot. As if sensing my intent, Vince grabbed my wrist, his eyes glinting with a warning.

"I've brought her here on urgent clan business." Vince's voice was firm and powerful. It almost didn't sound like him at all. He strode forward confidently and set the forged file on the table in front of the men. A few of them glanced at it warily, but most of them watched me like I was some feral animal about to strike. I crossed my arms and chewed on my lip, daring the old farts to make a move.

Go ahead, I challenged with my eyes. *See what happens when you do.*

"A hit has been ordered on one of our own," Vince went on, his eyes earnest as he leveled a gaze at each man. "Here's evidence."

Hector's eyes narrowed, but he snatched the file, his gaze flicking over the information. His eyes widened. "Where did you get this?" he hissed.

Several men stood, looking over Hector's shoulder to inspect the document. Fervent murmurs echoed around the table.

"From me," I said loudly.

Vince's eyes darted to me, but I ignored him. Stepping forward to face the men, I lifted my chin. "I live among a demon clan in Hinport. My name is Cora Covington, and I'm Damien Moretti's assassin."

My skin prickled as I felt Vince's shock ripple right through me. I kept my eyes fixed determinedly on the men. A few of them went pale, their eyes wide with fright. Others glared at me with intense hatred.

Hector, however, looked nonplussed. He merely raised his eyebrows as if responding to a small child. "Is that so."

"Damien ordered me to kill this Nephilim." I gestured to the file on the table. "When I failed to do so, he blackmailed me." I smiled without humor. "I didn't like that very much, so . . . here I am. He wants to take down your clan. He's branching out of Hinport. This is a threat you need to take seriously."

Vince sucked in a breath. I felt his eyes drilling holes right through me, but I clenched my fingers into fists and kept my gaze averted.

To my surprise, Hector scoffed, shaking his head in amusement. "I must say, I'm impressed you had the gall to come here, girl. You craft an entertaining tale."

"It's not a tale," I said, my tone icy. "Your clan is in danger. Will you really stand there and *mock* me when your people's lives are at stake?"

More men murmured to each other, their gazes no longer hostile.

Hector's eyes flashed dangerously. "What would you have me do? Incite panic among my people? Do something rash so you and your lover can make your move?"

I stiffened, my nostrils flaring.

A slow smile spread across Hector's face. "Ah, yes. I know all about Damien and his Blade. Don't pretend like you two don't have a *special relationship*."

Heat rose in my cheeks, and I gritted my teeth. "That has nothing to do with this."

"Doesn't it? You're a spurned lover looking for revenge. But as soon as you and your bedfellow make up, you'll turn on my clan and hand us over to him."

I lunged. In a flash, I drew my knife and pinned Hector against the table, holding the blade to his throat. Several men gasped, and a few reached for me, but I held the knife closer. Hector stiffened and grunted.

"Don't move, or he dies," I growled.

"Cora," Vince breathed.

Ignoring him, I leaned close to Hector and whispered, "I could kill you right here, right now, and it would make my job a hell of a lot easier." I withdrew, sliding the blade back in my boot. "But I won't."

Hector's eyes were wide as he stared at me. His chest rose and fell with quick breaths. The air was still and silent as we stared each other down.

Then, Hector started to glow. An ethereal white light filled his face and surrounded his body. In an explosion of pearly feathers, his wings stretched out behind him, raising him off the table and into the air. The vibrancy of his magic was so bright it stung my eyes, and I lifted a hand to shield them.

When Hector floated close to the ceiling, he bellowed down to me, "Do you think I couldn't take you down, girl? Do you think you are any match for me and my power? With one blow, I could send you to the depths of Hell."

My bones quivered from the power emanating from his voice, but I stood straighter. "I'd like to see you try!" I shot back.

Hector laughed, the sound echoing around me. "So be it."

"No!" Vince shouted. He darted in front of me, his hands raised toward Hector. "Don't, Hector. Please."

I almost shoved Vince out of the way, but the desperation and terror in his face was enough to stop me. Though he had every reason to despise me, here he was, trying to protect me. The plea in his eyes, the way his face was taut with fright, made my stomach coil, jolting me from my stubborn anger.

Then, a man stepped forward, his eyes wide and his face pale. "Hector, please." His gaze flicked from Hector to Vince.

Startled, I remembered Vince's father was among the Nephilim here. I hadn't even thought to look for him. As I focused on him, I saw the same bronze skin, firm jawline, and tall stature I recognized in Vince.

Something within me deflated. I couldn't do this.

I couldn't keep up this pissing contest with Hector. It accomplished nothing. He would never believe me.

Did I really need *Vince* to fight my battles for me?

The thought sent a mixture of shame and bewilderment coursing through me.

What am I doing?

My whole life, I'd only looked out for myself because I knew no one else would. My goal was simple: survive. Do whatever it took. Even at the expense of others.

My path had always been clear. Difficult, yes. But crystal clear.

Until now.

With Vince standing between me and Hector's angelic fury, it was like a fog creeping into my once lucid goal of survival. A variable I hadn't expected.

Someone *cared*—enough to get in harm's way to keep me safe.

A hard lump formed in my throat.

I'd stormed in here thinking only of myself. And when the Nephilim officials had sneered derisively toward me—as Nephilim are wont to do—I'd reacted like a child.

Just like they'd expected.

Disappointment and regret flared within me. I'd made a fool of myself. And Vince.

Slowly, I lifted my hands in surrender. Though the words felt like acid in my mouth, I said, "You're right. You could easily take me down. All of you. I'm outnumbered and outmatched. I'm sorry for lashing out."

A tense moment of silence passed between us. Hector's eyes blazed as he stared me down, but I looked at him unflinchingly. Vince remained between us, his arms outstretched in a plea for peace.

Finally, Hector descended. His luminescence faded until the room seemed pitch black in comparison, though the lights were on. I blinked as my eyes adjusted.

Feathers floated in the air as Hector's massive wings withdrew back into his shoulders. He crossed his arms with a smirk that made my blood boil.

My gaze shifted over his shoulder to the men behind him. Most of them stared at me with fury in their eyes—except for one. Vince's dad watched me with a mixture of curiosity and fear. His gaze kept sliding between me and Vince, and I knew he wondered how we knew each other.

A knot of guilt rose in my throat, but it pushed out all anger I felt toward Hector.

"Please," I said quietly. "If you know me, then you know my reputation. I never show my face. And I never miss my mark. If I intended to kill, I would've done it already. I beg of you to see reason. Your clan is in danger, and though you are powerful, Damien has all of Hinport under his thumb. He *will* bring this fight to you."

Another silence filled the room, punctuated only by the frantic breathing of Vince beside me. It took all of my restraint not to look at him.

"And where do you stand in this fight?" Hector asked softly.

I hesitated. "I won't take part in it."

"You are either with us," Hector said, "or against us."

I felt every man's gaze settle on me, and I knew they agreed with Hector.

But . . . fight with the Nephilim? Fight against my

coven? My friends? How could he expect me to agree to that?

As I stared into Hector's smug expression, I realized he was playing me. He knew I would never agree to fight with the Nephilim.

Lifting my chin, I stepped closer to Vince. I expected him to flinch away from me or cast me a disgusted look —and I wouldn't blame him—but to my surprise, he didn't. I could practically smell the confusion and shock rolling off him. We were close enough for our arms to touch as I said, "I stand with Vince."

Vince's dad stared at me with wide eyes, his mouth slightly open. A few of the men muttered to each other inaudibly. Surprise flickered in Hector's eyes before his expression smoothed into a blank mask. His gaze briefly dropped to Jocelyn's file on the table. He sighed and inclined his head.

"We will . . . consider this information, Ms. Covington. Thank you for bringing it to our attention."

Stunned, I gaped at the men, waiting for one of them to laugh at Hector's obvious joke. But then Vince started tugging on my arm, dragging me toward the exit. I stumbled after him, disoriented.

Hector's eyes remained pinned on me as we left. Even after I turned away, I felt him watching me.

My skin prickled with unease.

CHAPTER 20

VINCE

My whole body trembled as I stormed out of the meetinghouse with Cora right behind me. I didn't even register that I was walking down the sidewalk—*away* from my car—until Cora pulled on my arm to stop me.

"Vince, wait."

"What *was* that in there?" I demanded, whirling on her. "Were you trying to get yourself killed?"

Her head reared back. "No, I—"

"And what about me? I *trusted* you, and you challenged my clan leader like this is some competition!"

She blinked. "I know. I'm sorry."

"Were you telling the truth?" My voice kept rising, even though she wasn't arguing. "When you said you were sent to kill Jocelyn?"

Her mouth opened and closed as she stared at me.

My pulse raced, my heart quivering madly inside me. Every inch of me felt like it was on fire.

"No," Cora said at last. "I was lying."

I raised my eyebrows, unconvinced.

She sighed. "But I *do* know Damien Moretti."

"You're his assassin?"

A pause. "Yes."

"And his lover?"

Cora's cheeks turned pink, and she dropped her gaze. "Not anymore."

Rage and jealousy boiled within me until I felt like I might explode. A bitter laugh burst from my mouth. I turned away from Cora, running my hands through my hair. "This is just great."

"Vince—"

"*Why are you here?*" I shouted, waving my arms like a madman. "You weren't sent to kill Jocelyn, but you still showed up at *my* high school and keep popping up everywhere I go! If you aren't here on Damien's orders, then why are you here?"

"To take him down!" she roared, her eyes blazing. "He *betrayed* me, Vince. He knows all my secrets, and he's using them against me. So, now I'm using his against him."

"And my clan is getting caught in the crossfire."

She shook her head. "No, that's not—"

"You lied to me, Cora. I trusted you with *everything*, and you lied to me."

Despair filled her face, her blue eyes moistening. She stepped toward me. "Vince," she said in a broken voice.

"Just stay away from me." I turned and left her there, not caring that she had no way home or that the officials in the meetinghouse likely heard our shouting. All I felt was fury and betrayal coursing through me like a violent river.

My mind was a whirlwind of thoughts and accusations as I stalked down the street toward my house, ignoring the looks and comments of the other Nephilim on the street.

I didn't care. I didn't care about anything anymore.

When I reached my house, I stopped short. Jocelyn sat on the porch, reading a book. For a moment, I was reminded of Cora's incessant reading. But thinking about Cora got me angry again, so I shoved the thought from my mind.

"What are you doing here?" I asked, approaching Jocelyn slowly.

She glanced up at me with raised eyebrows. "You told me to meet you here."

I frowned. "No, I didn't." Confusion swirled in my head. "Or did I . . .?" I sighed, unable to remember when I'd last spoken to Jocelyn. "I'm sorry. I'm not myself right now."

"It's fine." Her tone was cool, but her blue eyes were kind. Forgiving.

Again, I thought of Cora and the steely edge to her eyes. Though they were the same color as Jocelyn's, they were so different.

"You look upset." Jocelyn stood, her brows pinching in concern. "What happened?"

Lilith, what hadn't *happened?* I opened my mouth to explain everything to her but then clamped my lips shut. How could I tell her I'd helped falsify evidence of an attempt on her life? Why had that seemed like a good idea at the time?

Because Cora had helped me with it.

A sour taste filled my mouth.

"I tried talking with the officials about the attacker," I said stiffly. "They said they'd look into it."

Jocelyn's eyes widened. "Really? So, they think it's a big deal?"

I remembered what Cora had said about Damien Moretti looking to expand to our city. Grimly, I said, "Yeah. It's a big deal."

Jocelyn crossed her arms, suddenly looking very small. "What do you think they'll do about it?"

"No idea."

"What do you *want* them to do about it?"

I stared at her, surprised by her question. People rarely asked for my opinion, especially regarding clan matters. "I want us to move somewhere safer. Somewhere away from Hinport."

Jocelyn cocked her head at me. "What does Hinport have to do with this?"

"Hinport sent the attacker."

Jocelyn's face went pale. "The . . . the *demons* . . .?" She sucked in a trembling breath.

I caught her by the arms and gingerly led her inside. "It's gonna be okay," I murmured, though I wasn't sure this was true. "It'll be fine, Joss. I've got you."

I eased her into an armchair and sat across from her, leaning forward to look into her eyes. Her face still looked wan, but her eyes were alert.

"What else did they tell you?" she asked.

"What do you mean?"

"About Hinport. How are they involved? Is my father looking into it?"

I opened and closed my mouth, the response dying on my lips. Her father . . . Of course. I'd forgotten he was there too. Clearing my throat, I shook my head. "They didn't know anything."

Jocelyn squinted at me. "Then, how did you know the attacker came from Hinport?"

"Because . . . because . . ." I trailed off as horror trickled into my stomach like a slow stream of icy water. My mind replayed the events in the meetinghouse, and Cora's voice echoed in my mind.

I never show my face. And I never miss my mark.

The attacker came from Hinport.

Damien ordered the hit.

Cora was his assassin.

Her words in the diner floated to the surface of my memory: *Power attracts enemies. What if someone comes after you?*

Nausea climbed up my throat. I suddenly felt dizzy.

"Vince?" Jocelyn asked, but her voice was far away.

I thought back to that moment between me and Cora in the park—when we'd almost kissed.

She'd smelled like lilacs. Just like the attacker had.

How had I not put this together?

Cora had attacked me and Jocelyn in the library. She hadn't been sent to kill Jocelyn—but to kill *me*.

"Vince, you look like you're about to puke." Jocelyn's hand on my shoulder jolted me from my stunned stupor.

"Joss," I rasped, looking at her through wide eyes. "The attacker . . ." *Merciful Lilith, what had I done?* I'd told Cora so much about me and my powers. How could I have been so stupid?

"I know," Jocelyn said, misunderstanding me. "I'm scared too."

I shook my head numbly, but I was too horrified to share the truth. If the clan found out what I'd done, they'd banish me. And my dad.

"I actually came here to tell you . . . I found something," Jocelyn said quietly.

"Found what?" I asked warily.

"It was in my dad's notes about Reapers. You were right to look there."

I stared at her in bewilderment. *Look where?* "Joss, what—"

She raised a hand to stop me. "It's okay. I'm not mad. I just . . . Vince, it's terrible."

The devastation in her eyes made my heart lurch. Alarm and anxiety pulsed through me. "What is it?"

Jocelyn exhaled. "There are no Reapers, Vince. It's a term the Nephilim clans invented to give the illusion of free choice."

I stared at her in confusion. "What?"

Jocelyn's hand trembled as it clutched mine. "Nephilim who don't pledge at the Ceremonial Rite aren't banished. They're—they're executed."

CHAPTER 21

CORA

Fuming, I stormed into my room at the inn and flung my bag on the floor. Rage pulsed through me, trembling down to my very bones.

How dare he? Didn't he know what I'd sacrificed today? If Damien found out what I'd done . . .

I shook my head, my hands quivering with fury. My movements were clumsy as I dug through my bag, searching for my Poisoned Balm. When I found it, I reapplied it to my lips.

This changed nothing. Damien still had a hold on me. He had the power to sic the entire demon population of Hinport on me with one word.

Bloodcaster.

Despite everything I'd told Vince, despite my desperate desire to protect him, I *had* to go through with this. My life depended on it.

My frantic pulse shot through me with urgency, making me restless. With an impatient growl, I overturned my bag on my bed to sift through the contents.

My blood was the most valuable thing in the world. Surely, I could come up with some spell to solve my problems. Something to get me out of this mess.

With shaking fingers, I leafed through worn pages of notes and spells I'd jotted down. Back in Hinport, I had a huge book of handwritten spells tucked away somewhere Damien couldn't find it. At least I'd had the foresight to keep *something* from that asshole.

I traced a finger over the symbol I'd etched into my notes a year ago. The symbol of eternal healing. The image was two intersecting triangles that almost looked like angel wings.

My fingers curled into fists at the thought. *Those damn angels and their self-righteous bull—*

A pounding on my door interrupted my thoughts. I lurched to my feet and snatched my knife. "Who is it?" I demanded.

"It's Vince. Let me in."

I stilled, my heart racing madly. There was something off about his voice. It almost didn't sound like him.

Which made me insanely suspicious.

Still gripping my knife in one hand, I slowly edged toward the door and peered through the hole.

It was definitely Vince. He had his arms pressed up against the door and his head bowed.

My instincts prickled against my skin, warning me that something was wrong. Why was his head bowed? Was this *really* Vince?

"Cora," Vince growled. "Open the door."

I remained frozen. This didn't sound like Vince at all.

"What do you want?" I snapped. My voice was level, despite my frantic thoughts. *Who could impersonate Vince? Who would come here pretending to be him?*

Damien would. If not him, then one of his goons.

"I need answers," Vince said. "Come on, Cora, you owe me that much."

I bit my lip, contemplating. If it *was* Damien or one of his men, I knew I could handle them. With a sigh, I unlocked the door and swung it open, still brandishing my knife.

Vince stared at me, his eyes dark with rage. He panted as if he'd run straight here. A sheen of sweat coated his face.

He strode forward so forcefully I backed away from him. Swallowing my unease, I lifted my chin. "Ask your questions."

Vince slammed the door shut. The door frame rattled from the impact. My brows knitted together as I stared at him.

Then, I figured out what was different about him. He

was *angry*. I'd never seen him this angry. He'd been upset when we argued earlier, but that seemed more like bewilderment and shock.

But this . . . this was almost terrifying. Vince was usually calm and chill. He was laid-back even when he didn't mean to be.

"Were you sent here to kill me?" he asked in a hard voice. His tone had the commanding authority of the demons I'd been surrounded by my entire life.

Another thing that unsettled me. I liked Vince because he was *different* from the trash I was used to.

But right now, he sounded just like them.

"Yes." My voice was calm. I knew he would've figured it out. I'd practically spelled it out for him.

"Why?" he asked through clenched teeth, taking a step toward me. It took all my resolve not to back away again.

"I don't know."

"Don't lie to me!"

"I'm not!" I shouted. "Damien gave me the hit. He didn't tell me why."

Vince shook his head, his nostrils flaring. "I don't believe you."

I raised my arms and let them fall by my sides. "Sorry. It's the truth. I can't tell you what I don't know."

Vince crossed his arms, his breathing sharp and

uneven. "Then, why do you *think* he ordered the hit? You're clever. I'm sure you've thought about it."

"Vince, I—"

"*Answer* me, Cora."

My mouth clamped shut, my head spinning with possibilities. Though I longed to defend myself, to explain what Damien held over me, I knew Vince had a point.

I owed him this much.

I took a breath. "Damien has only ever been concerned with owning Hinport. Usually, I take out his major competitors. People who get in his way.

"But the Nephilim?" I shook my head. "That one was new. He's *never* targeted light casters before. And he's never expressed interest in branching out of Hinport. Something has changed. Something recent." A lump formed in my throat as I remembered how he'd spoken to me the day he'd given the order. Like I was something he *owned*. Something to be tossed around and discarded when he got bored.

Hot fury raced through me again. My gaze hardened as I looked at Vince. "Power. Damien is after power. It makes him drunk. Turns him cold-hearted the more powerful he gets. He must've come into something big lately that made him hungry for more."

Damien had been like night and day. One day we were comrades like normal. The next day, he turned on me.

I'd wondered if he'd been planning it all along. But now I was almost certain he'd struck some kind of powerful deal and didn't need my loyalty anymore.

Vince stared at me, his eyebrows lowering and his jaw rigid with anger. "When did he order the hit?"

"One week ago."

Vince's mouth twisted. His eyes drifted away from me, and his expression grew distant. "What day . . . exactly?"

"Saturday."

Vince blinked. Though his expression remained cold like stone, something shifted in his eyes. "That was the day . . ." His mouth closed, and he looked at me as if just noticing I was there.

"What?" I asked.

"I have another question for you," he said as if I hadn't spoken. "And this time, I swear to Lilith, if you don't answer truthfully, I'll fight you." He edged closer to me, his eyes glinting. "We both know I bested you last time."

I straightened, bristling at his implication. He'd only won because he *cheated*.

Not that I was above cheating.

"What's your question?" I hissed.

"Why. Are. You. Here?" Each word was a breath against me, a sharp gust of icy wind. I knew what he wasn't saying.

Are you here to kill me? Or help me? Is anything you said the truth?

My instincts screamed at me to remain silent. To keep my secrets locked away.

But I was floundering. I couldn't count on Damien. I couldn't count on my fighting skills. If Vince *did* attack me, I didn't even know if I could kill him to save myself.

Why was I here? How was I supposed to answer if I didn't know?

"I originally came here to kill you because Damien blackmailed me," I said quietly. "He knows I'm a Blood-caster, and he has powerful friends. He threatened to expose me, to put a bounty on me if I didn't follow this through.

"But . . ." I took a shuddering breath before continuing. "I want out. I don't want to be his Blade anymore. So, I planned to expose *him*, just like he threatened to do to me. I thought if the Nephilim knew he was after one of their own, they'd hunt him down and take care of my problem for me."

Vince's mouth grew thinner. "You used me."

"Yes."

"You used my clan."

"Yes."

Vince inhaled a breath that sounded more like a hiss. He took a step closer so our noses were almost touching. "You're no better than the bastards you work for."

"You're right."

Vince's expression slackened in brief surprise. His lips parted.

"You're right," I said again. "I'm just like them. Because they're all I've ever known. I've lived my entire life looking over my shoulder, relying only on myself. I've done despicable things, Vince. Things that would make you shudder.

"But I don't regret any of it. It kept me alive. It made me stronger." I swallowed. "I never had *any* regrets . . . until now."

Vince blinked. Emotion stirred in his eyes, unreadable and disorienting. "What do you regret?" His voice was terse, as if he didn't care about the answer. But the gleam in his eyes suggested otherwise.

"I regret using you. I've never missed a mark. I've also never cared about anyone the way I . . . the way I . . ." I couldn't finish. Sure, I could butcher the toughest demon into a million pieces. But I couldn't tell this boy I liked him.

Stupid, stupid Cora.

Vince's face hardened again. "Is that little speech supposed to move me?"

"No. But you asked for the truth. And there it is. I don't know what I'm doing here anymore. I can't go back to Hinport. And I can't go through with killing you. That's what I know."

There it was. The truth I'd been hiding from. The real reason I'd struggled with this task—the reason I couldn't go through with it. Not because of Damien and his secrets. Not because I was curious about Vince's powers.

But because I cared about Vince. I cared so much I was willing to throw away my life and risk Damien's wrath.

Vince stared at me, his expression unyielding and his body stiff. I stared right back. My heart raced, but my breathing was calm and even. My years of training to use the adrenaline of battle to my advantage had kicked in.

This was a battle. Just like all the others. I was still in control.

Vince sighed, his frame drooping slightly. "You aren't who I thought you were."

"I know."

"You and I, we're strangers."

"I'm a stranger to you, yes."

He frowned.

"You didn't deceive me, Vince," I said. "I know you. You're good to your core. You fight for others. You show courage in ways I never could. I'll always admire that."

His jaw ticked back and forth as conflict warred in his eyes. "You can't win me over with compliments."

My mouth twitched with the ghost of a smile. "I know."

He raised a hand to my face, tracing the length of my jaw with his finger. His touch was feather soft. I closed my eyes, my breath hitching. A line of fire burned through my skin from his touch. "I believe you," he said.

His breath was a whisper against my skin. My pulse drummed an erratic beat against my body.

I was no longer in control.

"Good," I rasped, feeling lightheaded.

"But that doesn't mean I trust you."

"I know."

His fingers slid under my chin, lifting my face to meet his.

My insides coiled. My battle instincts failed me. I couldn't win this one.

His breath tickled my skin. My hands pressed into his chest.

The most surprising part about all this was how desperately, achingly, I *wanted* this. My body cried out for him, begging for his touch. Deep within my core, a flame ignited, scorching every part of me with need.

Vince leaned in.

I sucked in a breath, suddenly remembering my Poisoned Balm. "Vince, don't . . ."

He dropped his hand and ran it through his hair. He turned away from me, and disappointment flared inside me. I pressed my back against the wall behind me, closing my eyes to catch my breath.

"I need your help," Vince said, facing me again.

I straightened. My breathing was still ragged, and my face felt hot. But I met his gaze. "With what?"

"The Ceremonial Rite is coming up soon. After that, my dad and I will be safe."

I nodded, then faltered. "Does . . . does that mean you're pledging?"

His eyes were grim. "I have to."

A lump formed in my throat. My mind screamed, *Don't do it, Vince!* But I kept quiet.

"Until then, this new power of mine . . ." He trailed off and sighed.

"You want me to keep you safe," I guessed. "From Damien."

Vince looked at me. "No. I want you to help me use my power one last time. While I still have it."

I cocked my head at him. "To do what?"

"To bring my mom back."

CHAPTER 22

VINCE

To be honest, I hadn't come to Cora to ask for help. I'd planned on interrogating her. Demanding to know what she knew—*why* Damien was trying to kill me.

It didn't make sense. Cora had planted the idea in my mind that someone would be after me to figure out how to use my time travel powers.

But . . . how would *killing* me accomplish that?

I wanted to yell at her. To hurt her like she'd hurt me. But then I'd looked into her cold blue eyes and saw something she was trying to hide.

Emotion.

Arguing with me had made her *feel* things. When I touched her, I'd felt that spark between us. I knew she felt it too.

But she was a killer. And soon, I would pledge to

become a Nephilim for eternity. Nothing could happen between us.

Something in me snapped. I felt lost and overturned like a rowboat in a stormy sea. Nothing made sense to me anymore.

Oddly, it was my mother's face that popped into my head during that moment of overwhelming insanity. She was the one thing that had felt safe in my life.

And in all the madness of this past week, I'd forgotten my original plan to go back in time and save her.

Now, it grounded me. It was the only thing I could cling to. If Mom were still alive, everything would realign. She'd be the leader of the clan. She'd lift the ridiculous custom to pledge and forswear all other magic.

Most importantly, she'd be *here*. Dad would be safe. Mom would help me live a life as both a warlock and a Nephilim.

I was sick of being everyone else's pawn. Sick of having things decided for me. I'd given up on keeping my powers, but I'd be damned if they took away my chance at saving Mom.

I didn't care anymore. Just for now, I was determined to do what *I* wanted.

I was going to bring my mom back. Even if I needed Cora's help to do it.

As if our argument hadn't happened—as if she

weren't an assassin sent to kill me—we sat at her desk to make a plan. Cora sifted through notes of various spells she'd written. I squinted at her fine, curly handwriting, trying to make out the words.

"You wrote all these yourself?"

"Yes." Her tone was matter-of-fact. "Where else would spells come from?"

"A Grimoire?" I arched an eyebrow at her.

Cora glanced at me. "I don't have the luxury of using one of those."

Curiosity nibbled at me, but I didn't ask. Cora had spent her entire life hiding who she was. Asking around for a Grimoire would've drawn too much attention.

"What's that one?" I asked, gesturing to a strange symbol of two triangles overlapping.

Cora snatched the paper and slid it back in her bag. "A healing rune."

"What does it do?"

She cut a hard glance at me. "It heals."

"Yeah, I gathered that. But I've never heard of using runes for healing before."

"I haven't had the chance to test it yet. It involves applying my blood topically to a wound." She shrugged one shoulder, but her eyes stirred with curiosity. "I rarely show my blood to anyone, so . . ." She trailed off, but she didn't need to go on. Mixing her blood in a potion was one thing—the other ingredients would mask her identity. But using her blood directly on someone else? That seemed far too personal. Too intimate.

My throat felt hot, so I shoved these thoughts away.

"Here it is," Cora muttered, pulling out a worn sheet of paper that had a few grubby stains on it. "An Enhancement Elixir."

"What does it do? And don't just say *it enhances*," I added quickly.

Cora smirked. "It enhances a certain ability. I'll have to rearrange the wording in the spell to direct it to your time travel power." She placed a hand flat on the desk and turned to face me. "But first, we need to practice."

"Practice," I repeated in a flat voice.

"Yes." She looked at me in bewilderment. "Have you *ever* successfully done this before? Intentionally?"

I opened my mouth, then closed it. She was right. The two times I'd time traveled had both been accidents.

"Exactly," she said. I hated how smug she looked. "Jumping back a day or an hour is one thing, but ten years? We definitely need to practice."

I glanced at her door. "Do we have time? What if—"

"Damien won't come knocking. Don't worry."

"How do you know?"

"Because I know *him*. Even if he's caught wind of my betrayal, he needs time to gather forces and make a plan. He isn't impulsive. He ties up loose ends and calculates *everything* before making a move."

"Sounds familiar," I muttered.

Cora shot me a dark look. Her eyes cut right through me like a razor-sharp icicle. I stared right back, unflinching. Tension swirled between us before she finally looked away.

"Adrenaline is key," Cora said, jotting down notes as she spoke. "Fear, excitement, that kind of thing. So far, we know that envisioning lacrosse helps you get in the *zone*."

I nodded.

"The question is, how do you determine length of time?"

"It's how long I hold on," I blurted without thinking.

Cora stared at me. "What?"

My mouth fell open as shock rippled through me. I had no idea how I knew that. But it made sense. I'd held the bookshelf in the library only a few seconds, hence traveling backward a half hour. And in the park, I'd held onto the picnic table for longer and gone back several hours.

I guesstimated the math in my head and frowned. "So I'd have to hold on to an object for roughly . . . an entire *week*?"

Cora shook her head. "With my elixir, it won't be that long. A full day at most."

My eyes widened. "I can't just sit there holding something for an entire day."

Cora raised an eyebrow. "There are worse things, Vince."

"Yeah, well, when you're being hunted, grounding yourself in one place for that long is kind of dangerous." I rubbed the back of my neck. "Besides, I don't know if I can keep up my concentration for that long."

"I'll help you. And the elixir will boost your ability too."

I shook my head and covered my face with my hands. The more we discussed this, the more unlikely the scenario seemed. This plan was doomed.

But you won't know until you try, said a small voice in my head. And after the Ceremonial Rite, this power would be gone forever. How could I *not* try?

"What's the connection between the object you hold onto?" Cora asked.

I dropped my hands and sighed. "It's linked to the time I travel to. Whatever I hold onto, I travel back to that object in time. It kind of . . . grounds me."

"Like an anchor," Cora said thoughtfully.

"Yeah."

Cora blinked and looked back at her notes. "So our issue is not only timing, but location. Obviously, we aren't in New York City right now—"

"I can Jump us there."

"No, you can't," Cora said sharply. "Once you take us back in time, you'll be too drained, even with my elixir. A

Jump like this could kill someone, Vince. We aren't taking that chance."

I stared at her, stunned. Her tone was harsh and unyielding. I knew there was no arguing with her.

But why did she *care*? Sure, it would mean she'd be stuck in the year 2011 with no way back, but wouldn't my death solve all her problems?

"Besides," she went on, avoiding my gaze. "It's more probable for us to find an object linked to your past when you lived in New York City. You didn't live *here* in 2011, so it would make more sense to focus on the location of your home."

I nodded. "Dad kept everything. It's in the attic. I can look through it."

Cora suddenly looked up, her eyes flashing. "Don't go home. I'll go."

I frowned. "What? Why?"

"After what happened with your leaders, it's not a good idea. You need to lie low. And if Damien *does* come after you, your house is the first place he'll look."

"But my dad——" I said, panicking.

"I'll take him somewhere safe."

Discomfort wriggled through me. "Cora, I don't——" I stopped. *No, she needs to hear this,* I thought firmly. "I don't trust you."

Cora looked at me for a long moment. A mixture of emotions crossed her face. I recognized some—regret, hurt, confusion—but others were an enigma. Finally, she said quietly, "You trust me enough to help you with this. You trust me enough to give you an elixir with various ingredients—some of which could be poisonous. If you can't trust me with your dad, then we can't succeed."

Irritation flared within me, but I knew she was right. I clenched my teeth together. Trusting Cora around myself was one thing. But my dad? If something happened to him, I'd never forgive myself. Or her.

"Where will you take him?"

"A safe house in Hinport."

"Hinport?" My eyes widened. Panic rushed through me. "Cora—"

"It's safe, I swear on my life," Cora said. "Damien doesn't know about it."

I gave her a flat look. "Really."

Her nostrils flared. "*Yes,* really. Despite what you might think, I didn't share *everything* with him. I still like my privacy."

"How do you know he doesn't know about it?"

"Because I used my blood to seal the entrance. Only someone with my blood can enter."

I stared at her. *Blood magic?* The idea made my stomach roil.

"Even if Damien *did* know about it, he can't get in," Cora went on. "I'll bring your father there and come back for you when he's secure."

"And what am I supposed to do, just sit around and wait until you're done?"

Cora's eyes flashed, her gaze lethal. "No. You need to practice using your power while I'm gone. And if you can manage to go back in time and do something beneficial, then that'd be great."

"I—you—like *what?*" I sputtered.

"I don't know." Cora threw her notes and a few potion bottles into her bag. "Just don't screw anything up. Don't let Damien find out where you are. Keep your head down. Don't attract too much attention." She slung her bag over her shoulder and leveled a gaze at me. "Can you get back here on your own?"

I crossed my arms. "Of course I can. I'm not a child."

Cora rolled her eyes. "Never said you were, Vince. But you don't exactly have a glowing track record when it comes to time travel."

I scowled. I knew I was being immature, but I couldn't help feeling sour.

Cora was right. I was pretty much useless. I *had* to master this time travel ability.

"Tell me what I need to grab from that box in the attic." Cora raised her eyebrows.

I sighed, dropping my arms. "A small chain with a key on the end. It was my mother's. It's gold, but it's probably corroded by now."

Cora nodded stiffly and turned to go. "Keep the door locked. If anyone tries to get in, Jump to safety."

She pulled open the door.

"Wait," I blurted.

She turned to face me. Her face was impassive and stoic. Though her blue eyes blazed, every other part of her was firm and unyielding.

She was in killer mode right now.

"I . . ." I faltered, unsure of what to say to her. Something wrenched in my stomach at the thought of seeing her leave, though I didn't know why. I should despise her. Part of me still didn't trust her.

So, why did I feel this way?

I touched her shoulder, and she tensed. Emotion stirred in her eyes.

"Be careful," I murmured.

Her mouth curved upward in a half smile. "You too."

And then she was gone.

CHAPTER 23

CORA

CONFLICT SWIRLED WITHIN ME AS I HEADED BACK TO Vince's neighborhood. I thought of the way his gray eyes had sparkled with concern when we'd parted. His gentle touch on my shoulder.

Sometimes he hated me. Other times he seemed to care. I couldn't make sense of it.

My grip tightened on the strap of my bag as I walked. The weight of my weapons and elixirs in the bag comforted me.

I could do this.

But anxiety still gripped my heart. I'd never been in charge of keeping another person safe before. I'd lived my whole life just looking out for myself.

Now, I had to ensure the safety of Vince's dad, who was essentially as powerless as a mortal.

You can do this, Cora, I told myself again.

I kept a brisk pace as I walked down the sidewalk, keeping to the shadows cast by the slowly darkening sky. Vince's neighborhood wasn't too far, but it was at least half a mile. Impatience thrummed in my veins, and I quickened my stride. Part of me regretted not borrowing Vince's car, but it would be easier to slip past the guard at the gate on foot.

I rounded the corner, and the gate came into view. Just before I reached it, a small *pop* stopped me in my tracks.

I froze. *Damien.*

"Cora," rasped a voice.

Stiffening, I turned. My eyes widened.

Not Damien. Vince. But he looked . . . different. His clothes were ripped and smudged with dirt. A long cut ran across his forehead, and his hair was matted with grime.

My heart jolted in my chest. I surged forward as he fell to his knees. My hands caught his shoulders just before he collapsed.

"Vince?" I whispered, stroking the hair out of his face. I touched his cheek, and when he lifted his face to look at me, my blood ran cold.

His lips were purple. The color had drained from his face, leaving him sickly and ashen.

He'd been poisoned. I knew the symptoms well.

"Don't . . ." Vince whispered. His breathing was sharp and ragged.

"Don't what?" I asked in a trembling voice.

Vince's eyes looked hollow and haunted. "Don't . . . kiss me."

My mouth fell open. Horror sank in my stomach like an anchor.

Vince shifted. I tried holding him, but he scooted away from me before turning. With a *pop*, he vanished.

I sat on the sidewalk, numb from shock as I stared at the spot where Vince had vanished.

Don't kiss me, he'd said.

A hard lump formed in my throat. It wasn't hard to guess what he meant.

The Poisoned Balm.

This Vince wasn't the one I'd left at the inn. He had to have come from the future.

Meaning . . . Vince and I would kiss. And I would poison him.

A mixture of emotions swirled in my chest. My face felt hot at the idea of kissing him, followed immediately by shame and guilt. I lifted a shaking hand to my lips, allowing my fingers to barely brush them. Even the briefest of touches sent a flare of sharp heat searing through my skin.

The poison was still intact. I couldn't just rub it off. I

needed to make a special ointment with the antidote that would remove it.

Panic raced through me. I didn't have *time* to mix the ointment. Vince needed my help now.

My eyes burned as I blinked rapidly. I sucked in a breath, but it felt like I was getting no air. I couldn't breathe.

I can't kill Vince, I thought. *He has to survive this.*

I wasn't sure why. Killing had become as easy for me as breathing.

But not this time. Vince was the first person to learn who I was—and *what* I was—without seeing me as a threat or a prize. He might still be angry with me, but he'd accepted me.

No one else had done that before.

Resolve washed over me. I stood, dusting my hands on my pants. I took a deep breath. One thing at a time. Find Vince's dad first. Then warn Vince. If there was time, I would mix the ointment. And if there wasn't, I could keep a healing elixir on me to heal him if I accidentally . . .

I didn't let myself finish the thought.

Hopefully, my warning would suffice. I'd tell him what I'd seen. We'd both be on guard.

And we wouldn't, under any circumstances, come close to kissing.

Just before I reached the gate, I strode to the fence

and climbed over it. I dropped to the ground on the other side, barely making a sound. Even so, I held perfectly still for a long moment to see if anyone noticed.

Nothing happened.

I kept close to the fence, edging toward the nearest house to blend in with the shadows. A child giggled nearby. Voices echoed down the street. I waited until they faded before emerging and hurrying across the street toward Vince's house.

Occasionally, I had to stop and hide while more Nephilim passed. Each delay made me swear under my breath. Did these Nephilim *have* to be outside constantly?

Finally, I made it to Vince's small house. My eyebrows rose as I took in the shabby vinyl and unkempt yard. It was like Hector went *out of his way* to put Vince and his dad in the crappiest house possible.

What a douchebag.

Instead of approaching the front door, I crept around back and tapped on the kitchen window. For a moment, nothing happened. Then, the back door opened, and a man glanced around before his dark eyes settled on me. Now that I was closer, I noticed more similarities to Vince. Their eyes were the same shape. Their noses and jawlines were identical. The same dark hair fell across their foreheads, though Vince's dad had gray streaks in his.

"It's . . . *you*," the man said blankly.

"It's urgent," I hissed, stepping toward him. "I'm here for Vince. Can I come in?"

"Yes, of course." He didn't hesitate before stepping back and letting me in. Unease crept through me. It felt odd to be so . . . *trusted*.

When Vince's dad closed the door, he turned to face me, his eyes worried. "Is Vince all right?"

I grimaced. Where to begin? "He's safe for now. I can explain more on the way."

"On the way?"

"I'm getting you out of here."

The man scoffed. "Whatever for? I'm not exactly a threat."

"Look, Mr. Delgado—"

"Call me José."

I sighed with impatience. "Fine, *José*. Vince is being targeted. We aren't sure why. But your Nephilim clan isn't doing much to keep him safe. And honestly, I'm not convinced they will. You guys aren't exactly a top priority here." I gazed doubtfully at the peeling wallpaper and stains on the ceiling.

José remained eerily quiet, his gaze unreadable as he watched me. "Is this about his Mimic?"

"His what?"

"His—his . . . *abilities*?" José widened his eyes meaningfully. I could tell he was trying to give me a hint without directly saying his son could time travel.

"Manipulation of time?" I said quickly. "Yeah, that's my best guess." I set my bag down and sifted through it before finding a pistol.

José gasped. "What the hell's that for?"

"In case we meet trouble on the way." I handed him my dagger. Though I was more comfortable with a blade, I trusted myself more than José to handle a gun properly.

José took my dagger but kept it away from him like it was highly contagious. "I . . . haven't held a weapon in a long time."

"That's not true," I said. "Anything's a weapon if you make it one." I tucked my gun into the back of my pants and stood. "Where's your attic?"

José's brow furrowed. "Why? I thought we were leaving."

"Vince asked me to grab something. A gold chain with a key?"

José swallowed, his eyes tightening. "Cecile's." His eyes grew distant and moist. "I—yes. I know where it is."

To my surprise, he turned and strode down the hallway to one of the bedrooms. Frowning, I peered after him, but I couldn't make out anything in the shadow of the hall.

I restlessly drummed my fingers on the small counter

while I waited. My gaze fell on a book sitting on the barstool. I froze and leaned over to read the title.

Persuasion.

My cheeks warmed, and a slow smile spread across my face. It was a different edition than the one I carried. This one looked newer as if it had just been bought.

I pictured Vince reading it, and my chest turned soft at the thought.

Pull yourself together, Cora, I chided myself.

Quiet footsteps made me jump, and I straightened, edging away from the counter. José emerged with something small and shiny in his palm. He stood before me, staring at the chain in his hand and gently brushing his fingers against it. I looked at the small thing and gasped. It was so polished it gleamed in the fluorescent light. It looked as flawless as if it belonged on a shelf in a jewelry store.

Vince had thought it would've been tarnished. But . . . perhaps he hadn't known his father was holding onto it.

My mouth felt dry as I looked at José. Wrinkles formed along his forehead, and his eyes were closed. Despair was etched into his face.

My stomach knotted together as I stretched my hand to take the chain. As much as I wanted to leave this man to his grief, we didn't have much time.

José hesitated before handing it to me. "What do you need it for?" Desperation tainted his tone.

"Nothing dangerous," I said. "I'll take care of it."

José's lips pressed together in a thin line before he nodded. Once again, I was struck by the odd feeling that this man *trusted* me. Though I had no idea why.

"All right," José said with forced nonchalance. "Let's go."

A heavy pounding on the door made us both look up in alarm. Our gazes met, and José's panic and confusion told me he wasn't expecting anyone. I quickly shoved the chain in my pocket and drew my pistol.

More knocking. Then Hector's booming voice. "Open up, José! I need to speak with Vince."

Grateful Vince had been smart enough to stay behind, I widened my eyes at José and shook my head slightly.

"He knows I'm home," José whispered. He cleared his throat and shouted, "Just a sec!" He looked at me and jerked his head toward the door in the kitchen.

I nodded, gripping my pistol firmly as we edged toward the back door. José's face paled at the sight of my gun, but he made no objection. I carefully eased open the door, and it creaked loudly. Wincing, I shot José an exasperated look. Was *everything* in this house a piece of junk?

Hector knocked again. "It's urgent!"

"Out of time," I hissed, grabbing José's elbow and urging him to run. We sprinted out the backyard and toward the yard next-door, our footsteps silent in the grass. As we darted away, I caught a glimpse of half a dozen figures in front of José's house.

And one of them spotted us.

"There!" a man shouted.

"Move!" I cried, tugging José with me as we quickened our pace. But his movements were sluggish, and he quickly lagged behind me. I turned to urge him onward and found a blond man racing toward us, gaining speed.

"Go!" José panted, waving his hand. "Leave me!"

Like hell. I grabbed his arm and pulled, shoving him behind me while I raised my gun. I fired two rounds, and my ears throbbed afterward. The man chasing us dived out of the way, and distant screams echoed nearby.

I snatched José's arm again and kept running, crossing to the other side of the street. A burst of magic crackled in the air, and a blinding white light shone behind us.

Not good.

"Stop them!" someone shouted.

A stitch formed in my side as I pressed on, still dragging José behind me. His breathing turned ragged and faint. Still another block to go.

We wouldn't make it.

A gust of wind burst around me, tousling my hair. An

ethereal glow appeared in front of us as a figure material-
ized, his giant wings outstretched behind him.

José and I stopped short as the glow subsided to
reveal Hector, his eyes blazing. Behind him, four other
Nephilim appeared with pearly wings and hardened
expressions.

I raised my gun again.

"Don't bother," Hector sneered. "Our Nephilim
magic will only heal us."

"Not if I send one straight into your skull," I
snapped.

"Where is Vince?" Hector demanded.

"I don't know," I said.

Hector smiled coldly. "The Delgados are under my
protection. We will not harm them. But you? You, my
dear, have been hostile and unpleasant from the moment
I met you. Your presence here is unwelcome. Now, tell
me where Vince is or I will extract the information from
you by force."

I smiled too. "I'd like to see you try."

We stared each other down. José still gasped for
breath behind me.

After a tense silence, Hector barked out a laugh.
"Very well." He waved his hand toward us. "Take them."

CHAPTER 24

VINCE

For half an hour, I paced and poked around Cora's room, trying to distract myself from the crippling fear that something had happened to my dad. The space was immaculate and spotless as if it had been vacant for years. It was almost *too* tidy. I eventually found a large bag stashed under the bed filled with all sorts of weapons ranging from wooden stakes to rusted metal chains. There were also jars of herbs and other spell ingredients, plus vials of purple liquid, which I assumed was Cora's blood.

It made me deeply uncomfortable . . . but also curious. Why would Cora leave me here with her blood if it was so precious?

Did she really trust me that much?

Or maybe she knew what a moron I was. Even if I

wanted to use her blood, what would I do with it? I didn't know how to cast spells.

The thought set my teeth on edge. I wouldn't be in this mess if I weren't such a damn idiot. If I knew *anything* about my Teleportation powers or if I had the common sense to try to fit in with my clan . . .

I shook my head. Thinking about *what if* and *if only* wouldn't do me any good. Running my hand through my hair, I exhaled through my lips and gazed around the room, looking for an object to practice with. But all these items belonged to Cora . . . If I tried Jumping through time with them, who knew where I'd end up?

I needed something I recognized. Something I could control.

My eyes settled on a book on the table. I drew closer, squinting to read the title.

Persuasion.

A slow grin spread across my face. I'd just bought myself a copy and, in spite of myself, I was enjoying it almost as much as *Pride and Prejudice.*

Which, of course, I would take to my grave. I could just picture the torture Luke would inflict on me if he found out.

I carefully held the book in my hands. It seemed old; its leather-bound cover was worn with use and practically fell off in my hands.

This book was well-loved. I stared at it as something

warm filled my stomach. Slowly, I opened the cover and saw the name *Cordelia Cox* scribbled in a child's handwriting on the title page.

Stunned, my mouth fell open. Was this Cora's real name? Had she carried this book around since she was a kid?

A lump formed in my throat. She hadn't lied when she'd said it was her favorite. This wasn't part of her con.

This was the truth. It was *real.*

What else had she been truthful about?

I didn't want to think about this. The safest option would be to assume everything had been a lie.

I cleared my throat and sat at the desk, clutching the book tightly in my hands. Cora carried this book everywhere. So, when in time did I want to travel to? This was just for practice, so it couldn't be *too* far back in time. I could try Jumping to the school, but appearing in front of hundreds of witnesses didn't seem like a very good idea.

I closed my eyes, my mind traveling to the lacrosse field again. The focus was effortless this time. Perhaps with practice, I'd gotten better at it.

Instead of a book in my hand, it was a lacrosse stick. Instead of a bedroom, I stood in front of a grassy field filled with my teammates.

Luke was there. He cocked his head at me and said, "Where to?"

I gripped my crosse with sweaty hands. "The park," I said. "This morning."

Cora had the book then. Lilith, had that only been *this morning?* So much had changed since then . . .

Luke nodded and winked at me. "You got it." He swung his crosse and lobbed the ball toward me. I lifted my stick to catch it—

And suddenly, I was back in Cora's room, lifting the book instead. My eyes flew open. Energy thrummed around me. A sharp citrus smell stung my nostrils. I clutched the book so tightly my hands shook.

Even though my awareness wasn't on the field anymore, I still heard Luke's voice in my head. *Here we go, Vince.*

A small *pop* burst in my ears. The room shifted. I clung to the book as everything turned upside down. I was falling and rising all at once. Nausea swirled in my stomach. I wanted to close my eyes, but I had to watch— I had to know when to let go.

Distorted shapes spun in front of me. I squinted, trying to make them out.

Don't, Luke's voice said. *Listen.*

I closed my eyes, my ears straining. Her voice was distorted, but I heard Cora say, "He *betrayed* me, Vince. He knows all my secrets, and he's using them against me. So, now I'm using his against him." The smell of light magic and angel wings filled my nose.

The meetinghouse. After the incident with Hector. No, keep going.

More sounds and scents slammed into me like a sensory overload. I struggled to focus on each one as it passed. A car honked its horn. The sun burned against my eyelids. The smells of grass and dirt surrounded me.

The park! Without thinking, I let go of the book.

Gravity slammed into me so hard my head throbbed. I tumbled, colliding with something rough and concrete. My hands flew out to break my fall, and the ground cut into my skin. Hissing in pain, I rolled and jumped to my feet.

I stood on a sidewalk next to a small row of bushes. To my left was a road I recognized.

I was in my neighborhood.

Cora stood just a few feet away from me. Her back was turned, but she stiffened. Like she *knew* I was there.

Panicked, I dived into the bushes, ducking down low and holding perfectly still. My heart thundered loudly in my chest, and I held my breath so I wouldn't give away my hiding spot.

I felt like an idiot. At this point, Cora *knew* about my ability. But something in me warned me to stay hidden. I didn't want to mess with the laws of time.

Cora stepped closer to me. I clenched my teeth, shutting my eyes as if that would somehow keep her away from me.

Something scraped against the concrete. I opened my eyes, leaning forward to peer through the bushes. Cora stooped to pick something up off the ground. I frowned before realizing what it was: her book. I'd used it to travel, so, naturally, it would've been here.

Cora was probably suspicious as to how it had fallen out of her bag. I wasn't entirely sure how it worked either. But the book I'd held in my hands just seconds ago was gone. It must've disappeared when I'd traveled.

My head spun as I tried to work this out in my head. *So whatever anchor I use vanishes after I travel. It takes me to a different point in time when it existed and then . . . I don't know, merges with itself? Otherwise there would be two books in the same place.*

This made my brain hurt.

After a long moment, Cora turned and strode away from me. I waited until I couldn't see her anymore before rising from the bushes and looking around.

Okay . . . *not* the park. I was in front of the meeting-house, and Cora had just gone inside.

The incident with Hector hadn't happened yet.

Cursing, I ran a hand through my hair. I let go of the book too quickly. I wasn't thinking. *Of course* I hadn't traveled that far. Thinking of the sounds and scents during my Jump, I realized there hadn't been that many. If I'd wanted to travel back to this morning, I would've experienced the fight between Hector and Cora, our meal at the diner, and whatever she'd done after we'd seen each other in the park.

Curiosity filled me until it was almost unbearable. What *had* Cora done after the park? She'd seemed rattled.

Because we'd almost kissed.

Again, I achingly wondered what was real and what wasn't. Had that just been part of her con? Had she been trying to seduce me?

Well, if that were true, then why leave? Why not let me kiss her?

My face burned as I thought this through. *You're an idiot, Vince,* I snapped at myself. *Focus.*

I crept closer to the meetinghouse, keeping my head down in case someone looked out the windows. Again, I was struck by a sense of urgency: *Don't let anyone see you.*

I couldn't explain it. But I felt it down to my bones.

Stay hidden.

I edged around the building to where I knew the dining hall was. Already, I could hear muffled shouts. And then, Cora's voice: "Will you really stand there and *mock* me when your people's lives are at stake?"

When I reached the window, I cautiously peered inside. There were the clan officials—and Cora and me. The men surrounded us, but Cora stood tall and erect like someone regal. Someone with authority.

I couldn't believe I never noticed it before. The confidence. The finesse.

Hector said, "What would you have me do? Incite panic among my people? Do something rash so you and your lover can make your move?"

I flinched at the word *lover.* It still made me ill, imagining Cora sleeping with that demon bastard.

My jaw ticked back and forth as I leaned away from the window and looked around. A small copse of trees surrounded the meetinghouse, so I was still out of sight. But what could I *do*? I could just Jump back to the present . . . but Cora mentioned doing something beneficial. Something that could help us.

I couldn't exactly barge into the meetinghouse. As much as I wanted to erase the events that happened here, I had to stay out of sight.

Where could I go? My house was empty. Except—

I stiffened. *Jocelyn*! In my mind, I heard her perplexed voice.

You told me to meet you here.

No, I didn't . . .

I blinked, my mouth falling open. It all made sense now. She'd spoken to my Mimic!

I strode away from the meetinghouse just as an ethereal glow burst from the window. Hector had just spread his wings. I didn't have much time. Breaking into a jog, I hurried down the street, gasping for breath by the time I reached Jocelyn's house.

I didn't know why I was here. But I knew it was important.

With a deep breath, I knocked on the door. Jocelyn opened it, her eyes guarded. "Hey." Her tone was icy. Vaguely, I recalled our argument in my car. It felt like ages ago. She was probably still upset.

I didn't blame her.

"Hey," I panted, wiping sweat from my brow.

She frowned. "You okay?"

"I need to look in your dad's office," I blurted.

Her eyes narrowed. "Why?" Her voice was laced with suspicion.

I remembered what she'd said earlier today: *It was in my dad's notes about Reapers. You were right to look there.*

"I need to know more about Reapers," I said quietly. "Please, Joss. I have to know the truth before the Ceremonial Rite. Before I sign my life away forever."

Jocelyn's eyes tightened, and she inhaled sharply. For a long moment, she looked at me as if scrutinizing me. I tried not to fidget or glance over my shoulder. Had Cora and I left the meetinghouse yet?

"Aren't you the least bit curious?" I asked, stepping closer to her. "I know your mind's made up, but pretend you're indecisive like me. Wouldn't you want to know for sure?" Even as I said the words, curiosity burned within me. Why were Reapers executed? What threat did they pose?

Jocelyn sighed, her eyes softening. "All right. But be quick. Dad will be home soon." She stood back to let me in.

Relief surged through me, and I hurried inside. Jocelyn led me to her dad's office, which was more disorganized than I'd remembered. Then again, I hadn't been inside this house since I was a kid.

"It'll be in the file cabinet," Jocelyn said.

We both slid open drawers and started leafing through things. Each file was alphabetized, but when I searched for "Reapers," there wasn't anything there.

Jocelyn's brow furrowed as she noticed the same thing. "That's weird." She reached her hand inside, feeling along the bottom of the drawer as if a file had slipped underneath.

But I knew better. The officials wouldn't keep this kind of thing out in the open. It would be hidden somewhere.

I searched higher up the alphabet, wondering if maybe they'd used a code word for it, when my fingers froze. *Delgado, Vince.*

My blood turned to ice in my veins. There was an entire *file* dedicated to me? A quick glance at the other files told me no one else had the same privilege. Not even Jocelyn.

My hands shook as I pulled out a sheet of paper from within the file. There was my dorky freshman picture. My eyes widened as I scanned the information next to it.

Timewalker . . . Jumper . . . Reaper connections . . .

And then, underneath it all, in bright red ink, the words: *viable threat.*

"We shouldn't be doing this," Jocelyn hissed, startling me so badly I dropped the paper. When she glanced at me, I hastily shoved it back in the drawer, hoping she hadn't noticed. My hands still trembled, and my entire body felt cold.

Viable threat. The words were burned into my brain. I couldn't unsee them.

Reaper connections? What the hell did that mean?

"Vince?" Jocelyn asked.

I shook my head, feeling sick. "You're right. I—I shouldn't have come here." I stood, just as a door slammed somewhere in the house.

I stilled. My heart stopped for a full beat.

"Out the back," Jocelyn hissed, hastily ushering me out of the office.

"Joss?" called a deep voice—Peter Wilkes, Jocelyn's dad. "We have company."

I froze. Jocelyn did too. Her face drained of color. "C-coming!" she called before shoving me toward the kitchen. I hurried to the back door and turned to face her.

"I'm sorry," I whispered. "I'll meet you later, okay? At my house."

Jocelyn nodded before shoving me out the door. I heard her lock it behind me, and I leaned against the brick exterior of the house, trying to calm my heart rate.

Viable threat. Reaper connections. Timewalker? What did all of it mean? And how did they *know?*

" . . . business to take care of," a muffled voice said from the open window. "We won't be long."

"Okay," came Jocelyn's timid voice.

Soft footsteps. A door shutting. And silence.

My skin prickled with unease. Who was with Mr. Wilkes? And what business did he need to discuss so quickly after seeing me and Cora?

I carefully crept around the house toward the window to the office. The window was shut and the curtains drawn. I swore under my breath and pressed my ear to the window.

" . . . gone too far," said a deep voice I recognized. Hector.

"What do you want to do?" Peter Wilkes asked.

I held my breath, waiting.

"We have to end this before it exposes everything," Hector said. "Prepare what you need. Then, send some men to grab Vince. And his father. They can't be allowed to leave."

Horror numbed my body, freezing me in place.

"The girl will still be with him," Mr. Wilkes said.

"Wait until she's gone. Use José as leverage if you need to."

Bile crept up my throat. *Dad.* And Cora was supposed to get him out of there. What if—

I broke into a run before realizing what I was doing. I sprinted through the Wilkes' yard and onto the street, pumping as far as my legs would take me. My lungs burned. Sweat coated my body.

Before I realized it, I'd run across the street to my house. My steps faltered. What was I doing here?

Urgency pulsed through me, and I strode toward the back, using the spare key under the potted plant to get into the kitchen. Hurrying to my room, I reached under my bed and found what I was looking for.

Cora's dagger.

I wasn't sure why I kept it. I hadn't even known it was hers until recently. It had just been a relic. Evidence of the attack in the library.

But this belonged to Cora. And if she was in trouble, then she'd need all the weapons she could get her hands on.

I flew out the back door, sprinting through the back-yard just as Jocelyn's voice floated from the porch. "You told me to meet you here."

I briefly considered trying to use my wings, but I didn't have time.

Besides, there was no room for error here. I was better at Jumping.

But what could I use as my anchor this time? I couldn't use Cora's dagger because she didn't have it. I needed something that would bring me to her and my dad.

After jumping the fence, I glanced around to make sure no one could see me. My gaze fell on a lamppost on the sidewalk, and I stopped short. My eyes grew wide. Reaching forward, I gripped the lamppost and closed my eyes. There was Luke, standing in the field with his crosse as if waiting for me.

"You ready, Vince?" he asked.

"Take me forward," I said.

He grinned and nodded.

I turned in place, still gripping the lamppost, and vanished with a small *pop*.

CHAPTER 25

CORA

My fingers were slick with sweat as I gripped my pistol. I knew bullets wouldn't do any good. Knives wouldn't either, but I found myself wishing for my dagger anyway.

The Nephilim closed in on us.

I fired a round. Several figures dodged out of the way. Then, I flung the pistol forward so it cracked against another Nephilim's head. He staggered back in surprise.

That was all I needed. I snatched José's hand and uttered a spell.

"Magic above, and powers that be,
Protect us from this enemy.
Hide us so we can flee from here
Away from the foes who draw near."

My hands glowed purple, and several Nephilim

gasped. Hector took a step toward me. As the spell burst from my fingertips, I met his gaze.

He registered no surprise at the color of my magic. He *knew*.

Which could mean only one thing: Damien had told him.

Purple smoke engulfed José and me, obscuring us from view. It swirled and swelled like a storm. I felt José tense next to me, but I gripped his arm firmly as we backed away from the Nephilim. A narrow beam of light appeared from within my magic smoke, piercing through the haze like a beacon. It grew until a small tunnel of clarity highlighted the street ahead of us—like a flashlight amidst the darkness.

"Come on," I said, urging José onward. We rushed down the street, following the clear path through the fog. Shouts echoed behind us as the Nephilim struggled to see through the smoke.

"Purple . . .?" José panted in bewilderment.

"Later," I muttered.

A small *pop* echoed next to me, and I stiffened, raising my hand to stop José. Unease spread through me.

"Vince?" I whispered tentatively.

Someone grabbed my arm and twisted, wrenching me away from José. I cried out as pain shot through my shoulder.

"Guess again," hissed a familiar voice in my ear.

My stomach dropped. Damien. "So what, you're working for the light casters now?" I snarled. "Are you their hitman? Oh, how the mighty have fallen."

Damien twisted my arm harder, and I sucked in a gasp.

"Cora!" José cried.

"Stay back!" I shouted. If he got too close, I had no doubt Damien would kill him.

"Lose the fog, Cor," Damien said. "Or I'll break your arm."

"Go to hell," I spat.

Crack. A scream ripped from my throat as crushing agony swept through me, momentarily blinding me. Fire shot up my arm, and when I tried to move it, the pain intensified. I collapsed to my knees, and Damien strode toward José.

"No . . ." I moaned.

"Let's try this again," Damien said, snatching José by the throat. José clawed at Damien's fingers feebly as he choked. "Lose the fog, or he dies."

"All right!" I shouted, raising my good hand. "Let him go."

Damien raised his eyebrows expectantly.

I inhaled a shaky breath and closed my eyes, focusing on the tug of my magic. It crackled through me as the fog dispersed, settling within me once more. When I opened my eyes, the street was clear.

And the Nephilim drew closer.

White spots danced in front of my eyes as I tried to rise. My arm quivered, and each movement sent slices of anguish through me. Nausea swirled in my stomach. I gritted my teeth. I just had to hold on until I could get my healing elixir. Where the hell was my bag?

Damien cocked his head and grinned at me before drawing a knife from his pocket. He raised it to José's throat.

"No!" I screamed, staggering forward.

José elbowed Damien in the gut, then jerked backward against his face.

Damien grunted and dropped the knife, clutching his nose as it bled freely. José surged forward and touched my good shoulder. "Can you run?"

"He broke my arm, not my legs," I snapped, cradling my arm against my chest as we ran.

A blinding white light stopped us in our tracks. Wind burned against my eyes as Hector landed in front of us, his eyes glinting with triumph.

"Your efforts were impressive, Miss Covington," he said with a smile. "But it's useless. It will be easier if you submit to us."

"Why?" I roared. Fury blazed through me, fierce and merciless. "Why align yourself with *Damien*?"

Hector chuckled. "I wouldn't expect you to understand."

My nostrils flared, and my fingers itched to grab my blade. If I weren't injured, I knew I could take him down.

But not with my broken arm. And not when I had to protect José.

My eyes flitted around the street. Nephilim emerged from their homes, looking at the scene with curiosity. The Nephilim officials surrounded us, forming a large circle.

No way out.

Urgency pulsed through me. *There must be a way. There has to be.*

"Cora," José whispered.

"We're not giving in," I growled.

"*Cora.*"

I blinked and looked at José, whose face was pale. He pointed a shaking finger toward Hector.

Frowning, I followed his gaze. It wasn't Hector he pointed to—but something just over his shoulder. A figure edged closer. Someone I'd mistaken for a normal Nephilim. But as I looked closer, relief swelled within me.

It was Vince.

He spun in place, and with a small *pop*, he suddenly appeared right next to me.

"Grab him!" Hector bellowed.

"Get him out of here!" I shoved José toward Vince,

who glanced at me in concern before spinning and vanishing with his father.

I fell to my knees again, succumbing to the pain in my arm as the Nephilim advanced. But Vince and José were gone.

It was just me now. The knowledge sent a bolt of triumph through me.

Hector drew closer to me, his eyes blazing. "Where did they go?"

"Come closer, and I'll tell you."

Hector sneered. "You can't harm me, *girl*." Still, he approached.

A little closer, I urged him. *Come on . . .*

When he was within a foot of me, I slashed my good arm through the air. A jet of purple flame seared through him, knocking him backward. Hector fell over with an *oof*, and then I was running. Bursts of white light filled the air. A small *pop* echoed behind me, and I turned on my heel, sprinting hard to the left just as Damien lunged for me. My lungs burned and my arm throbbed with numbing pain, but still I ran.

Another *pop*, and I jerked to the right. Then—

"Cora!"

I froze at the sound of Vince's voice. He appeared next to me and grabbed my hand. Before we could Jump, someone else grabbed my injured arm. I cried out, trying to pull free, but the agony coursing through me made me go limp.

"You're not going anywhere," Damien growled. He jerked me forward, and I fell. His foot collided with my gut. I moaned. My body felt like it was on fire.

Vince surged forward, swinging a punch. Damien blocked it and hit him in the stomach. With a grunt, Vince hunched over, clutching his stomach.

"Vince!" I croaked, writhing on the ground.

"A cute effort," Damien said with a chuckle. I wriggled forward, trying to get close enough to touch Vince so he could Jump us out of here.

"What's this?" Damien asked, his voice dangerously soft.

I froze, my eyes fixed on Damien as he bent over and picked up something on the ground. My heart lurched when I recognized it.

The gold chain. It must've fallen out of my pocket.

My throat felt dry. "Damien—"

"It must be pretty important," Damien said. A slow grin spread across his face, and his eyes glinted. He tossed the chain in the air and caught it, then shot a malicious glance at Vince.

Vince went rigid. His eyes flashed, and his jaw hardened as he stared at Damien. "Give that to me," he said, his voice slow and hard. "Now."

Damien raised his eyebrows and laughed. "Impressive! You almost sounded intimidating for a moment."

Vince's hands shook as they balled into fists. In a burst of white light, his wings appeared from his shoulders, huge and magnificent. Damien's eyes widened, and he staggered back a step. My jaw dropped as Vince floated into the air, his great wings beating and billowing behind him. He raised a hand, and a strike of white lightning speared straight into Damien's chest. He pinwheeled backward, dropping the chain.

Sucking a breath through my teeth, I climbed to my knees and edged forward before snatching the chain. Something hot gripped my uninjured hand, and I cried out.

"It's all right," said an ethereal voice next to me. It sounded like several voices layered into one. The whisper was so soft it caressed my ears. "Come with me."

My pulse quickened as I stared at Vince. This was it. This was the vision I'd had of him. He glowed like a ghost. I felt if I reached for him, my hand would pass right through him.

I thrust the chain into his hands and cradled my injured arm against my chest again. "Get us out of here, Vince."

Vince glanced down at the chain, his expression shifting slightly. He gently took my hand again and spun in place. The air squeezed out of me, and gravity pressed inward, smothering me. A small *pop*, and we were gone.

I wasn't sure where Vince meant to take us. But when we Jumped, a deafening *boom* shook the ground. Dirt and gunpowder filled the air so all I saw was smoke. Shouts and screams surrounded me. In the distance, I barely made out the peaks of skyscrapers.

Panic raced through me. This wasn't Ravenbrooke. Where were we?

"Vince—" I turned to find him when something exploded in the air in front of me. I went flying, my body weightless, my mind numb with terror, before I crashed to the ground. Then, everything went dark.

CHAPTER 26

VINCE

THE SMOKE IN THE AIR WAS SO THICK I BARELY SAW what was happening.

Until Cora went flying like a rag doll.

I watched her land a few yards away from me. She didn't get up.

Panic coursed through me like a powerful current, and I sprinted toward her. Shots fired around me. Growls and moans filled the air.

She's not dead, I told myself again and again. *She's a Bloodcaster. Her magic will protect her. She's not dead.*

I ducked as someone lunged for me. Narrowly avoiding his blade, I punched him in the face—only to realize he was a demon. Some kind of scaly, scabby-looking gargoyle. My fist came back covered in slime. Revolted, I backed away from him as he advanced again. I dodged another blow and kicked him in the chest.

While he was down, I struck him in the head over and over until he didn't get up again.

Breathing heavily, I straightened and rushed to find Cora before someone else attacked.

I found her partially buried in rubble. A huge hunk of concrete covered her legs. Dirt smeared her face along with purple blood.

She wasn't moving.

"Cora," I whispered, hurrying to her side. I tried to lift the concrete, but it was too heavy. After several deep breaths, I tried again. My muscles strained and my arms burned, but I finally managed to shift it off her legs. I brushed her hair off her face and leaned close to feel for a pulse.

Nothing. She wasn't breathing.

No, no, no, I thought numbly. My pulse thundered so loudly in my ears that it was all I heard.

"You're not dead," I said, my voice trembling. I carefully scooped her up and held her close to my chest. Her head lolled backward, her arms hanging limply by her side. A thick knot formed in my throat at the sight of her so frail and helpless.

Cora was never like that. She was always strong.

She wasn't dead.

I couldn't revive her in the middle of a battle. My gaze roved over the debris-filled street. Buildings crumbled, and more explosions shook the ground. A crowd of demons and casters fought in the middle of the road. A burst of white light indicated a Nephilim was nearby.

But I couldn't watch.

Instead, I turned away, carrying Cora as far from the fray as possible. After jogging two blocks, I found a building still in one piece. The doors were locked, but I smashed the glass and brought Cora inside. It looked like it had once been a bookstore. Shelves had long since been emptied, but several loose sheets of paper lingered.

Nervous that someone would find us, I carried Cora to the back of the store to a cramped supply closet—also with empty shelves. Gingerly, I lay her down on the floor and leaned close to listen for a pulse.

Still nothing.

Alarm and anguish tore through me like a riptide. I sucked in several sharp breaths, but my lungs still felt like they weren't getting enough.

"You *can't* be dead," I said through gritted teeth. "I'm still angry with you! You aren't allowed to die until I've forgiven you." I pressed my lips together, closing my eyes as tears threatened to fall. Shaking my head, I said, "No. *No.* I'm bringing you back, Cora."

I straightened and pressed my hands against her chest, counting each compression as I went. When I reached ten, I pulled her lips apart and pushed air into her. Again. And again. Then, back to compressions. I kept a rhythm in my mind as I counted. Compressions. Mouth-to-mouth. More compressions.

I wouldn't give up until she started breathing again.

Unease prickled through me the more I did this. Was I doing it right? I hadn't practiced since the CPR class Coach insisted we take two years ago.

Still, I kept going. Sweat trickled down my brow, and my lips felt numb, but I wasn't going to let her die.

"Stay with me, Cora," I whispered.

Cora sucked in a deep, rattling breath. The sound was so stark against the silence that I jumped and scrambled backward, my heart racing a mile a minute. Eyes wide, I edged closer to her, afraid I'd imagined her breath, not daring to hope . . .

Her chest rose and fell with labored breaths. She coughed, her head turning this way and that as if she were in a fitful sleep.

"Cora." I leaned over her and touched her cheek. "Cora, can you hear me?"

She coughed again, her eyelids fluttering. "Vince," she rasped.

A laugh of disbelief bubbled from my lips. I bent my head as a tear rolled down my cheek. "Merciful Lilith, you scared the *hell* out of me!"

"I didn't—I wanted—I feel fuzzy," she murmured, her speech slurred like she was drunk. Slowly, her eyes opened. Her pupils were dilated.

"Come on, let's sit you up," I said, trying to sound casual. But I knew her disorientation and the state of her eyes weren't a good sign.

I had to keep her conscious so she wouldn't get a concussion. Enough lacrosse accidents had taught me that.

I eased my hand behind her back and pulled her forward, propping her up on the shelves behind her. She grunted and grimaced as if the movement caused her pain.

"You're warm," she said with a soft sigh. "And minty."

I chuckled nervously, thrown off by her forward and slightly unnerving chatter. "Thanks. I think."

She reached for my hand, and I wound my fingers through hers. "Blood witch . . . I smell blood."

With my free hand, I gently touched the bleeding wound on her head. She hissed in pain. "Sorry," I muttered.

"It's okay. I heal fast. Faster than lightning. Faster than *you*." She laughed. Her blue eyes found mine, holding my gaze like a magnet. Though I knew she was loopy, her eyes burst with a sudden clarity that kept me transfixed. Heat swirled in my head, and my mouth felt dry.

"How come your wings don't rip through your shirt?" she asked, her voice a little too loud as she gazed at the fabric of my shirt.

I cleared my throat. "Uh, the enchantment of the wings allows it to pass through. Same reason it doesn't shred through my skin every time."

"Ow," Cora said suddenly, wincing again. "I can't—I can't move my arm." She shifted the left half of her body and cried out, then burst out laughing. "That's so weird."

I grimaced. "Yeah . . . Damien broke your arm."

Cora's eyes widened. "Really? That bastard. I never liked him. Well, that's not true. I *really* liked him, if you know what I mean, but then he manipulated and black-mailed me like I was his *property* and . . ." She blew air through her lips and cocked her head at me. "Well, he's not like you, Vince. He doesn't see me as a person like you do."

I stared at her, stunned into silence. Part of me knew I should do something about her injury, but the other part was eager for more. Cora was never this open with me. "Everyone should see you as a person," I said quietly.

"Right?" Cora said, giggling. "I *am* a person. I'm not just a blood bank."

"No, you aren't."

She leaned closer, scrutinizing me. "Your eyes are like a storm."

Her warm breath tickled my skin. I swallowed. "Cora—"

"I'm not supposed to kiss you," she blurted.

My face burned, and I cleared my throat. "Uh, what?"

Cora giggled again. "I can't remember why. My brain —so fuzzy."

"We need to get you somewhere safe." I shifted, prepared to carry her if I had to, but she grabbed my arm.

"Don't," she said, her face sobering. "I'm safe with *you*, Vince. I've never felt safer."

I stilled. "I can't protect you, Cora."

"You've done a fabulous job so far." She flashed a dazzling smile that lit her entire face. I'd never seen her smile like that. "I'd like to—can I . . ." She trailed off, her eyes roving over my face as if trying to memorize it. "Can I touch your hair?"

I was so startled that I laughed. "Uh, sure."

She smiled again, leaning closer and running her soft fingers through my hair. It fell forward into my eyes, and I closed them, relishing the feel of her fingers caressing my scalp. The smell of lilacs filled my nose, and my hands itched to grab her waist and bring her closer.

She's injured, I reminded myself. *Don't take advantage of her.*

She ran her thumb along my lower lip. I gasped, my eyes flying open. Cora was only a breath away, her nose touching mine.

"Is this okay?" she whispered.

I couldn't think. Couldn't breathe.

"What about this?" She brushed her lips against

mine. My heart stopped, my stomach coiling into a tight knot. Flames exploded inside me.

Cora drew away, her eyes opening to peer into mine. "Is that okay?"

The fire enveloped my chest, consuming everything. "Yes," I said, my voice low. "That's . . . more than okay."

A slow smile spread across her face. She leaned in again, and this time, my hands grasped her waist and brought her against my body. Her lips met mine, gentle and warm. That familiar lilac scent filled me, mixing with soot and sweat. Her hot breath mingled with mine. She curled her uninjured arm around me so our chests pressed together. My fingers traced her face, her neck, her hair. She wrapped her legs around my middle so our bodies were fully entwined. Her lips trailed up my jaw until she nibbled on my ear. A strangled groan rose in my throat, and Cora laughed.

"I'm not supposed to do this," she whispered.

"I don't care," I breathed.

She drew back to brush the hair out of my face, her blue eyes glowing with tenderness. "Vince, I—" She went still, her face slackening in shock. "Your—your lips are purple."

I blinked. "What?"

Horror flooded her eyes. The color drained from her face. She raised a shaking hand to her lips. "Oh, no . . ."

CHAPTER 27

CORA

By the time my sluggish brain had caught up, it was too late. The damage had been done.

I was achingly aware of my body wrapped around his. Blushing, I scooted off him, and my legs throbbed, sending shooting pain up my body. Somehow, I hadn't felt it until now. Adrenaline? Or maybe my incoherent self just hadn't cared.

I ran my hands through my hair as I tried to think. "I —we kissed?"

"Uh, yeah, but—"

I swore loudly, covering my mouth. "Vince!"

He raised his hands, his expression bewildered. "I don't understand! Cora, you—you're injured, and I—"

"Dammit, dammit, *dammit!*" I dropped my hands and inched closer to him. His eyes burned with heat, and I knew what he was thinking.

I tried not to think about it too.

I felt his forehead. No fever. Yet. So far, the only symptom was purple lips.

That was a good sign. Usually, the poison was instantaneous.

"How—how long?" I asked. "How long were we kissing?"

"Just for like a minute." He was blushing now too.

"And how do you feel?"

"I mean, it was great, Cora—"

"*No*, I mean, do you feel sick? Feverish?"

He frowned. "My lips are burning a little, but . . ." He trailed off, his face now beet red.

I couldn't remember the last time I reapplied the balm. Maybe it had worn off? Maybe it was a less concentrated dose of poison . . .

"Cora, what's going on?" Vince asked.

My hand flew to my forehead. "I . . . I wasn't supposed to kiss you."

"I know. You said that. But why not?"

"Because there's poison on my lips."

Vince's mouth fell open. His face paled, and his eyes grew round as saucers. "*What?*"

"I—I'm sorry! It was a precaution against you, against Damien—"

"Against *me*? I wasn't a threat to you, Cora!"

"I know, I just—"

"How could you not *tell* me?" he demanded, his eyes blazing. "All those moments we had, when we almost—" He cursed, raising a hand to his hair and gripping it firmly. "Cora, I gave you mouth-to-mouth."

Horror pooled in my stomach. "You what?"

"Well, how the hell was I supposed to know you had *poisonous lipstick* on?"

I covered my face with both hands. How could I have been so *stupid*? Vince had come to me from the future, *warning* me not to kiss him!

But then I'd been knocked out. That hadn't happened to me in years.

"When a Bloodcaster loses too much blood, it's like . . . inebriation," I said quietly. "Like being drunk. It's one of the reasons I had to learn self-defense. I become a liability."

"Yeah, I gathered that," Vince snapped.

"Vince, I—I'm sorry." Tears pricked my eyes, and I swallowed. Regret and guilt swirled in my stomach, so thick I couldn't breathe. "I can heal you! I just have to—" With my good hand, I patted my pockets, searching . . .

But then I remembered the fight with Damien. I'd lost the bag with all my potion vials.

I couldn't heal Vince without an elixir.

"I feel fine, Cora." Vince's tone was still harsh. "Let's just find a way back home first."

I blinked. *Back home.* The ground rumbled with a

nearby explosion. Vague memories of battles and gunfire surged to the front of my mind. "Where are we?"

Vince's eyes were grim. "The Demon War. The year 2011."

I gaped at him. "You—you *did* it? But I thought—"

"I know. I thought it would take a whole day. But . . . I don't know, my wings were out, my Nephilim magic was activated. There were lots of other variables."

"You were holding the gold chain," I said numbly, remembering handing it to him. My eyes fell to my outstretched hand. It was covered in purple blood. "Merciful Lilith . . . I was *bleeding*. My blood—" With wide eyes, I stared at Vince. "We might have accidentally cast a spell. Made a kind of elixir with your magic and mine."

Vince's brow furrowed. "Can we do it again? To get back?"

I nodded. "If we replicate the ingredients, we'll reverse the effects. Where's the chain now?"

"Gone."

My heart froze. "What do you mean?"

"The few times I've traveled, whatever I've used as an anchor kind of . . . merges with itself. Otherwise there would be two chains in the same place."

I frowned. "So it's . . ."

"With my mom right now."

A lump formed in my throat, and I swallowed hard. "Okay, so we'll just have to find another anchor to use."

Vince remained silent, his eyes far away.

"Vince?"

"She's out there somewhere," he said softly.

I shook my head. "Vince, the *poison*—"

"I can't just let her die again!"

"But if we wait, you won't be well enough to travel and we'll be stuck here!"

"I don't *care!*" he roared, slamming his fist against the wall so forcefully that a shelf snapped in half and crumbled to the floor. "If I can save my mom, I don't care if I die here."

His eyes burned into mine, and I heard what he wasn't saying. *I don't care if you die, either, Cora.*

I read it in his face. And I didn't blame him one bit. I deserved it.

To be honest, it wasn't the *worst* way to die. At least I was away from Damien and Hector.

"How—how do you know she's still alive?" I asked.

"It's midday," Vince said, his expression stony. "Dad saw it happen in the middle of the night. Mom kept the gold chain on her as a good luck charm. We found it in the rubble after . . . after it was over."

My throat felt tight. I swallowed. "What do you need me to do?"

He looked at me as if just realizing I was there. "You can stay here." His voice was flat. Emotionless.

My mouth fell open. "*Stay here?* Vince—"

"Your arm is broken and you have a head injury. Plus, I know you can't walk right after that concrete fell on you."

"What're you gonna do, go out there and *fight*?" I said angrily, waving my good arm toward the door.

His jaw went rigid. "You think I can't?"

"No, I don't. You're not a killer, Vince. And this is a *war*."

"Just because I'm not as cold-hearted as you," he said, "doesn't mean I can't take care of myself."

He stood, glaring down at me. With a grunt, I scrambled to my feet as he strode toward the door. My knees buckled, and I teetered. Pain sliced through my right leg, but the left one felt fine, so I kept my weight on it.

"Vince!" I called after him. He didn't turn around. "*Vince*! What about your dad?"

He stilled and slowly turned to face me again. "He's safe."

"W-where did you take him?" I sputtered. "How can you be sure Hector won't find him?"

"He won't," Vince said shortly before darting out the door.

I stomped my uninjured foot and gritted my teeth. "Son of a bitch!" With an angry huff, I limped after him, still cradling my arm against my chest.

As soon as I stepped onto the street, gunfire and explosions surrounded me. I winced, my head throbbing violently, and edged away from the street, hoping to avoid getting blasted again. Squinting, I searched for Vince. He couldn't have gone far.

Unless he'd Jumped.

"Idiot," I hissed, hurrying toward the sounds of battle. Gunfire, shouts, and screams echoed around me. I'd fought with worse injuries than this. I'd be fine.

But what about Vince?

A small voice inside me wondered why I even cared. *He hates you,* the voice reminded me. *And you're supposed to kill him.*

But I'd ignored that voice a long time ago. I wasn't certain when, but at some point, I'd shut off all my instincts and chosen Vince instead of my own self-preservation.

It had been the only time in my life I'd put someone else first.

And here I was again, risking my neck to make sure he didn't die.

"I'm an idiot too," I grumbled, turning down another road and looking around frantically. Vince was tall—he was sure to stand out.

A blast of white light burned against my eyes, and I sucked in a breath. But as the light faded, I realized it was another Nephilim. I inched closer, trying to make out the Nephilim's features.

It was a man. Not Vince's mother. I almost turned

away before I did a double take and scrutinized the Nephilim again.

It was Hector Moses.

He looked exactly the same. His black hair was smooth, even in the heat of battle, and his dark eyes blazed with a cold fury. He wielded a dagger in each hand, and his magnificent wings were outstretched behind him. Demons surrounded him, and he slashed and stabbed, his arms a blur as he took down his enemies.

My body itched to turn away, to keep searching for Vince . . .

But if I killed Hector right here, what would happen? Would the future be altered?

Vince and his dad would be safe. Damien would have no ally.

A bolt of longing coursed through me, so intense I took a shaky step forward—

And then realized what a moron I was. I couldn't even beat Hector when I was uninjured. He'd kill me in an instant.

Leaving Vince to fend for himself.

Swearing under my breath, I turned away and hurried in the opposite direction where a larger crowd of demons and casters fought. I glanced upward toward the sky. Ash and smoke filled the air so thickly it was hard to tell what time of day it was. But the sun winked feebly from behind the smog, so I knew there was still time.

A demon lunged for me. I ducked, swinging my good fist so it collided with his jaw. He howled and staggered backward. I stared at him. The lower half of his body resembled a huge gray wolf, but the top half was human. He bared fangs at me, his eyes gleaming yellow.

Some kind of mutated werewolf. I almost pitied him.

Until he attacked again.

My left arm lifted instinctively, sending a flare of pain up my body. I crumpled, and the werewolf collided with me. We fell to the ground in a heap of fur and claws. I kicked him off me and rolled away. He snapped his teeth hungrily, the motion sickeningly disturbing on a human face. His eyes gleamed with malice.

I slammed my forehead against his, and he stumbled. My uninjured foot connected with his hind legs. I kicked again and again until he stopped moving. Wiping sweat from my brow, I hobbled away before he had the chance to heal.

My head throbbed while I pushed forward, half-limping. I glanced over the chaos around me as I searched for Vince. My arm was in agony. Exhaustion pulled at my body.

I have to find him, I thought, pressing on. *I have to find him.*

Sucking in a shaky breath, I surged forward.

Something heavy collided with me, dragging me backward. I kicked and flailed as my assailant pushed me against a pile of wreckage that had once been a building.

I raised my good arm, preparing to shove my fingers into my attacker's eyeballs, and then froze.

It was Vince. His eyes blazed, and a streak of blood stained his cheek.

"What're you doing?" he growled.

I dropped my arm, breathing heavily. "Looking for *you*."

"I told you to stay behind."

I laughed without humor. "And you expected me to listen? I don't answer to you."

"No, just to your demon lover."

My nostrils flared. "Are we really gonna do this now? Here?"

Vince stared at me, his jaw rigid. His lips were still purple, reminding me of what I'd done to him. My resolve flickered and died.

I swallowed. "Have you found her yet?"

Vince shook his head. "Found my dad, though. I'm staying close."

"I saw Hector," I blurted.

Vince's eyes snapped to me. "Where?"

I jerked my head in the direction I'd come. Vince followed my gaze and stared hard, his jaw ticking back and forth as he contemplated. I had no doubt he faced the same inner conflict I had.

"I don't know if Hector was there when it happened," Vince said quietly. "For now, let's leave him. My mom is the priority."

"What does she look like?" I asked.

Vince looked at me, his eyebrows lowering.

Before he could object, I said, "I'm helping you. Don't try to stop me."

Vince sighed. "Her name's Cecile. She's got blond hair. Average height, maybe a little short. Gray eyes."

"Like you."

"Yeah. Like me."

He held my gaze for a long moment. I wanted to apologize—for poisoning him, for deceiving him, for dragging him into this mess with Damien. But something told me that would only make things worse.

Instead, I said, "I never thanked you."

"For what?"

"For saving my life."

Vince watched me, his eyes softening.

"Thank you," I whispered, leaning closer. "I didn't deserve it, but I'm still grateful." My voice broke on the last word. I wasn't used to being indebted to someone. A lump formed in my throat, and I dropped my gaze. I couldn't look at him anymore.

His fingers gently grasped my chin, forcing me to

meet his eyes, which were tender and bright. "I'd do it all over again, Cora."

My mouth felt dry. The memory of our kiss, hot and passionate, floated to the surface of my mind. I knew he remembered it too. His eyes sparked with desire.

Determination pulsed through me, strong and powerful. Fire burned within me. "I swear to you," I said, "I will make sure you and your mom get out of here alive. Even if it kills me."

CHAPTER 28

VINCE

Cora's pledge to help me still rang in my ears even after we'd plunged ourselves into battle. After taking down a shapeshifter—one-handed—she grabbed the demon's discarded dagger and tossed it to me.

Surprised, I caught it by the hilt. "But . . . you need this more than I do." I offered it back to her.

Cora shot me a hard look and shook her head before tackling another demon who lunged for her. Even with her broken arm, her body moved with elegance and grace. It was almost like a dance.

She's incredible, I thought, awestruck. Though I longed to simply watch Cora in action, I kept my mind focused on our goal.

Find Mom. Keep her alive.

Cora and I fought side-by-side for hours. A few yards

away, I made out the black hair of my dad as he fought. I didn't want to get too close, just in case. But I had to make sure he stayed nearby.

Sweat and blood covered my face. I kept glancing at Cora to make sure she was all right. She was fading. Her movements became sluggish. A gargoyle sliced into her shoulder, and she cried out.

I kicked the demon I was fighting and buried the dagger in his throat. Then, I slammed into the gargoyle, pinning him to the ground. While he was down, Cora took my blade and drove it into the demon's neck. He choked on his own blood before he went completely still.

Panting, I looked at Cora. Her eyes were haggard, and her face was sticky with blood—but it was red, so I knew it wasn't hers.

Even if it kills me, she'd said.

As I stared at her, a painful desperation tore through me, fierce and powerful. *I don't want her to die.*

The small, logical part of my brain knew her death would make things easier for me. Being around her only made my life more dangerous.

But I couldn't lose her. My entire being was tethered to her. No matter what she'd done—no matter how much I shouldn't want her.

She had to survive this.

I stepped closer to her and cupped her face in my hands. "Don't die," I whispered. "I need you, Cora."

Shock flitted across her face, and her lips parted. Emotion stirred in her eyes.

A pair of werewolves leapt for us. We both ducked. Claws raked down my arm, and I cried out. Cora slashed the dagger and cut into both of them. Blood dripped onto my shirt, but I couldn't tell if it was mine or not. Pain flared through my body.

Cora raised her good arm and shouted,

"Vile demons of unholy crimes,

I banish you 'til the end of time!"

Her hands glowed purple, and the werewolves shuddered. The magic surrounded them until a bright light momentarily blinded me. The werewolves howled before vanishing.

Cora fell backward into my arms, and I held her against me. She felt ice cold and limp.

"Cora?" I said.

She didn't answer.

Panic pulsed through me. I glanced around, worried another demon would try to attack while Cora was unconscious. But for now, we were alone.

Conflict swirled in my mind. Find Mom . . . or get Cora to safety? I glanced upward at the darkening sky. It wasn't quite dusk. We still had time, but not much.

I hoisted her up in my arms and ran across the street to the sidewalk, using the shade of a nearby building for cover. Gingerly, I set her down on the dusty ground, propping her up on the brick wall.

"Cora," I whispered, touching her cheek. Her head lolled to the side. I searched for a pulse. It was there, but it was faint.

I hung my head, groaning in agony. This was my fault. I should've taken her back home right away. She was injured, for Lilith's sake. She'd lost so much blood she was delirious and chatty, and then I'd made her fight with a broken arm.

With a heavy sigh, I fished through my pockets, looking for something to use as an anchor to take us back home. Wedged in my back pocket, I found Cora's dagger. My breath caught in my throat. How had I forgotten about this? For a moment, I ran a finger along the decorative swirls on the hilt, marveling at its beauty.

I swallowed hard. Hopefully, the dagger would be a strong enough anchor to bring us home. This wasn't worth getting Cora killed. No matter what she'd done to me, I couldn't lose her.

Even if it meant not saving my mom.

What had Cora said? If we could replicate the spell . . .

I needed the same ingredients as before. The anchor, Cora's blood, and my wings.

Damn. That was easier said than done. My wings

tended to pop out on their own. I couldn't always control it.

"First things first," I muttered. I brushed my fingers against the injury on Cora's shoulder. Bright purple blood gleamed on my fingertips.

"What're you doing?" Cora croaked.

I jumped, my heart skittering madly. Cora's eyes fluttered open. Her face was losing color.

"I'm getting you home," I said. "You'll die here."

Cora let out a raspy chuckle. "I'll die back home too. Damien and Hector are waiting for me."

"You can take them." I tried to keep my tone light.

Half her mouth quirked up in a tired smile. "Leave me, Vince. Go find your mom. You can take her back."

I stared at her. "What about you?"

"I won't make it."

"Cora—"

"Don't." Her eyes flickered with that same intensity I was used to. "I'm tired of running, Vince. It's better this way. I've finally found something worth dying for."

I stilled, my heart thundering in my chest. She couldn't mean that. It was just the blood loss talking.

But she looked at me with clarity in her gaze. "I'm sorry," she whispered. "For everything."

"I'm *not* leaving you," I said through gritted teeth.

"I need to heal," she said, leaning her head back

against the wall. "I can't heal in the middle of a battle. If I hadn't lost my bag in the fight with Damien, I could use my healing elixir."

"What are the ingredients?" I asked. Hope sprang to life in my chest. "Maybe I can make a potion for you."

"Eye of newt, wormwood, angelica," she said with a smirk. "Not exactly stuff you'd find lying around."

"I'm a Jumper. I'll just Jump to an apothecary and come right back—"

"Vince, *no*. You need to save your strength."

I barked out a laugh. "You're one to talk."

"I'm serious! What happens if you Jump and you accidentally go back further in time? Or you return to the future *without* your mom?"

My hope deflated like a balloon. "I can't just do *nothing*."

"You can do something," she said. "You can find your mom."

"I'm not—"

"Don't let this all be for nothing."

"No, *listen* to me," I growled, leaning forward and placing both my hands on her cheeks. "You're staying with me even if I have to drag your ass around this city. *I'm* the one who's been poisoned, remember? If anyone dies here today, it's me."

Cora frowned at me. "That's right. You were poisoned." Her eyes widened. "Ah. Nephilim magic."

I blinked. "What?"

"It has healing properties."

I stiffened. I knew this. How often had I seen Hector or one of the other officials heal someone? "I can heal you."

Cora sighed sleepily. "No, you can't."

"I can try!"

"Vince, you can't even control when your wings come out. Healing is a precise and delicate art. You can't just do it on a whim."

"How would you know?" I snapped. "Have you used Nephilim magic before?"

"Yeah. I made a potion once—"

"Forget it," I said quickly. "Let me just try, okay? What have you got to lose? Worst-case scenario, I kill you, and you get your wish."

Cora chuckled hoarsely. "All right, fine. Take your best shot."

I took a deep breath and lifted my hands, unsure of where to put them. After some deliberation, I put them on her head, then felt ridiculous when she laughed.

I closed my eyes, envisioning the lacrosse field again. My crosse was in my hands. The smell of grass surrounded me. My opponents flanked me.

I looked around for Luke, but he wasn't there.

Shaking my head, I thought, *It's fine. It's just your imagination. You can do this.*

I swung the crosse, tossing the ball. My opponents surged forward. Adrenaline pulsed through me. Magic crackled within me. A beam of light shone on the field, and I focused on it. With my stick in hand, I rushed toward it. Energy roared within me until I felt my bones rattling.

Cora gasped, jolting me from my vision. My eyes snapped open, and I looked at her expectantly. My hands were glowing an ethereal white, and my wings were stretched out behind me.

But her injury remained. The dried blood formed a deep purple splotch on her head like a grape jelly stain. Her face was still pale, her body weak and limp.

I dropped my hands in frustration. It hadn't worked.

But I felt different. My Nephilim magic swelled within me, ready to burst.

Cora stared at me with wide eyes, and I frowned. "What is it?" I asked.

"It's just—you're glowing," Cora murmured, awestruck. "It's breathtaking."

Heat flooded my face. "Oh. Um, thanks."

"I had a vision of you like this," she said. "Well, I had a vision of you from earlier. Right before we traveled." Then, she grimaced. "It was from my Seeing elixir."

"Seeing elixir?" I repeated warily.

"Yeah. You drank it too."

My head reared back. "What?"

"The hot chocolate I gave you. Remember?"

"What . . . what did it do to me?" I wasn't sure I wanted to know.

"Just made you have visions about me. That's all."

My brow furrowed. "But why?"

"Visions can show me things I can't find out on my own. In order to ensure my visions were only of you, we both had to take the potion. I figured it would give me more information about you." Her cheeks turned red, and she dropped her gaze.

My brow furrowed as I struggled to remember. *Had* I had a vision of her? Then, my blood ran cold. I looked around at the carnage and chaos around us. "This," I whispered. "I saw *this*. Remember? I told you I saw you standing in the middle of a battle. Not doing anything."

Cora watched me for a long moment before she laughed. "I remember. I was confused at the time, but now it makes sense." She exhaled slowly. "Go find your Mom."

I blinked. "Cora—"

"The healing didn't work. Go find her."

I swallowed, glancing over my shoulder. We were still alone, but a pack of demons fought a Nephilim nearby. They would spot us soon. I looked back at Cora and clasped her hand in both of mine.

"My mom can heal you," I said. "I'll find her and bring her here. I swear it, Cora."

She offered a small smile. "I'll be fine."

"Take this. We can use it to get back to our time." I placed the hilt of the dagger in the palm of her hand. For a moment, Cora stared at the dagger, her eyes sparking with recognition. Her lips parted, and she looked at me in surprise.

I brushed a kiss along her fingertips. "I'll come back for you."

She smiled again, but it didn't reach her eyes. "Be careful."

I nodded before rising to my feet and hurrying away from her. My stomach churned with unease, but the thrum of Nephilim magic coursing through me gave me strength. I stretched my arms and shoulders, trying to find the muscles of my wings. The weight behind me dragged, slowing me down. I cracked my back, rolled my shoulders, and flexed my arms before I finally found it. My wings twitched in response, and I closed my eyes, sensing the muscles. I pushed and pulled, and my giant wings flapped behind me. Just the singular motion left me gasping for breath. The wings were so damn *heavy*.

Again, I urged myself. I flexed the muscles again, and my wings flapped once more. This time, it felt easier.

Whoosh. A gust of wind tousled my hair. Whoosh.

My feet lifted off the ground. Whoosh. My arms and back burned, but I was flying now.

When I hovered several yards above the ground, I leaned forward, still flapping my wings. I soared fast—too fast. I tried to slow down, but I didn't know how. A building grew closer and closer. I was about to smash into it—

With a grunt, I swiveled to the side, struggling to keep myself in the air as I did a ridiculous somersault to avoid crashing. My eyes roved over the battle below me, searching for the bright blond hair of my mom. Bursts of white light drew my attention, but as my eyes fell on each Nephilim, my stomach sank with disappointment.

Not her, I thought in frustration after checking the tenth Nephilim. *Where the hell is she?*

A mass of demons huddled together about half a mile from where I left Cora. Squinting, I turned slowly, flapping my wings to carry me closer. A small beam of light pierced through the center of the demons, momentarily illuminating the figure in the middle.

My heart stopped. It was her.

Mom.

Her long blond hair was a tangled mess behind her, falling out of the bun she usually kept it in. Her gray eyes blazed. Enormous white wings were outstretched behind her, but several demons grabbed hold of her feathers, tearing her down so she couldn't take flight.

Dread coiled in my stomach. My mom was completely outnumbered. There were no other Nephilim nearby.

This was it. Her life would end here, among this circle of demons.

I relaxed my wing muscles, drifting in the air as I slowly descended. Arching backward, I lifted my legs, landing with a kick in the face of the demon closest to my mom. The demon howled in pain as I fell on top of him, rising to my feet and punching him in the face.

Mom gaped at me, pausing only for a moment before slashing at a demon with a bolt of white magic. "Who are you?" she cried.

The sound of her voice jolted memories buried deep within me, making me falter. A demon wrapped his fingers around my leg and tugged, knocking me off my feet. With a roar, I thrust my arms forward, and a jet of white magic burst into the demon's chest, sending him flying.

"A friend," I said, hopping to my feet and kicking another demon away from my mom.

Together, we fought, and the crowd of demons slowly thinned. When they spread far enough for Mom to access her wings, she swung around, flapping wildly so a strong gust of wind whipped toward the demons. Several of them fell over from the impact, and dozens of feathers swirled in the air.

Another burst of white light, and a pair of demons fell.

I almost got stabbed because I was so distracted. A demon swung a blade toward me, and I was too slow to duck. It cut into the top of my shoulder, and I yelped as pain exploded down my arm. I aimed a punch, but the demon caught my arm and twisted. Remembering my wings, I focused on those muscles, which throbbed and ached from my flight. Gritting my teeth against the agony coursing through me, I flapped my wings and focused on the demon who still gripped my arm.

Wind spiraled behind me. My magic glowed, and white light assaulted the demon. He released me and fell backward with a shrill cry.

Mom took down the last remaining demon, leaving us standing amidst a pile of corpses. She wiped sweat from her brow and turned to face me. Aside from a minor cut above her eyebrow, she looked unharmed. Her eyes were bright, and she grinned at me.

"You're not a soldier, are you?" she asked.

I laughed. "What gave me away?"

She shrugged and stuck out her hand. "Either way, thanks for your help."

I shook it, wishing I could cling to her hand forever. Swallowing, I said, "I could use your help. My friend is mortally wounded. Can you heal her?"

Mom frowned. "Why can't you do it?"

"I—I can't."

Mom's eyes widened in understanding, her gaze roving over my face. I knew she was taking in my appearance, probably noting how young I was. Her brows knitted together, and curiosity sparked in her eyes. "Right," she said slowly. "Yes, of course I'll help. Lead the way."

CHAPTER 29

CORA

Playing dead, as it turned out, was a very effective survival strategy.

I was fading. I knew I wouldn't be able to hold my own in a fight. Though I clung to the hilt of my dagger like it was a lifeline, I remained slumped over and kept my eyes closed.

Demons just passed me by, assuming I was already dead.

It wasn't hard. My body held on by a thread, barely clinging to life. I knew I had to stay awake—because if I didn't, I might never wake up.

But exhaustion tugged on me like a heavy weight, trying to drag me down to the depths of unconsciousness.

And oh, how I longed to submit.

Vince needs you, a small voice whispered in my head.

Does he? I whispered back. *I've only made his life worse. I can't even fight right now, and that's the only thing I'm good at.*

Throughout my life, I had a clear goal: kill to survive. Look out for myself and no one else. Never look back.

But meeting Vince had turned everything upside down.

Suddenly, I wasn't just looking out for myself. I was looking out for him. And now I was making all these crazy decisions that put my neck on the line.

For what? For suddenly developing a conscience? For falling for the man I was supposed to kill? We could never be together; I knew that.

So *why?* I wanted to scream at myself, to shake my shoulders and knock some sense into my muddled brain.

Perhaps death was easier. Vince's life would be better. I could finally rest and stop running. Stop fighting.

I'd fought my whole life. I was tired.

Well, it's nice to know that the person responsible for my undoing is an inexperienced, kind-hearted Nephilim who's never taken a life before, I thought bitterly.

But picturing Vince sent a tendril of warmth through my chest, and I realized I didn't regret it at all.

The blood loss was making my head spin. I wasn't moving, but I felt my surroundings shift and swirl like a kaleidoscope. Nausea rose in my stomach.

Just take me already, I silently begged Death.

A thin beam of light glistened in front of me, burning

through my eyelids. I grimaced, flinching away from it. Another Nephilim, perhaps?

No . . . This wasn't a white light.

Slowly, I cracked open my eyes and gasped. A warm red glow surrounded a winged figure. But instead of the usual pearly white wings, this Nephilim had black wings, like a giant raven.

My mouth fell open as I stared at the Nephilim in awe. A *dark* angel? I'd never seen one before.

As my eyes adjusted to the light, I made out the face of the man in front of me.

It was Vince.

My mouth felt dry as he approached me and knelt at my feet. His eyes were soft, but there was something different about him. His hair was cut short so it no longer fell in his eyes, and his face was hardened by something I couldn't explain. There was a grimness in his expression that I often saw in my own reflection.

It made me feel strangely sad.

"Not yet, Cora," Vince whispered, brushing his knuckles against my cheek.

I blinked, and he vanished. The eerie red light was gone. I was completely alone, tucked away in the shadows as I hid from the battle.

My heart skittered in my chest. Had I imagined it?

Of course I had. I couldn't trust my brain right now.

But the smooth caress of his fingers on my face had

felt so real . . .

And it wouldn't have been the first time a different version of Vince had visited me.

But . . . a *dark* angel? Like a Reaper?

My body felt numb with shock as I remembered what Vince had said. *If I leave the clan, I'll become a Reaper. Reapers are more susceptible to dark magic. No one's met a Reaper before. They just . . . vanish.*

My throat went dry, and my head throbbed. This wasn't possible. Reapers didn't exist, right? No one had ever seen one.

I must've been hallucinating. That was the only explanation.

"Cora!" a voice shouted.

I started, my eyes widening as Vince and a blond woman approached me. Vince touched my face—similar to how Reaper-Vince had done just moments ago. But this time, his fingers were sticky with blood and caked with dirt. His white wings were outstretched behind him just like the woman.

I stared at the woman, suddenly realizing who she was. Cecile—Vince's mother.

A lump formed in my throat, but I was too weak to say anything.

"Lilith, are you all right?" Vince asked, peering into my eyes. He held my face in both of his hands and turned me so I looked at him.

I blinked slowly at him, and his face drained of color. Not a good sign. I must've been worse off than I thought.

"Can you heal her, Mo—" Vince's mouth clamped shut as he turned to his mother. "Can you?"

Cecile nodded and crouched in front of me. Her skin was pale and smooth, and her soft features seemed elegant enough to belong to a queen. I recognized the gold necklace hanging from her neck—the chain with the key.

"Head injury?" she asked. Her voice was deeper than I'd expected.

"Yeah," Vince said.

Cecile touched my forehead and frowned. I winced when she gently brushed her fingers against my wound. Her hand came back coated in my purple blood.

Cecile stared at the blood for a long moment. Something unreadable stirred in her eyes. She looked at me, her shrewd gaze missing nothing.

She knew what I was.

Slowly, Cecile turned to face Vince. "Who are you?" she demanded.

Vince blinked. "What?"

"I can't just heal her without knowing who you two are. I don't even know whose side you're on."

"I'm Nephilim," Vince said indignantly.

"But *she* isn't." Cecile jerked her head toward me.

Vince shook his head. "We aren't a threat to you.

We're only passing through. You—you won't see us again, I swear it."

He can't mean that, I thought. *He can't just leave her here to die.*

"Please," Vince begged, his voice cracking. "She can't die. She's—she's too important to me."

He doesn't mean that, either, I thought, closing my eyes. Perhaps I was hallucinating again.

Cecile sighed. "Very well." Her gentle hands touched my head again, and I grimaced as a fresh wave of pain flooded through me.

"By the power of pure Nephilim magic in me,
I summon white light to banish impurity from thee."

A white glow surrounded me, blinding me even with my eyes closed. I squinted, trying to turn away from the blazing light, but Cecile held me in place. Warmth tickled my head, tingling along my body as it spread. It coursed through me like a river, and strength returned to my body. I breathed deeply. The ache in my head vanished. The feeling in my arm returned as my bones mended themselves.

I sucked in a sharp gasp when Cecile broke contact. A sudden chill swept over me as the warmth left me.

But I was healed. Energy pulsed through me, and though I was still covered in dirt and blood, I felt like I could run a marathon. Clarity burst in my mind, strong and refreshing.

"Thank you," I breathed, looking at Cecile in wonder.

Her lips pressed together in a thin line. I knew she still had reservations about healing me.

Vince dived forward, crushing me against his chest in a tight embrace. His hand cradled the back of my head like I was something precious. The urgent, affectionate gesture made my eyes burn and my throat feel tight.

"Thank Lilith," Vince whispered against my hair. He drew back to look me over and laughed in amazement.

My lips parted as our eyes locked. Our faces were only a breath away from each other. The joy in his eyes was so alluring I found myself leaning closer . . .

"If you'll excuse me, I must return to the battle," Cecile said, rising to her feet.

A cold brush of reality swept over me. Vince's smile faded as he looked up at his mother.

"Wait," Vince said, jumping to his feet. "Please don't go. I—I have to talk to you."

Cecile huffed in exasperation. "It'll have to wait. As I said, I don't even know you. And my people are *dying*. I've wasted enough time already." She turned away.

"No, *please*—" Vince cried.

"Cecile!" boomed a voice.

I stilled, my blood running cold. I knew that voice.

Vince stiffened as he looked toward the interruption.

Hector approached, his great wings fluttering behind

him. He drew closer to Cecile with outstretched arms. "There you are. I was worried you'd been killed."

Cecile straightened. "Do you have so little faith in me?"

Hector smiled without humor. "Of course not." He bowed deeply. "I'm relieved our leader is unharmed." His gaze slid to Vince, and suspicion sparked in his eyes.

Something wasn't right.

I tried to rise, but Vince shifted, blocking me from Hector's view. Shielding me.

I froze. Why was he protecting me? I was healed—I could *help*.

"Who are you?" Hector asked Vince.

"A friend," Vince said. "Just passing through."

I couldn't see Hector, but I knew this answer didn't satisfy him.

"Strangers aren't welcome here," Hector said sharply. "Especially not here in battle where foes are lying in wait."

"He's with me," Cecile said, her voice sharp with authority. "Don't question him, Hector."

An awkward silence fell between them. I held my breath, my eyes wide as I waited for a response.

"Of course," Hector said in a tight voice.

More silence. My palms were sweaty as I curled my fingers into fists.

"Where are the others?" Cecile asked. "Where is my

husband?"

"He's well. I saw him fighting earlier. He can handle himself."

"Take me to him."

"Of course," Hector said again.

But no one moved. Again, that eerie feeling of suspicion settled in my bones.

And slowly, the pieces slid together in my mind.

Hector, the clan leader intent on sealing his people off from the world. Damien, who could take out those who stood in the way. Like Vince.

And Cecile. The clan leader who died, leaving Hector in charge.

"Vince—" I jumped to my feet.

A screech tore through the air as a horde of demons appeared out of nowhere, surrounding Cecile. I grabbed Vince's arm and dragged him back into the shadows with me. He struggled, but I held him tight.

"Be quiet," I hissed in his ear. "Not yet."

Gargoyles, werewolves, and vampires crowded around Cecile, their bodies restless and their eyes hungry.

Cecile backed away from them uncertainly, but there was nowhere to go. She was completely surrounded. "Hector, what is this?"

"I'm truly sorry," Hector said softly. "It isn't personal. But it must be done."

"*What* must be done?" Cecile demanded, her tone icy.

Her hands formed tight fists, and her wings quivered in anticipation.

Vince went taut, the tendons standing out in his arms and neck. I squeezed his hand. "Not yet," I said again. For now, Hector had forgotten about him. We had to keep it that way.

"It's for the good of the clan," Hector said. He raised his hand in the air, and the demons howled with excitement before surging forward.

Cecile blasted several demons with a burst of bright light. But the horde kept coming.

"Now!" I shouted.

Vince and I joined the fray. I passed him the dagger, feeling confident enough without it since I'd been healed. I ducked to avoid a demon's blow and aimed a kick into his chest. He staggered backward, and I landed a punch in his jaw. Another kick, and he was unconscious. I swiped his knife and buried it into the throat of another demon.

A soft *pop* sounded behind me, and I whirled around in alarm. Then, Vince reappeared behind the demon he'd been fighting. The demon was so surprised he didn't react when Vince sliced his throat. Another *pop*, and Vince disappeared again.

A slow smile spread across my face. Warmth and awe spread through me. *Look how far he's come,* I thought to myself.

He certainly wasn't perfect. With his next Jump, he stumbled, and a demon hit him in the shoulder. But Vince was resilient. He popped back up, dodged another blow, and easily overcame the demon.

Hector's minions weren't bright. We could easily defeat them. But there were too many. A dozen crowded Cecile, and though her Nephilim magic was powerful, it drained her. Each blast of white light grew more and more feeble. The demons never stopped.

"Vince!" I shouted, looking around wildly for him.

Pop. He appeared next to me, his face covered in sweat. "What's wrong?" he panted.

I kicked another demon down and jerked my head toward Cecile. "She needs help. She's fading."

Vince nodded and Jumped again, reappearing alongside his mother. They fought back-to-back, forming a powerful duo. I stopped to watch for a moment. The mother-son team was impressive—their great wings stretched behind them, and their magnificent white magic assaulted their foes. For one strange moment, I found myself wistful and almost *jealous*. What would it be like to have that kind of power?

My distraction cost me. A gargoyle raked his claws down my back, and I cried out before smashing my forehead against his. While he was disoriented, I grabbed his head and twisted, snapping his neck easily.

Vince's shout cut through the battle, ringing in my

ears. I froze, straightening as I searched for him. He'd gone down—he was no longer standing with his mother.

"Vince!" I cried, shoving past demons to get to him. Panic raced through me as I scanned the crowd frantically. Where was he?

I finally found him crouched on all fours, breathing heavily. Blood ran freely down his arm. His lips were still purple, and his face had drained of color.

Ice hardened in my stomach. *No.* Could the poison finally be affecting him? His wings shook. His eyes rolled back.

I dropped to the ground next to him and grabbed his shoulders. "Vince, look at me."

He groaned feebly before meeting my gaze, his eyes vacant and lost. "I'm f-fading," he whispered.

Desperation coursed through me. I touched his cheek, holding his face in my hands. "*No!* You have to hang on. Just a little longer. Please."

"My . . . wings," he rasped. "My Nephilim magic . . . won't last much longer."

I stilled, staring at him. "The poison?"

He shook his head. "Not that. I'm underage. It doesn't last long. Keeping my wings out . . . I can't . . ." He trailed off with a groan, hanging his head.

I stared at him, numb with shock. A demon lunged for us, but I stabbed him in the stomach before turning back to Vince.

If his Nephilim magic was fading, then how would we get back home?

I shook my head. Surviving this battle was the priority. Saving his mom was more important. We could return home anytime. We could wait until he was fully recovered and travel tomorrow or the next day. It didn't matter as long as we survived this.

I brushed his hair behind his ears and pressed my forehead to his. He smelled of sweat and mint. "Stay down," I breathed. "I've got this."

Jumping to my feet, I spun and sliced through two demons at once. I kicked another in the face. A punch to the throat. A stab in the gut. Sticky demon blood coated my arms. The thrill of the fight consumed me. I was unstoppable.

An explosion of white magic filled the air, rippling through the crowd like a sonic boom. Everyone teetered and collided with each other, including me and Cecile. I grabbed her to keep her upright. She looked me over in brief confusion, as if surprised I was fighting alongside her. I glanced around, relieved to find Vince still huddled on the ground. His face looked ashen.

"Enough!" roared a voice.

The demons all froze, looking up in fear. The white light intensified, blinding me. I raised a hand to shield my face. The air crackled with the ashy smell of light magic.

Hector.

"I don't know who your friends are," he said, his voice drawing nearer. "But they've made this exceedingly difficult for me." He sighed, and the light faded as he approached. My fingers gripped the hilt of my knife. He was almost close enough to stab . . .

"I don't want to kill you, Cecile," Hector said.

So close, I thought. *Just one more step.*

"Then *don't*," Cecile said. "You have a choice, Hector."

Hector took a step closer. "I know. That's—"

I lunged, swinging my blade. He sidestepped me, but I nicked his collarbone. I advanced again. A blast of white magic hit me in the chest. With a grunt, I toppled backward.

"Foolish girl!" he bellowed, raising his hands toward me.

"Stop!" Cecile rushed forward, putting herself between us with her arms raised. "It's me you want, Hector. Leave her be."

Hector's eyes blazed as he glared at me. Slowly, his gaze moved to Cecile, and his face slackened. "Very well," he said through clenched teeth. He shifted so his hands were outstretched toward Cecile. "*Cecile Delgado, by the Nephilim power within me, I—*"

"No!" I shrieked, scrambling to my feet. Cecile spread

her arms, blocking me from reaching Hector. "Cecile, *no!*" I shouted.

Shouting over me, Hector continued, "*I strip you of your light magic and banish you to the realm of the Reapers! May you—*"

A strangled roar tore through the air, cutting off Hector's words. Sparks exploded in the air, and a figure tackled Hector, pinning him to the ground.

My heart lurched into my throat. *Vince.*

He clawed at Hector's face, landing a punch to the older man's jaw. Light magic whipped in the air, and Vince went flying. In a panic, I lifted my hands, and my purple magic surrounded him like a cloud, easing him gently to the ground.

Hector's angry eyes fixed on me. "Blood witch," he whispered.

I faced him, my nostrils flaring. My entire body quivered with rage. "Bring it on, old man."

Hector bared his teeth like an animal before lunging. I ducked, stabbing him in the thigh before rolling under him. Another slice in the back. And again in the arm. White light blasted around me, but I turned my head, rolling again to escape the heat of his magic. A hand reached for me, and I couldn't dodge in time. Fingers grabbed a fistful of my hair and yanked me to my feet. I cried out, reaching fruitlessly to free myself from Hector's grip. I felt like a child about to be spanked.

"Cora!" Vince cried. His voice sounded weak.

"You are a thorn in my side, girl," Hector snarled. Raising his free hand, he sliced his magic into my chest. A white-hot pain cut through me. My body was on fire. Hector released me, and I crumpled. I couldn't breathe. My throat was scorched. My chest throbbed with fresh agony. Stars danced in my vision. I staggered, trying to rise, but the pain was too intense. My arms shook. Nausea roiled in my stomach.

Distantly, I made out Hector's voice as he continued his spell.

"May you live out the rest of your days as a Reaper among the dead. With the white magic within me, I banish you from this realm."

"No," I moaned feebly.

Magic crackled in the air. A pearly glow consumed Cecile, and she screamed. Red magic bled through, swirling sinisterly with Hector's magic. A massive crevice formed in the ground with a mighty *crack*. Crimson smoke pooled from the abyss, swallowing up Cecile. Her screams faded, echoing in the endless pit as she fell. The ground rumbled, and the crevice sealed itself. The red and white magic slowly vanished, leaving Vince, Hector, and me standing among a throng of demons.

Cecile was gone.

CHAPTER 30

VINCE

A TORRENT OF AGONY CONSUMED ME. EACH MUSCLE ached and burned. My wings felt like they were tearing through my flesh with each breath I took.

My mom's scream echoed around me. But when I tried to rise, my vision darkened, threatening to take me down again.

I blinked, struggling to see. Something glinted on the ground next to me.

Mom's gold chain.

I wasn't sure how it had fallen off. But the sight of it sent an explosion of agony splitting through me. My face crumpled, and I grabbed the chain. It was speckled with dirt and blood.

No, I thought weakly. *Mom.*

I collapsed with a groan, succumbing to the pain.

Something nudged me. My eyes flickered open to find Hector crouched over me, his expression curious.

My blood ran cold, and I hastily dropped the chain, then shifted to hide it from view. I tried to stand again. Hector pressed his boot against my chest, crushing me. I choked, struggling to breathe.

"I don't know who you are," he hissed. "But I swear on Lilith's name I will end you for getting in my way."

I coughed and sputtered before croaking, "I'd . . . like to see you try."

A fierce cry split through the air, and Hector went down. I blinked, looking around in alarm.

Then, I saw her. Cora tugged Hector away from me, dragging her blade through his shoulder. Hector roared in pain and shoved Cora away from him.

On your feet, Vince, I told myself. I stood, teetering slightly. A demon was there, baring his teeth at me. He landed a punch on my face, and I staggered backward.

Stay on your feet, I ordered.

The demon aimed another punch. I ducked just in time.

"Vince!" Cora shouted.

I'm here. But I couldn't speak. It required too much brain power. Another blow hit me in the gut. I hunched over. I wouldn't last much longer. Cora grunted, and a burst of purple light filled the air as she fought Hector.

Suddenly, she was in front of me, holding my shoulders. "*Now,* Vince," she gasped.

"What?" I whispered.

Cora raised my hand to the blood trickling from her shoulder wound. My fingers came back coated in purple. "The dagger?"

I stared at her, dazed.

Cora swore and pressed the hilt of her dagger into my palm. "*Focus,* Vince. Just one more time."

She twirled, kicking a demon out of the way. Hector lunged, but Cora spun out of his way, as elegant as a ballerina.

I closed my eyes, gritting my teeth against the pain. *One more time,* I thought to myself. *You can hang on for one more.*

In my mind, I was on the lacrosse field again. Once more, Luke was absent. But I knew I could do this without him. I *had* to.

I gripped the crosse in my hands tightly. *Go forward,* whispered a voice. *Go forward in time.* I lunged, dodging my opponents. The ball soared toward me, and I raised my crosse to catch it.

Forward, the voice whispered.

The ground shifted beneath me. "Cora!" I shouted.

Her warm hand found mine and gripped it tightly. My other hand still held the dagger. It was slick with sweat and blood. The air spun, and we lost our footing, but I held Cora's hand like a lifeline. Gravity left me. I was weightless. Floating. My stomach dropped, and bile crept up my throat. Voices and shapes distorted around me.

Then, everything slammed back into place so violently my head throbbed. A mind-numbing pain wracked through me as my wings finally gave in, receding back into my shoulder blades.

Cora's hand slid out of my grip.

Agony pulsed through my head like it had its own heartbeat. *Pain, pain, pain,* it seemed to say.

"Vince," whispered a voice.

Cora. Thank Lilith she'd made it.

"Nice of you to join us," the voice said.

Unease crept through me. Something wasn't right.

I shivered, my entire body trembling. The nausea in my stomach intensified until I heaved, vomiting on the ground.

"Lovely," the voice said in disgust.

Not Cora. I tried opening my eyes, but they were cemented shut. My skin felt hot and cold at the same time. I shuddered, wrapping my arms around myself to keep warm, but it did no good.

The voice chuckled. "Poisoned balm." Whoever spoke was male.

Where was Cora?

"Nasty stuff," he went on. "I've seen it firsthand. It

isn't pretty. If you like, I can end you right now. Spare you the torment."

A feeble spark of clarity shot through my mind. *Damien.*

Since I couldn't see, I tried using my other senses to figure out where I was. The sun warmed my skin. Concrete scraped against me. I sniffed the air. Faint gunpowder. The ashy scent of magic. And a familiar whiff of pine tree mingled with Nephilim wings.

I was back in my neighborhood. I must've traveled right back to where we'd left off—the fight with Damien.

"Where . . . is . . . she?" I said hoarsely.

Damien laughed again. "I don't think you should be so concerned about the bitch who poisoned you."

A roar of fury ripped through me, and I lunged. In a flash, my warlock magic surged to life. A faint *pop* echoed, and the ground shifted. My vision blurred, and I slumped over.

"Cora," I moaned faintly.

"Vince?"

I tried looking around, but I was blinded. The poison coursed through me, fierce and strong. "Don't . . ."

"Don't what?" she asked.

"Don't . . . kiss . . . me," I whispered. But a small part of my brain registered that it didn't matter. It was too late.

I'd given her mouth-to-mouth. And even if I'd known

her lips were poisonous, I would've done it all over again. I wouldn't have let her die.

Another *pop*, and the ground shifted. I heaved and vomited again.

"What the hell?" Damien said. I heard some scuffling, and then a rough pair of hands turned me over so I lay on my back on the concrete. The sun blazed overhead—it warmed my face.

But I still couldn't see anything. Just a blinding white light.

"Where did you get that?" Damien murmured. His voice was soft and dangerous. It made my skin crawl.

Hands reached for me again. A small clinking sound made me frown. What was that?

"Did she give this to you?" Damien said sharply. "Where is she?"

I shook my head, confusion swirling within me. What was he talking about?

"Well, it doesn't matter now," Damien went on. "You can't heal without this. And I'd wager your Nephilim magic has run out, so you're as good as dead anyway."

Nephilim magic. Of course. It had healing powers.

But I'd used too much of it. I had a limited supply since I was underage. And now it was gone.

Allowing the poison in my body to run its course.

"Vince!" shrieked a voice.

Cora. I tried to rise, but my body wouldn't move. I

felt nothing but icy chills quivering through me. Black spots bled through the white nothingness of my vision. Sickness swirled in my gut, and I knew I would puke again.

Before I could, I passed out.

"Vince," whispered a voice.

I groaned. In my mind, I saw my mother's fierce expression as she battled demons. Her glowing blond hair and steely gray eyes. The way she held her ground in the face of danger.

She didn't even flinch.

It achingly reminded me of someone else I knew. Someone with chilling blue eyes . . .

"Vince," the voice said again.

"Mom," I mumbled, turning my head. My eyes wouldn't open. It was like they were cemented shut. As consciousness slowly sharpened my mind, a crippling pain wracked through my body. I shuddered, wrapping my arms around my stomach.

Something warm pressed against my cheek. I sighed, relishing the soft feeling of comfort that washed over me.

"Wake up, Vince."

I blinked. Black crept into the corners of my vision, but I could see again. Everything was fuzzy. I could barely make out a figure sitting next to me in a dark room.

But she wasn't Mom.

Disappointment swelled within me, and I shivered against the chills that overcame me. "I feel . . ." I said hoarsely.

"I know. It's the poison. I'm so sorry, Vince."

I frowned. Gradually, my mind caught up. I faintly registered the familiar smell of lilacs as the figure drew closer. "C-Cora?" I asked.

"Yes, it's me."

I swallowed. A mixture of emotions filled me. Relief. Regret. Anger. Confusion.

"Where are we?" I tried sitting up but groaned when agony consumed me, freezing me in place.

"Shh," Cora said. Warmth pressed into me again. "Lie still. We're in a prison cell in Hinport."

Hinport. The city of demons.

"Damien?" I asked.

"Yes. He cuffed us with dampeners. We can't use our magic."

I huffed a feeble laugh. "I couldn't use it anyway. Too weak."

"I know." Cora's voice was heavy with anguish. "I found my healing elixir. It was in the bag I'd dropped during the fight with Damien. I . . . I tried sending it to you. I was too far away, but I thought if I could cast a spell, I could get it to you quick enough. It was in your hands, Vince. But Damien found it first."

My brow furrowed as I struggled to remember. Damien's suspicious voice. *Where did you get that? Did she give it to you?* The clink of glass.

Damn. If I'd only been coherent enough to uncork the vial and drink it . . .

It also explained how I'd Jumped. Had I time traveled to a different version of Cora? My mind had been too foggy . . . It was hard to remember.

Cora inhaled shakily. "Vince, I'm so—"

"Don't say it. I already forgave you."

She fell silent. I squinted, trying to make out her face, but my vision was still blurry.

At last, her voice thick with emotion, she said, "I don't deserve that. You should *hate* me."

I laughed again, but it sounded more like a wheeze. My stomach quivered with nausea again. "I know. But I don't." I paused as memories slowly seeped into my mind like molasses. My mother. Hector. Damien. The Demon War. I took a shaky breath. "Without you, I never would've learned the truth about Hector. Or my mom."

Cora hesitated before asking, "What *did* happen to your mom?"

Pain filled my mind, but I couldn't stop the memory from consuming me. A bright white light, mingling with red. The crevice in the ground swallowing her up. Mom's screams.

And me, just sitting there and letting it happen.

"He banished her from the clan," I whispered. "Stripped her of her light magic. Made her a Reaper."

"A Reaper," Cora repeated, her voice hushed.

I nodded, though the motion made me feel sick again. "Jocelyn told me there were no Reapers. That it was just a cover-up for the clan to kill anyone who refused to pledge. But . . . but it's not true. There *are* Reapers. They're tied to the Underworld." The words of Hector's spell echoed in my mind. *I strip you of your light magic and banish you to the realm of the Reapers. May you live out the rest of your days as a Reaper among the dead.*

Hector had recited that spell as if he knew it well. As if he uttered it all the time.

Reapers weren't dead. They were just unable to live in the mortal realm. Forever banished to live among the dead.

A lump formed in my throat. Heat burned my eyes, and I closed them against the anguish threatening to swallow me whole. In a choked voice, I said, "My mom . . . is alive."

CHAPTER 31

CORA

Vince slumped against the stone wall, his face clammy and covered in sweat. His eyes were dazed.

It killed me to see him like this. So weak. So ill.

And all because of me.

"We'll find her," I said quietly. "I swear it, Vince. We'll get out of here and find your mom."

Vince chuckled hoarsely. "Don't lie, Cora. I'm lucid enough to know I'm dying. And without access to my magic, I can't heal. Neither of us can do anything to stop this."

My mouth trembled, and I hung my head. Sobs quivered through me, but I shoved them down. I would *not* lose it in front of him. I had to be strong.

"Cordelia," Vince murmured.

I stilled. My blood turned to ice in my veins. I hadn't

heard that name in years . . . My voice trembled as I asked, "What did you say?"

"Cordelia Cox. That was your name, wasn't it?"

My mouth turned dry. I could barely breathe. A mixture of emotions filled me. Regret. Fear. Yearning.

Cordelia had been a completely different person. Someone with hopes and dreams.

But she'd also been feeble and weak. An easy target.

"Yes," I breathed. "A long time ago."

Vince was silent. His breathing turned ragged. "I like the name. It's beautiful."

I huffed a laugh. "Sure it is. That's not why I changed it."

"I know."

"Besides, Cordelia Cox doesn't exactly inspire fear. I figured Cora Covington was more . . ."

"Fit for an assassin?"

I laughed. "Yeah."

"I can see that." A pause. "But I still prefer Cordelia."

I smiled. Warmth filled my chest.

"Do you regret it?" he asked. His voice was feeble and wispy.

"Regret what?"

"Giving everything up. If you'd just killed me, things would be so much better for you."

"True." I paused. "But no, I don't regret it. Not at all."

"Even if it means you'll die here with me?"

I stared at him. He wasn't looking at me, though I remembered one of the side effects of the poison was blindness. His eyes were vacant but soft as they gazed emptily at the wall in front of him.

"I don't regret anything, Vince," I whispered. "Least of all dying here with you."

Vince was silent, but his lips quirked upward in a small smile.

"Actually, I take it back," I added. "I regret using the Poisoned balm. And I regret not getting that healing elixir to you in time."

Vince grinned. "That's all right. I was surprised you had it on you anyway."

"To be honest, I found it on the ground. It had fallen out of my bag during the fight. I got lucky."

Vince said nothing. I suddenly stiffened as something pricked my mind. My heart raced frantically inside my chest. I gazed up and down my body, looking for fresh wounds. But no—everything had dried.

"What is it?"

My eyes flicked to Vince, whose brow was furrowed.

"I—I might be able to heal you," I said.

"How? You can't use your magic."

"My blood *is* magic, Vince."

"But won't you need ingredients?"

I shook my head. "Not if—not if I try that healing rune."

Vince sucked in a breath. "I thought you weren't sure that would work."

"I'm not. But what have we got to lose?"

Vince pressed his lips together. "Have you ever used runes before?"

"Once."

"What happened?"

I hesitated. "He died."

Vince made a strangled noise that sounded like a half cough, half laugh.

"But . . . it was a death rune. He was *supposed* to die."

"Still not comforting."

I sighed, leaning my head against the wall. "I can't just sit here and watch you die, Vince. Please let me try."

Vince was silent for a long moment, his expression unreadable. At long last, he asked, "Why?"

"Why what?"

"Why are you doing this for me?"

I swallowed. "Because I don't want you to die."

He shook his head. "I need something more than that, Cora. Why have you given up everything for me? Why are you so desperate to keep me alive?"

Knots formed in my stomach. I shifted my weight, suddenly feeling warm. "Vince, I—"

"I need to know. I need to hear you say it."

My eyes closed. Emotion climbed up my throat, suffocating me. *I can't,* my body screamed. *I can't expose my vulnerabilities like that.* I'd trained my whole life to shove them down deep where no one could find them.

But meeting Vince had changed all that. My instincts were different now.

I inhaled a shaky breath. "Because I love you." My voice cracked, betraying my fear. I kept my eyes shut tight, unwilling to look at his face and see the disgust or unease I would inevitably find there.

A scuffling sound made me open my eyes. Vince wriggled on the ground, shifting closer to me. I straightened, my arms itching to reach out and steady him as he teetered. But these damn restraints kept me from helping.

At long last, he leaned his head against the same wall I was propped against. Our faces were inches apart.

"I . . . love you too," he rasped. Then he chuckled. "Damn it all, but I love you, Cora. Even if you're the death of me, I'll always love you."

Tears filled my eyes, and I sniffed. "You're an idiot."

He laughed, and I joined in.

I leaned closer. A sheen of sweat coated his face, and his skin looked sickly and green. I leaned my forehead against his. He felt warm. Too warm.

"I'd kiss you," I breathed, "but I don't want to put more poison in your system."

Vince grinned. "I'm tempted to say it'd be worth it."

My cheeks burned, and I found myself smiling again.

"Okay," Vince said, leaning away from me. "I'll do it. Try this . . . rune thing."

I nodded, testing my restraints once more. They cut into my wrists, unyielding. With a sigh, I said, "I know this is going to sound weird . . . but I need you to bite me."

Vince burst out laughing, which turned into a coughing fit. "You're right," he choked. "That *does* sound weird."

"I'm serious, Vince. I need fresh blood. And with my hands tied, I can't get it myself. It's the only way."

Vince groaned and closed his eyes for a moment. "Fine. Where?"

"My shoulder."

Vince edged closer to me. He stared blankly at me, his face conflicted. "Your sleeve—"

"You'll have to drag it down with your teeth," I said. "Unless you want to risk getting fabric in the wound."

Vince's face reddened. "Right." He cleared his throat and swallowed. "Um, you ready?"

"Yes."

Vince leaned in, struggling to nibble on the collar of

my shirt. His teeth grazed my neck, and I suppressed a shiver of pleasure.

Now's not the time, Cora, I thought, closing my eyes.

He caught my sleeve and slowly dragged it down. A chill swept over me as my shoulder was exposed. I kept my eyes closed, but I sensed Vince's hesitation.

"Go ahead," I said quietly.

Vince swore under his breath before leaning in again. He bit down on my shoulder. I gasped—but not from pain. He didn't even break skin.

But it made a bolt of heat sear through my stomach. My body arched, aching for him. I took a deep breath.

"Harder than that," I said in a strained voice. "Please."

Vince made a low sound in his throat that only aroused me further. Damn him.

He bit down again, hard, his teeth scraping through my flesh. I clenched my teeth as pain lanced through me. Blood dripped down my shoulder.

Vince spat on the ground and panted, "Like that?"

"Yes. Now lie down."

With a grunt, he shifted and wriggled until he lay on the ground in front of me, his gaze fixed on the ceiling. His face was still red.

Wincing against the throbbing in my shoulder, I inched toward him, leaning forward until my face hovered over his stomach. "I'm going to, uh, pull up your shirt now."

His face turned a darker shade of red. "Um—"

"The rune needs to be on your bare skin. This is the most accessible point for me."

"Right. Ah, okay. Go ahead."

I held my breath, trying to squash the twisting and turning in my gut. *Get a grip, Cora.* Slowly, I caught the hem of his shirt in my teeth and tugged upward. I lost it a few times and had to try again. Vince's body stiffened in response, and he made several small noises of protest. Finally, my face hot and my body covered in sweat, I managed to roll the shirt up to his chest. I took a moment to appreciate the rigid muscles of his torso and abdomen.

"Like what you see?" he said hoarsely.

I wanted to shove him, but I laughed.

"What now?" he asked.

"Now, I test my painting skills."

"With *what?*"

"My nose."

He barked out a laugh, and I joined in. Yes, it truly sounded absurd.

But we had no other options.

Turning my head toward my wound, I dipped my nose into the blood that still welled from Vince's bite. Then, I leaned over, my back and arm muscles straining.

Slowly, I painted onto Vince's stomach with my blood. His body stiffened, and his stomach quivered.

"Stop that," I said through my laughter.

"I can't help it—you're tickling me!" I stopped, ducking my head to succumb to giggles for a moment.

"Okay, be serious," Vince said thickly. "My life is at stake."

Silence fell. Then we both laughed again.

I cleared my throat. "For real this time. I swear it."

Vince snorted, and my lips twitched, but I dipped my nose in blood once more and tried again. In a few minutes, I'd painted one of the triangles on his stomach. It was a little lopsided, but it would do. I buried my nose in the injury, trying to get more blood.

"You may have to bite me again," I muttered.

"Don't tempt me."

I grinned and leaned over to paint the second triangle. My arms shook. I held my breath as I worked, careful not to tickle him with my breath.

At long last, it was finished. Gasping for breath, I withdrew to admire my handiwork. It looked as if a two-year-old had painted it. But the rune was recognizable. That was all that mattered.

"A masterpiece, I presume," Vince said.

I gently kicked his leg. "I'm going to try the spell now."

"I thought you couldn't do magic."

"My blood has the magic. I just have to activate it somehow."

Vince nodded and closed his eyes. "Go ahead."

I shifted, sitting up straight and focusing on the rune, the magic within me, the power in my blood. After a deep breath, I murmured,

"I summon the spirits gathered near,
Seal my essence. Heal this body here.
Answer the call of the Blood Witch.
Make this man whole and enriched."

For a long moment, nothing happened. Despair filled me, and my stomach dropped to my knees.

Then, a purple glow filled the tiny room, warming my face. Vince cried out as the magic consumed him, no doubt burning his skin. My body itched to reach for him, to touch him, but the restraints held me back. A heavy thrumming shook the walls. Energy crackled in the air. A sharp gust of wind burst against me, tousling my hair.

A blinding white light filled the room, and I shut my eyes. As it faded, the purple glow vanished. Soon, the light disappeared, leaving us alone with our quickened breathing.

Anxiety pulsed through me, and I quickly looked at Vince. His eyes were closed, his expression taut with agony. He breathed in deeply, and it sounded clear, unlike the rasping from before.

His lips were no longer purple.

"Vince?" I asked, afraid to hope.

Vince slowly opened his eyes. Clarity burst in his gaze as it settled on mine, freezing me in place. Warmth stirred in my belly. There was such heat in his expression that it made me blush.

"I'm all right," he said in a low, throaty voice. "It worked. You healed me, Cora."

CHAPTER 32

VINCE

As good as it felt to finally be free of the poison in my body, it didn't change our predicament.

We were still imprisoned. And we were still cuffed.

Cora mentioned that, in the past, she'd broken her thumbs to get free of handcuffs. But these magic dampener cuffs separated our hands, so that was out of the question.

Plus, it made my stomach roil just thinking about it. As if me biting her hadn't been bad enough.

"Can we do something with your blood?" I asked, struggling again to see if I could wriggle free. "I mean, obviously the cuffs don't affect your blood. Can you cast another spell?"

Cora shook her head. "Even if I knew the right rune, my magic is drained. I gave you the rune of eternal healing." She quirked an eyebrow at me. "Kind of a big deal."

I blushed. "Right. Sorry. And thanks . . . again."

Cora grinned.

"You're oddly chipper, given our situation," I said, though I couldn't stop the slow smile from spreading on my face as well.

Cora's eyes were soft as she gazed at me. "You aren't dying. Things don't seem so grim now." She paused. "Besides, they have to let us out sometime. That'll be the best moment to strike."

"Speak for yourself," I said with a hollow chuckle. "I'm no fighter."

Her expression sobered. "I saw you fight in the Demon War, Vince. You're better than you think."

I stared at her. A lump formed in my throat. She couldn't mean that. But as our eyes met, she stared at me with such fierce affection that it made my stomach spin.

"Your best bet," Cora said, "is to play dead."

I choked on my laughter. "What, like a dog?"

"They think you've been poisoned. They won't know I've healed you. It worked for me in the Demon War. And I have a death elixir that does it too."

My smile faded as I remembered her lying there, bleeding out on the street while I raced to get my mom to heal her. I swallowed. "Uh, a death elixir?"

"Yeah. A potion that mimics death. Stops the heart, paralyzes the body . . . I don't like using it too often. It feels like a coward's way out."

I fell silent, knowing how frustrated Cora would be to just lie there instead of fighting her way out.

"Hector will try to kill you," she said quietly. "Are you prepared for that?"

I didn't answer. Though I'd always felt animosity toward Hector, I'd never figured him to be the murderous type. But *why*? What had I ever done to him?

I stilled as I remembered his enraged expression in the Demon War when I'd foiled his plans to eliminate my mom. *I don't know who you are, but I swear on Lilith's name I will end you for getting in my way.*

A jolt raced through me. I'd been his mark for over a decade. He *remembered* me.

When had he realized who I was? Had he known from the beginning, when I was only eight years old? Or was it when I first Jumped that he recognized the ability —and then recognized my face?

A sour taste filled my mouth as I thought of the years I'd lived in the clan, right under his nose. Had he just been biding his time, waiting for the proper moment to execute me? To exact his revenge?

No, there had to be something else. Some other piece I was missing. Why would Hector align with Damien? What did the demons gain from my death?

And why was Hector willing to eliminate my mother to accomplish it?

"Tell me about Damien," I said suddenly, sitting up straighter. "Why would he work with Hector?"

Cora frowned as she considered this. "Damien wants power. He wanted to figure out how you time travel."

I shook my head. "Hector wouldn't just hand over a Nephilim like that."

An uncertain expression flashed across Cora's face.

Before she could argue, I added, "No, I mean, whether or not he likes the Nephilim, he wouldn't hand one of us over. There's too much power, too much light magic in us. He'd either kill us, or—"

"Strip your powers," she said. "Like your mom."

"Yeah." My throat felt tight.

"Maybe Hector intends to double cross Damien," Cora said.

"Or maybe there's some other bargaining chip we're overlooking."

Cora's eyes widened. "Vince, what if—"

A heavy, metallic creak interrupted her. Alarmed, we both wriggled and shifted until we were standing, prepared for whoever was entering our cell. I knew Cora had advised me to play dead, but I couldn't let her face the enemy alone.

The huge door swung open, revealing a pair of figures. The blinding light of the sun behind them made me squint as my eyes adjusted. Then, slowly, I made out a familiar gangly figure with dark skin and dreadlocks.

"*Luke?*" I said in bewilderment.

Cora went rigid, backing against the wall. "Benny?" Her eyes flicked from the light-haired man to Luke. "Did Damien send you?" Her voice was like ice.

Luke laughed. "No. He doesn't even know I exist. We're here to break you out."

"Is my dad—" I started.

"He's fine," Luke assured me. "He's with my parents."

Relief spread through me, and I stepped forward. But Cora remained where she was.

"I don't trust you," she said, her steely eyes on Benny.

I glanced at the man. He was tall and muscular, with light brown hair and yellow-rimmed eyes.

A werewolf.

"I'm a Thinker, Cora," Benny said in a deep, rumbling voice. He ticked his head toward Luke. "We both are. Like you, we've had to keep our magic a secret."

We both are. Shock numbed my body as I stared at Luke. A *Thinker?* Luke was clairvoyant? My mouth opened and closed, my body overcome with chills.

No. This couldn't be right.

"Look, we can talk about this later," Luke hissed, glancing over his shoulder. "Someone's coming."

I didn't ask how he knew that. My head was still reeling. Luke? A *warlock?* And all this time, he'd pretended not to know about magic . . . pretended to find my life *fascinating.*

Had everything in my life been a lie?

A torrent of questions and emotions swirled in my mind. I couldn't see straight.

Warm fingers grasped my arm, bringing me back to reality. I glanced up and found Cora looking at me, her eyes full of concern. I hadn't even registered Luke cutting our cuffs off. My wrists itched and ached from the restraints, but I focused on the comfort of Cora's touch. I swallowed and nodded, answering her unspoken question: *Are you going to be okay?*

Luke touched my shoulder, his brown eyes searching mine. I resisted the urge to flinch away from him.

"I've got your back," he said quietly. "Just like on the field."

This isn't like on the field, I wanted to scream at him. *Because our entire friendship has been a lie!*

During lacrosse games, I'd trusted him. Because I'd *known* him.

Not anymore. This person in front of me was a complete stranger.

"They freed us," Cora muttered, rubbing her wrists. "I say we follow them. Worst-case scenario, they lead us to a trap, but at least we can fight."

I nodded again. "Fine." My voice was strained. Luke easily picked up on it and shot me a guilty expression.

He'd always been able to read me. Now, I understood why. And it made me feel nauseous all over again.

Was he reading my thoughts right now?

I tried wiping my mind clean, but it was like telling my body to stop breathing.

"Come on." Cora took my hand in hers and squeezed. Reassurance spread through me, and I focused on what I knew: Cora loved me. I loved her.

And we would get out of here alive.

Determination quelled my thoughts of betrayal and confusion. I gripped Cora's hand firmly in mine and shared a solemn look with her. Her eyes blazed, fueling the fire within me.

We emerged in a small courtyard with the afternoon sun beating down on us. Benny waved us over to the edge of the courtyard where the shadows would conceal us. But we were still too exposed.

Luke suddenly raised a hand and frantically pointed toward a hedge of bushes. We dived to the ground, using the foliage as cover, and held perfectly still.

Footsteps echoed nearby, drawing closer. I held my breath, my heart hammering in my chest. *We'll be caught for sure.*

Cora stiffened beside me, and I looked at her in alarm. She was watching Benny, her expression tense. My gaze flicked to the werewolf, whose eyes were shut, his face completely rigid. The tendons stood out in his neck.

Alarm raced through me. Was he having a fit? I

shifted to reach for him, but Luke touched my shoulder and shook his head.

The footsteps suddenly stopped. A low voice murmured, "Did you hear that?"

Silence blared against my ears. My pulse thundered so loudly it was sure to give us away.

"I heard it too," said another man. "This way!"

They rushed off. Their footsteps slowly faded until silence fell in the courtyard. Benny exhaled, his face pale and his arms shaking.

"What the hell was that?" I hissed.

"He communicated with them telepathically," Luke muttered. "Made them believe they heard something. It takes a lot of strength, and he probably won't be able to do it again. Let's get out of here before they come back."

"This way." Cora jerked her head toward a sidewalk curving to the left. I frowned until I remembered she knew this place.

We were in Hinport. This was her territory.

We followed the sidewalk, which wound between two impressively tall buildings that cast helpful shadows for us to hide in. The sidewalk opened up to a grimy parking lot filled with cars that looked like they belonged in a junkyard.

When we reached the lot, Cora lifted her hand to stop us. Her head whipped back and forth as she looked around. She sniffed deeply.

"What is it?" I whispered.

Cora straightened, her eyes widening in alarm. "Go back. *Go!*"

"Did you really think," boomed a voice, "it would be that easy to escape?"

A chill raced down my spine. In the middle of the parking lot, a figure emerged from the shadows.

Damien.

Behind him stood several other demons I didn't recognize. I scanned each of their faces, looking for Hector.

He wasn't here.

"Do *you* really think you can beat me?" Cora challenged, her voice echoing in the lot. "I'm the Blade of Hinport."

"Only because I made you," Damien snarled.

Cora laughed coldly. "If that's true, then what's stopping you? Go ahead and *unmake* me, Damien. I'd love to see you try."

Damien stood stiffly, his eyes blazing. A few demons shifted uncomfortably behind him, eyeing Cora with wariness and trepidation.

Interesting.

I glanced at Luke, whose face was slack with shock. When I looked around for Benny, he was nowhere to be found.

Perfect.

"Weapons?" I whispered to Luke.

He shook his head slowly, his face ashen.

Great, I thought. With a deep breath, I closed my eyes, concentrating on the magic within me.

Come on, I urged. *Come on.* I pictured myself on the lacrosse field, stick in hand. A thrill of adrenaline raced through me.

And across from me was Luke, his face as blank and horrified as when I'd just looked at him.

A jolt rippled through me, and I staggered back a step.

This was *really* Luke. Inside my head. I'd thought he was just part of my imagination.

He grimaced apologetically. Shock numbed my body, and the fire within me died.

Luke had been in my head this entire time. He was linked to my time travel ability.

I stared at him, dumbstruck. *More lies,* I thought.

Luke shook his head. "Don't think like that, Vince. You can still do this. You have to trust me."

"How can I trust you?" I shouted. "I don't even *know* you!"

Luke raised his hands in surrender. "I know. You're right. Just—just picture the Luke you *did* know. The one you trusted on the field. He's the one who helps you with your magic. Focus on him."

I gritted my teeth. That was easier said than done.

How could I just bury all the lies that had come between us? All the secrets he'd kept?

I couldn't just force myself to forget.

Cora grunted, bringing me out of my imaginary lacrosse field. I blinked, focusing on the parking lot, and found her fighting Damien. The other demons surged forward to attack.

Luke turned to me with wide eyes. "*Now,* Vince!"

I closed my eyes again, my mind a tangled mess of emotions and thoughts. *The game,* I told myself. *Think of nothing but the game.*

My crosse in my hand. Sweat on my face. The smell of grass and dirt.

My eye on the ball.

I lunged. My arm flew forward, grasping Luke's wrist as I spun in place. With a small *pop*, I arrived in front of his house. Gravity pulled me forward, and I collapsed with Luke by my side.

Luke scrambled to his feet, his mouth falling open. "What—"

"Stay here," I growled. "Take care of my dad."

I spun again and arrived back in the parking lot. A dozen demons crowded Cora, but she spun and kicked, keeping them all at bay without even breaking a sweat. I frantically searched for a weapon, but there was nothing but the beat-up cars in the lot.

Suddenly, an idea filled my mind. I rushed forward,

gripping the bumper of the car closest to Damien. One demon turned toward me, but before he could attack, I spun in place, still gripping the bumper.

Shapes shifted in front of me. Instead of squeezing my eyes shut, I kept them wide open, focusing on the blurry images. I made out Cora's dark bob of hair as she raced toward Damien. Then, as if on rewind, Damien and his minions retreated to the shadows. Luke, Cora, and I emerged from the sidewalk.

Now. I released the bumper and collapsed to the ground. Urgency pulsed through me, and I scrambled to my feet, hurrying to hide behind the car and wait for Damien to show up. I'd time traveled only a few minutes backward. My mind spun with sharpness and clarity as I remembered what I'd seen. Damien, surrounded by a dozen other demons. Benny had vanished. The demons were armed, but Cora wasn't. And—

Take me, a voice said in my head.

I blinked, whirling and expecting to find Damien's shadowy form. But no one was there.

Take me, the voice said again. *Get me out of here. I'll send for help.*

My blood ran cold. Who was speaking? And *how?*

Soft footsteps echoed on the other side of the lot. Damien and his goons had arrived.

Vince, the voice said in my head, more insistent. *You*

have *to Jump me away from here. No one knows you're here. Let me go get help before the entire coven kills you!*

I finally recognized the voice. It was Benny.

Benny, who had mysteriously vanished right as we'd entered the parking lot.

Gritting my teeth, I spun in place and reappeared on the sidewalk, a few yards behind Luke, Cora, Benny, and myself. As if sensing me, Benny turned and looked at me. After ensuring the others kept going without him, he approached me, his yellow eyes gleaming.

I grabbed him by the collar and shoved him against the wall of the building next to us. "How did you know?" I hissed.

"Know what?" But he grinned widely. He knew exactly what I meant.

I shoved him harder, raising him off his feet. He choked and sputtered. "Okay," he rasped. "Okay, put me down."

I slowly lowered him but kept a firm grip on his collar. "Talk," I ordered.

"Luke and I," he croaked. "We're linked to your mind. I saw what you saw."

My eyes narrowed. "How?"

Benny shook his head. "I don't know. It happened years ago. Someone cast a spell on our minds, and then we had access."

"Luke—"

"Luke doesn't see everything I do. He's still harnessing his powers."

I swallowed, shoving down my feelings of betrayal. "Why should I believe you?"

"Like I said, I'm linked to you. I know you're outnumbered. I can use my link to send help. But I have a short range. I can't reach anyone from here."

"How do I know you aren't just abandoning us to die?" I said through clenched teeth.

"You don't," Benny said, his expression grim. "But you know I'm right. Can you really take on Damien and his throng of demons? He has powerful allies."

I stared at him, my jaw rigid and my mind racing. I was running out of time. Swearing under my breath, I released him, then snatched his arm. "Where to?"

"Werewolf pack in east Hinport. Just past Glen bridge."

I nodded, then spun in place. With a small *pop*, we disappeared and arrived about half a mile away from the bridge that led to Ravenbrooke. Benny teetered, and I didn't bother trying to catch him before he collapsed to the ground in a heap.

"If you abandon us," I said, pointing a finger at him. "You're a dead man."

Benny jumped to his feet and raised his eyebrows. "Don't worry. I know better than to make an enemy of the Blade of Hinport." He flashed another grin and hurried off, leaving me gaping after him.

For a moment, I stared at the space where he'd stood, sifting through the information circling through my head. Ever since I'd tapped into my warlock magic, it was like a spike of caffeine surging through me. My mind was alert. My body was prickling with energy.

And I could see things so much more clearly.

I know better than to make an enemy of the Blade of Hinport.

That explained it. Cora had been shocked to see Benny. She knew him better than I did, but I knew enough. She didn't trust *anyone* in her coven, least of all Damien.

But Benny had come to our aid. Why?

Because of Cora.

A deep voice chuckled behind me. "Fancy meeting you here, Vince."

I turned and found myself face-to-face with Hector.

CHAPTER 33

CORA

DAMIEN'S DEMONS SWARMED AROUND ME, CLOSING IN. I kicked Damien in the chest, then ducked as he swung a blow. Punch in the kneecap, then again in the groin. He howled, bending over. But as I turned, another demon lunged. A third grabbed me from behind, pinning my arms. A fist collided with my jaw, and I grunted. Pain spiked through me.

I couldn't take them all. I was good, but not *that* good.

With a roar of fury, I bashed my forehead against the face of another demon, who I vaguely registered was Kip.

I knew him. I knew *all* these demons.

They didn't seem to care that they were attacking one of their own.

Well, I didn't care either. I didn't care what they did or what they knew.

It was time to end this once and for all.

Power thrummed through my body, and I arched backward. My skin tingled. It didn't matter that I was still pinned, that they could easily dismember me right here.

And then I unleashed the Bloodcaster magic within me.

A shrill cry pierced the air. Purple fog exploded from my chest, engulfing the men in front of me. Several of them gasped and cried out in surprise. I closed my eyes, focusing on the sweat and fear of the man still holding my arms in place. I felt his pulse. Heard his breathing.

I stiffened, and my magic lunged for him, slicing right through him. With a guttural choke, he released me and slumped to the ground.

The shrieking continued, chilling and brutal. With a jolt, I realized it was coming from me. I stopped, but the thrumming in my body continued as if a roar still built in my throat.

The eerie mist still surrounded me, but I opened my eyes and saw the figures around me perfectly. It was just like my shadow elixir. It obscured me from view, but I could still see.

A slow smile spread across my face.

The demons scrambled around, confused as they bumped into each other in their efforts to grab me. I ducked under the arms of one demon and punched him in the gut. Elbowed him in the face. Swung around and snapped his neck.

A small *pop* echoed behind me. Was that Vince . . . or Damien?

I hoped Vince was hidden. I hoped he was smart enough to avoid this. It didn't take a genius to figure out I had feelings for him. Damien would certainly use that against me.

Another *pop*. The smell of alcohol and ash.

Definitely Damien.

I spun to face him, aiming a high kick. He caught my foot and twisted. Pain shot up my leg, and I grunted. With a twist, I shoved him away, using both feet to slam into his chest. We fell to the ground. My purple smoke was fading. I didn't have much time.

Damien spun in place, but I lunged, grabbing his ankle before he jumped. The air pushed against me, squeezing the breath out of me. Gravity shifted, and shapes distorted.

We reappeared across the lot, several yards away from the faint purple fog of my magic and the disoriented demons still trapped inside.

Damien roared in fury and grabbed my head before slamming his forehead against mine. Spots danced in my vision, and my head throbbed, pulsing with agony. I scrambled away from him, barely dodging a knife in the chest.

With my head still spinning, I jumped to my feet. Damien hit me in the shoulder, then the stomach. I bent over, coughing as pain coursed through me. Swinging around, I aimed a kick at him, but he spun in place, reappearing behind me. His arms circled me as he gripped my head in his hands again. I knew with one quick motion, he could break my neck.

"This is pointless, Cora," he hissed in my ear.

I sucked in a breath and flipped him over, my arms and shoulders screaming in protest. Damien landed flat on his back, sputtering and choking. I kicked him in the face, then again in the groin for good measure. He howled in agony. Hovering over him, I pressed my knees into his chest and swiped the knife from his hand.

"Son of a bitch," I growled, raising the knife. It was *my* dagger. The one Vince had used to bring us back to the present.

Damien had stolen it. The bastard.

I raised the dagger to his throat and hissed, "Why? Why work with Hector?"

Damien laughed hoarsely, his teeth glinting with his blood. "It must be mind-boggling for you, Cora. To be betrayed like that."

I buried the knife into his shoulder, and he screamed. A quick glance around the parking lot told me I was out of time. Damien's buddies were racing toward us.

"Tell me now, or I slit your throat," I said.

Damien only laughed again. "You won't. I have too much value."

My eyes narrowed. The men were getting closer.

In a swift motion, I slid the blade along his throat. Blood gushed from the wound, flowing like water from a faucet. Damien's eyes widened in shock. A horrible choking sound bubbled from his lips, spewing flecks of blood on me.

Then, he went silent.

Slowly, I slid off him and wielded the bloody knife toward the demons that approached. They faltered when they noticed their leader lying in his own blood.

I raised my eyebrows. "Your boss is dead. So, what's it gonna be? Challenge me, or surrender?"

The demons glanced at one another uncertainly. Though they vastly outnumbered me—and my body ached at the thought of fighting all of them—I knew I could still take down a few.

And they knew it too.

One of them, Kip, stepped forward, brandishing his knife and baring his teeth at me. Rage filled his eyes. He'd been close to Damien.

A few others edged closer to me, spurred on by Kip's fury. A groan built in my throat, but I straightened, gripping my own knife tightly as they approached.

So be it.

"We stand with Cora!" bellowed a voice across the lot.

I stiffened. The demons and I whirled, searching for the interruption.

From the shadows emerged a figure with his arms outstretched, his yellow eyes gleaming.

Benny. I'd wondered where he'd gone.

Behind him was an entire pack of wolves ranging from light brown to inky black. All of them were as big as bears, standing on all fours and approaching slowly, their eyes hungry.

A few of Damien's men gasped as they backed away, their faces pale.

My mouth fell open. A *werewolf* pack? I'd just assumed Benny was a lone wolf. He was the only werewolf in our coven.

Apparently, he had some powerful friends.

Benny bowed to me and pressed his fist to his chest. "We recognize Cora as the Blade of Hinport and pledge to follow her." His eyes raked over the demons standing in front of me. "We challenge anyone who defies her." His eyes blazed as he stared down Damien's men, daring them to step forward.

Shock rippled through me, and I found myself gaping like a moron. *Pledge to follow her* . . . How could they? I was no leader. I didn't even have friends in the coven.

So why were they loyal to me?

Benny's gaze shifted to me, and something unreadable sparked in his eyes. Something he was hiding.

There was more to this story.

But for now, I was grateful for the support. I straightened. "And I stand with the werewolf pack of Hinport," I said loudly. I needed as many allies as I could get. "What about you, Kip?"

Kip flinched as if I'd slapped him. All anger had fled from him, and he visibly trembled as he stared frightfully at the wolves. He swallowed loudly and dropped his knife with a loud clatter. "I stand with you, Cora."

The other men dropped their weapons as well, raising their hands in surrender. I smiled. Triumph pulsed through me.

It felt too easy, though. Once again, I looked at Benny, who watched me intently. He would definitely be calling in a favor from me soon.

But for now, I needed to assert myself as the coven leader. It was all so unexpected. I'd planned on bolting as soon as this was finished because I'd expected every demon in the city to be after my blood.

If it meant stopping these demons from ripping each other apart—and possibly severing any ties to Hector—then I had to step in and clean up Damien's mess. I had to at least try.

I lifted my chin at Benny. "Can you have one of your guys escort Damien's men to the prison cells? I need to keep them contained while I figure out what to do with them."

Benny nodded and pointed to a gray wolf who immediately shifted to the form of a bulky blond with impressive muscles. The blond and two other wolves approached Damien's men and ushered them out of the parking lot toward the prison I'd escaped from earlier.

When they were out of earshot, I approached Benny. Unease swirled in my gut.

"Your allegiance is appreciated," I said quietly. "But definitely unexpected. I never intended to take Damien's place."

Benny's eyebrows lifted. "So, why'd you kill him?"

"Because he threatened me. He blackmailed me. He was dangerous."

"I agree."

I shook my head. "That still doesn't make me fit to lead the coven."

Benny glanced at the other wolves before responding. "We have something in common, Cora. We keep our identities a secret."

I frowned. "Your Telepathy? Why?"

"It's one of the most coveted powers in the magical world. I can't tell you the horrors I've witnessed from people trying to extract that kind of magic." He shuddered, his expression darkening. "I elected to become a wolf to disguise my warlock powers. No one asked what kind of demon I was after that." He leveled a hard gaze at me. "You protect your own. You protect secrets. Damien didn't. He had no loyalty. And he betrayed your secret when it best suited him. From what little I know about you, I know you would never do something like that."

I stared at him, unsure how to respond.

"Make no mistake, I will call on you for a favor in the future," he said. "But for now, my pack pledges loyalty to you because you have been loyal to the demons of Hinport."

My throat was warm. His words touched me. I'd never felt anything like this before. My entire life, I'd been looking over my shoulder, watching every step, expecting betrayal at every turn.

This was such a shock to me that I stood there, frozen, for several moments. Benny cleared his throat, obviously uncomfortable, and it jolted me from my stupor.

I rubbed my nose. "Thank you, Benny. I owe you a debt, and I fully intend to repay you." I exhaled long and slow, my body shaking. Not from the battle—but from shock. I glanced around the lot, and alarm quivered through me. "Where's Vince?"

"I thought you knew. He took me to the pack, and I assumed he came back here."

I looked around again in case I overlooked him, but

the churning in my stomach told me something was wrong. "Can't you sense him. Like mind-to-mind?"

Benny sighed and closed his eyes for a moment, breathing deeply. He frowned. "He's . . . near Glen Bridge. Right where I left him—where the pack lives. Why is he still there?"

Hector. I knew it down to my bones. He hadn't been here, which meant he had better things to do.

Like eliminate Vince.

"I've got to go," I told Benny before sprinting away.

I only hoped I wasn't too late.

CHAPTER 34

VINCE

MY ARMS FELT STIFF AT MY SIDE. MY ENTIRE BODY went rigid. I wiggled my fingers to ensure my magic still crackled with life within me.

It did.

Even though I faced Hector. Even though every inch of me screamed to run—because I knew I couldn't beat him—my magic still flared to life like a trustworthy companion.

"Why?" I demanded. Thank Lilith my voice didn't tremble.

Hector cocked his head at me like a predator eyeing its prey. "Why what?"

I spread my arms wide and let them fall at my side. "Why kill me? Why banish my mother? What do you gain from all this?"

Hector smirked, his eyes glinting. "So you finally did it, then. You finally traveled back to the war."

I stared at him. He'd been waiting for this. All those years he'd watched me, wondering when I'd finally travel back in time and thwart his careful planning.

And now we were here. Everything was out in the open.

"If you're going to kill me, I at least deserve an explanation," I said.

Hector inhaled deeply. "Your mother was a roadblock, unfortunately. She didn't see the potential for our clan."

"How so?" I couldn't keep the bite out of my tone.

"She wanted to mingle with lesser magic," Hector spat. "She wanted to taint our bloodline. Every alliance she forged dragged us downward. I simply wanted to raise us up again."

My brows furrowed with incredulity. "By *isolating* us from the world?"

"Precisely."

I scoffed, and his eyes flashed.

"You couldn't possibly understand," he snapped. "I've been around for *centuries*. I've seen what demons and even the lesser light casters do to our kind. We have immeasurable power, but around them, our magic is stifled. It cannot grow. If we keep the Nephilim bloodline pure, then we can thrive. We can embrace our true potential."

"And kill anyone who gets in your way," I said, my fists trembling with rage.

Hector gazed at me with patronizing sadness. His eyes remained cold, but his face twisted with false sympathy. "It's unavoidable, boy. Not only because of your dissensions and your doubts about the clan, but because of your power."

I stilled. *My power?* Then my blood turned to ice.

My time travel power.

"The moment your Mimic appeared to you in the school parking lot, we knew," he went on. "It triggered our defense mechanisms. This power of yours is too dangerous. Too volatile. As you've already witnessed, too much is at risk. We can't leave that power in your hands."

"It's not up to you," I growled. "This is *my* magic!"

"Yes, and if you'd committed to pledge yourself to the clan from the start, we wouldn't be in this mess. But you're a loose cannon, Vince. I can't trust you to keep the clan safe. You're too dangerous to keep alive."

"What harm have I done?" I roared. "I stopped you from *killing* my mom!"

"You interfered with carefully laid plans without a second thought. You're *reckless*. The clan deserves better than the likes of you."

I gritted my teeth so firmly my head throbbed and my jaw ached. Fury pulsed through me. "All right," I hissed. "Then, do it. Kill me." I spread my arms again, waiting.

Hector blinked, his face smoothing in momentary shock. But he recovered quickly. A burst of bright light exploded in front of me.

Before it hit me, I spun in place, reappearing behind Hector. I punched his lower back, then his neck. He fell over with a satisfying yelp.

I spun again, appearing in front of him. A kick to the gut. A punch to the jaw.

Again, behind him. I kicked his legs out from under him.

When I appeared in front of him again, he was ready for me. He sliced his arms through the air, and a bolt of white magic cut right through my chest, bringing me to my knees. I groaned, my chest on fire.

"That's a neat little trick," Hector said in a strained voice as he staggered to his feet. "But it's useless, I'm afraid."

Panting, I glared at him, my body still thrumming with power. When Hector loomed over me, his wings casting shadows on me, I grabbed his wrist and spun again.

Gravity yanked me forward. *Back,* I thought. *Go back in time.* Images blurred around me. Distorted sounds warbled in my ears. I focused on the shapes in front of me. The dark alley. Hector's blinding light. Benny and me arriving to find his pack.

I kept going, some innate instinct within me waiting for the parking lot to clear. For the witnesses to empty out—all except for Hector from the past. I saw his figure in the shadows, hiding while Benny and I spoke. He'd been waiting for me.

When Benny and I vanished, leaving only Hector, I let go. The present Hector and I toppled over, groaning. His entire body shuddered and thrummed. I gaped, my head still spinning.

I'd never used a *person* as an anchor before.

Dazed, I looked up and found the *other* version of Hector standing in front of us, his face ghostly pale. His mouth opened and closed as he looked between me and the first Hector.

Two Hectors? How did this help my situation?

Then, the first Hector shuddered again. A strange glow surrounded him, but it wasn't the intense glow of Nephilim magic. This glow was like a soft mist, a murky gray echo of his own body as it surrounded himself.

In a flash, First Hector surged forward, colliding with Second Hector. They both cried out, their voices echoing in the dark alley.

My eyes widened, and I scrambled backward, worried this strange magic would ricochet and hit me. The two

Hectors quivered so intensely they became a blur. His scream tore through the air, chilling me to the bone.

A burst of light seared against my eyes, and I raised a hand to shield them. A loud *thump* told me Hector had fallen over, though I wasn't sure which one.

Slowly, I lowered my hand. The glow was gone.

And only one Hector remained. He hunched over, gasping and covered in sweat.

What. The. Hell?

Then, I remembered what happened to the other anchors I'd used. Cora's book. Mom's necklace. They'd somehow merged with their duplicates.

And now, Hector had done the same.

My mouth felt dry, and I resisted the urge to approach him and ask if he was all right. He was the *enemy*, for Lilith's sake.

Shaking my head, I jumped to my feet and kicked him in the gut. He groaned and rolled over, sprawling on the ground. His wings had vanished, and he suddenly looked feeble and helpless.

I kicked him again. His face turned ashen.

"Stop," he rasped. "Please."

I hesitated. Could I really kill a defenseless man? Even if it was Hector, I wasn't sure I could.

My hesitation cost me. Hector snatched my ankle and pulled. I toppled to the ground, my arms scraping against the pavement. I tried wriggling away, but Hector dragged me closer to him. My legs flailed as I tried to kick him, but he held fast, dodging my feet.

Sudden energy rippled through me. A burst of magic flared to life, something I hadn't been able to recognize until now. It made my entire body tremble.

I sucked in a breath. My Nephilim magic. It had run out during the Demon War, but it must've somehow recharged with Cora's healing rune.

A slow smile spread across my face. In a burst of white magic, my wings sprang from my shoulder blades, fanning out behind me in all their feathery glory. They slammed into Hector, who flew backward, sliding several feet away from me.

An ethereal white glow surrounded me as I rose to my feet. Power pulsed through every inch of me. I approached Hector with a euphoric feeling of unquenchable strength.

Hector had the gall to look afraid for a split second. But he masked it quickly.

"Again, a worthy effort," he said, his voice weak. "But you're still no match for me on your own."

"He's not alone," said a voice behind me.

My heart lurched in my throat. I whirled and found Luke standing in the mouth of the alley.

Something lodged itself in my throat—a mixture of regret and agony. What was he doing here? I'd Jumped him home to keep him *away* from this mess.

"Luke," I warned.

He strode toward us, ignoring me. His hard gaze was fixed on Hector. I'd never seen my friend look so fierce. So intimidating. He was usually a goofball. All casual.

But right now, he seemed like a warrior.

Hector stared at Luke in confusion. "Who are you?"

Luke grinned. "You don't know me? Excellent. That makes this so much more enjoyable." His gaze shifted to me. "I felt you travel. It summoned me here."

I didn't know how to feel about that. Part of me felt relieved. Another part felt oddly violated. Like he'd intruded on my magic somehow.

"You shouldn't be here," I said. "It isn't safe."

Luke laughed. "Nothing is safe."

Hector grunted as he tried to rise. But something whipped through the air and sliced into his shoulder. He collapsed backward with a pitiful cry of pain.

I stared at the decorative hilt of the dagger lodged in Hector's shoulder. I *knew* that dagger.

My breath caught in my throat as I turned and found Cora standing a few feet away from Luke. Her eyes were steely, her body lithe and graceful as she drew closer.

She was magnificent. She, too, looked like a warrior.

And it robbed me of my breath.

Cora flashed me a brief grin that made my stomach flip. Her eyes shifted to Hector, and she frowned, no doubt noticing his sickly pallor. "What's wrong with him?"

"I traveled with him."

"So?"

"I used him as my anchor."

Cora's eyes widened, but confusion lingered on her face.

Luke, however, turned pale.

"What is it?" I asked him.

Luke rubbed his forehead. "I, ah . . ."

Hector groaned as he wriggled on the ground. I approached him, afraid he might try something.

Before I could reach him, a pearly glow enveloped him, momentarily blinding me. In a burst of magic, he vanished. The glow subsided, and nothing remained of Hector but a few lingering feathers drifting in the air.

My jaw dropped. "Where—where did he go?"

"He probably knew he was too weak to fight all three of us," Cora muttered, her eyes raking over the alley as if expecting Hector to reappear. Her gaze cut to me. "Nephilim can Jump?"

"The really powerful ones can."

Cora raised her eyebrows. "That's handy. How do we track him?"

"We don't," Luke said sharply. I'd never heard him speak like that before—with authority.

I stared at him. His face twisted in an uneasy grimace.

"Why not?" I demanded.

Luke's eyes darkened as he stared at me, unyielding. I felt so much distance between us, growing like a living thing. In that space, the secrets he'd kept festered and throbbed, tearing apart the friendship we'd built over the years.

He was a stranger now.

"*Luke*," I snapped. "Tell me."

He sighed. "Your anchor through time links you, serving as your gravitational force to pull you back down. Otherwise, you might end up in, like, outer space or something. Using a *living thing* as a gravitational force? Well, it throws their own center of gravity completely off balance. And usually your anchor creates a sort of double. Like, it appears in a place it once existed, and for one moment, there's two of them. Then, they merge together."

"Yeah. The two Hectors did that."

Luke's face turned ashen. "Oh, Lilith . . ."

I flinched. I'd never in my life heard him swear like that.

Only witches and warlocks did that. It was yet another reminder that my friend had lied to me for years.

Cora seemed unfazed. She shrugged one shoulder.

"What's the big deal? Even if it kills him, that still seems like a victory to me."

Luke shook his head. "It's not as simple as that. His body is now marked by time."

"What does that mean?" My voice came out harsher than I intended.

"It means other Timewalkers will see him," Luke said. "It's like you've labeled him as an anchor. Something others can use to manipulate time."

I merely blinked at him.

"He can travel," Luke said with a hint of impatience. "The mark allows one to travel freely."

"But he doesn't have the power," I protested.

"Not yet," Luke said ominously.

"So, what do we do when we find him?" Cora asked, flipping her dagger from one hand to the other.

"You can't kill him," Luke said quickly.

My mouth fell open. "Why *not*? Do you know what he's done? He's—"

"I know." Luke raised his hands as if that would appease me. "But once something is used as an anchor, it's linked to the timeline. Removing an anchor from existence risks altering any events that need to be preserved. If a Timewalker destroys an anchor, he breaks the laws of time."

I stilled, remembering what my dad had said about that. *We do not use our powers to alter the way the world works. Doing so will make you some powerful enemies. And they won't just come after you. They'll come after me, your friends, anyone who's associated with you.*

My mouth turned dry. "So, we're supposed to just *let him go?*"

Luke sighed. "This has never happened before, Vince. At least, not to my knowledge."

My eyes narrowed. "And what *is* your knowledge exactly? Please enlighten us." My voice dripped with sarcasm.

Luke shot me an exasperated look. "Vince—"

"I don't trust you! You have to explain yourself. Because right now, your argument holds no merit."

Luke groaned, running a hand down his face. "I work for the Timekeepers. They monitor the timeline and make sure fixed points are protected. They've studied Timewalkers like you for centuries, Vince. They know what they're talking about." He exhaled, his cheeks puffing out. "They'll have to bring him in."

"Bring him in?" Cora asked, raising an eyebrow. "What are you, a cop?"

Luke glared at her before raising his wrist. He pressed two fingers to his watch, and a strange green light lit up the alley. "I need some assistance," Luke said.

The green light flickered and then vanished. A moment later, a small *pop* signaled the arrival of three figures in dark green robes, like perky monks or something. Their hoods were raised, obscuring their faces, but they turned toward Luke and whispered something inaudible.

"He's escaped," Luke said in a normal voice. "He's marked as an anchor."

The figures whispered again.

Luke nodded. "I agree. Find him. Do what you have to."

"Hold on a minute!" I shouted. I was utterly fed up with this. "You can't just—"

The robed figures vanished with another *pop*. A strange, metallic smell filled the air. It wasn't light magic *or* dark magic. It didn't even smell like Cora's magic.

It was another force entirely.

"Where did they go?" Cora asked. Her body was tense as if preparing for battle. She didn't like this foreign presence, either.

"It doesn't matter," Luke said, his expression stony. "It's under their jurisdiction now."

Cora's nostrils flared, and she stepped toward Luke. "I don't care who the hell you are. Hector's committed crimes against Vince, the Nephilim, and my coven. He has to answer for it."

"It's not up to you anymore."

"The hell it isn't!"

My head was spinning. I was barely listening. Instead, the image of the hooded figures flashed in my mind.

Who were they? They were obviously Jumpers, but they used a different kind of magic.

Luke mentioned *Timekeepers*. Was that what they were too?

"There are bigger forces at work here!" Luke's voice was insistent. I'd never heard such urgency in his voice before. His wide eyes shifted to me, pleading, as if *I* could talk some sense into Cora.

I only stared at him, too numb to school my expression into anything but shock.

A door slammed from a building nearby, and I flinched. Somehow, the sound snapped me out of my haze, and I glanced from Cora to Luke. Cora's face was pale as she looked around, her body still in a fighting stance.

"You two need to leave," Cora hissed. "*Now.*"

I blinked. "What?" Instinctively, I drew closer to her.

Cora swallowed. Desire and regret mingled in her eyes. She gently placed a hand on my chest. "We're in Hinport. A city of demons. And you two have light magic. You *can't be here.*"

I searched her face. Vulnerability shone in her eyes, clear as day, burning right through me.

And I knew she was right. Even if there was no threat, I had to give her peace of mind. I had to let her take care of things—just like she always did.

The thought shook me to my core. Were we really

just going back to normal? Could I simply return to my Nephilim clan as if nothing had happened?

"Vince," Luke muttered. Footsteps echoed nearby, followed by urgent shouting.

I stared at Cora, holding her gaze, trying to convey everything I felt for her in that single look. Then, I snatched Luke's wrist—perhaps a bit too forcefully—spun in place, and we both disappeared.

CHAPTER 35

CORA

I MADE QUICK WORK OF CLEANING OUT DAMIEN'S office and destroying his things. I wanted no memory of him. And, as Benny frequently reminded me, it was important to establish myself as the coven leader right away to quell any unrest that might pop up from Damien's death. Already, several demons—who had been loyal to Damien—had left the coven.

But, to my surprise, the coven actually grew in size. Benny brought his pack with him. Though the idea of werewolves in my coven made me uneasy, Benny made it clear it wasn't up for discussion.

I couldn't exactly argue with him. Not when he'd come to my aid against Damien.

"Kip and the others are still causing problems," Benny reported, sitting in the armchair across from my desk. I sat back in my chair, gazing distantly out the window behind me.

"Keep them cuffed," I told him without breaking my gaze. "They'll need to earn our trust. Either they'll break, or we'll execute them."

Benny nodded. When he said nothing, I finally looked up.

"What is it?" I asked.

"A few demons are calling for your . . . Ascension. I'm not sure what to tell them."

I stared at him, keeping my expression carefully smooth. "And what do *you* think?"

Benny watched me for a long moment, his yellow eyes contemplative. "I think it needs to be addressed. But it's up to you whether or not you want to try it. Bloodcasters are so rare that no one really knows what happens when they Ascend. We don't even know if it'll work."

"Does the coven know?" I asked.

"Some of them do. I've heard them whispering about it. After you used your magic against Damien and his men, it was hard to keep it a secret."

My jaw ticked back and forth. "Am I in danger?"

Benny smiled. "I don't think so. They've seen what your magic can do. And even without it, you're still the Blade. With me and my pack behind you, no one will touch you."

My eyes narrowed slightly. Was that a veiled threat? A grim reminder of the consequences of severing ties with him? I smiled too, but it was cold. "Don't fret, Benny. I have a feeling we'll be allies for a long while."

Benny's eyes glinted, and he inclined his head. "Happy to hear it."

My eyes returned to the window as he left the room. My body relaxed, and I set my feet on the desk, swinging back and forth in my chair. Light poured into the room from outside, casting a gentle glow on the floor. Before, Damien had kept the curtains drawn, and the room reeked of cigarette smoke and alcohol. After ensuring the space was deep-cleaned and the furniture was replaced, it now felt a bit more open. More peaceful.

A *pop* echoed in the hall, and I dropped my feet, my heart jolting inside me. Footsteps drew nearer. Then, a quiet knock sounded at the door.

"Who is it?" I asked, my voice trembling.

"It's me. Vince."

My heart lurched again, but something hot twisted in my stomach. I stood, wiping my hands on my pants and straightening my shirt. My hands lifted to smooth my hair before I cursed under my breath and dropped my arms. *Idiot,* I chided myself.

"Come in," I said.

The door opened, and there was Vince, his hands shoved in the pockets of his hoodie. He looked just like a regular teenager. But his eyes were haunted. I considered everything that had changed for him. The secrets his best friend kept. The reality that his mother was probably alive somewhere in the Underworld.

My heart twisted with sympathy.

"Hi," he said, crossing his arms.

"Hi."

We stood there awkwardly, keeping several feet between us.

"Are you all right?" I finally asked.

Vince huffed a laugh. "I'm hanging on by a thread. But I'm alive."

"And your clan?"

"They're a mess. Most of the officials are gunning for Jocelyn's dad to take over, but he and Hector were working together, so it would just be the same all over again." He shook his head. "But it doesn't matter."

Dread filled my stomach. "Why not?"

He lifted his gaze to meet mine. Despair stirred in his eyes. He wasn't here with good news.

"I'm denying my pledge to the clan," he said softly. "I'm going to become a Reaper."

I stared at him. Though the news should've come as a shock, it didn't. I remembered him during the Demon War, standing in front of me with great dark wings.

I'd known he would make that choice.

But it wasn't until this moment that I realized what that meant.

"You'll go to the Underworld," I whispered.

"Yes."

"And you won't be able to come back."

"No."

A lump formed in my throat, but I forced myself to nod. "Right. That makes sense. Your mom is probably down there." I pressed my lips together and dropped my gaze. I couldn't look at him. "Uh, what about your dad?"

"He's leaving the clan too. Trying to find a job and a place to live."

I finally looked at him. "He can't go with you?"

Regret twisted his expression. "No."

My chest tightened. "I'm sorry." He'd been willing to give up *everything* for his dad.

But things had changed now that he knew about his mother. And I realized what an impossible predicament he was in: give up one parent to be with the other.

The thought dragged my heart down to my feet.

"I know I should be grateful," Vince said, his brows furrowing. "I'll finally get to know my mother, assuming she's still alive."

"She is," I said at once. "She has to be. From what I saw, she's strong."

The hint of a smile quirked his lips up, but it faded

quickly. "It's just—you shouldn't feel sorry for me, Cora. You lost everything once too." His eyes held mine.

Ordinarily, I'd brush it off. I never knew my parents, so what was there to lose? But the tenderness in Vince's gaze stirred something in the depths of my heart that I thought had been tucked away forever. A deep, aching yearning.

I swallowed, struggling to find my voice. "You have every right to be sorrowful about this, Vince. Just because I've suffered losses doesn't make yours any less painful."

Vince shifted his weight from one foot to the other. The space between us seemed to pulse like it was a living thing, wriggling and pulling us farther and farther apart. I longed to draw closer to him, but I couldn't bring myself to make that first step.

So, we stood there, avoiding eye contact and not moving.

At long last, Vince said in a low voice, "Come with me."

My gaze snapped to his. "What?"

He stepped toward me, and I sucked in a breath. "Come with me to the Underworld, Cora."

My mouth felt dry. "I—I can't. You just said your dad—"

"He's a mortal now. But magical beings can exist in the Underworld." His eyes glittered with excitement.

"You'd be safe from everyone chasing you. You could live with me among the Reapers."

Live with me. The idea sent a thrill racing through me. I licked my lips, my head spinning at the thought. "Vince, I—I—"

He took another step closer. "I know I'm asking a lot. And I'll understand if you refuse. But I *love you*, Cora. I want to be with you."

My breathing turned sharp and ragged. I felt like I wasn't getting enough oxygen. "How—how will I get back?" I whispered.

Uncertainty flashed in Vince's eyes, and in that moment, I knew he hadn't thought this through. Did either of us know *anything* about living in the Underworld? What if I disintegrated to ash as soon as I arrived? What if an invisible barrier kept me out?

What if the other Reapers executed me on the spot?

I took a deep breath. "I have responsibilities here, Vince. I can't just abandon my coven."

"You were ready to abandon them after killing Damien."

I flinched. He had a point. "Yes, but . . . they need unity right now. And strength. If I take off, the coven will crumble. I have to clean up Damien's mess."

"Why?" Vince challenged, his eyes blazing.

I held his gaze. "Because this is my home." The words resonated inside me with finality and purpose.

Hinport *was* my home. It had never felt like it until now.

Vince's lips spread into a thin line, and he stared hard at the floor, his jaw rigid.

This time, I took a step toward him. There were only a few inches between us. Slowly, I took his hands in mine, relishing the feel of his calloused palms. I raised his hand and pressed it to my cheek.

"I love you, Vince," I breathed, pressing a soft kiss to his fingertips.

"But not enough to come with me," he said in a broken voice.

I closed my eyes as regret threatened to consume me. "Would you stay? For me?" I opened my eyes to watch his reaction.

Surprise stirred in his eyes, followed by guilt and agony. He shook his head. "I can't pledge myself to the clan. Not if there's a chance they'll follow Hector's plans."

"Then, you understand."

Vince nodded, but the motion was stiff, his jaw still clenched.

I changed the subject. "What will happen to you?"

Vince exhaled, long and slow. "All I know is my wings will turn black and I'll leave this realm. It's all pretty vague, to be honest. And a little terrifying." He uttered a shaky laugh. "I've been researching everything there is to know about the Underworld so I can be prepared." His face sobered. "But since my mother never returned to us, I can assume there's no way back." His gray eyes sparked with an emotion so raw it made my chest ache.

We both drew nearer, closing the gap between us so our chests almost touched. I stared up at him, lifting my hand to sweep the dark hair out of his eyes. "Does that mean this is goodbye?" I asked.

Determination flared in his gaze. "No." He placed his hands on my waist, and heat sparked through me. "I swear to you, I will find a way to come back. I'll find a way to be with you, Cora." He pressed his forehead against mine, and I closed my eyes. "They say Reapers get to keep their magic. I'll still be able to Jump. To time travel. I can find a way back to you."

I smiled at the ferocity in his tone. My hand pressed against his cheek. "I know you will." I drew away to look at him. "Come back to me, Vince. I'll be here. I'll be waiting."

Desire flooded his eyes, making my knees go weak. He leaned in, his nose brushing against mine, and then stopped. "Are you—" he murmured.

I laughed lightly. "No Poisoned Balm. I removed it. See?" I pressed another kiss to his fingers.

Vince's eyes lingered on my lips, making my skin feel hot. I stood on my tiptoes, wrapping my arms around his neck and raising my eyebrows. "Well?"

Half his mouth lifted in a heart-stopping smile. He drew nearer, his lips meeting mine with the softest of kisses. I suppressed a shiver of pleasure and pulled him closer, arching against his body. His mouth searched mine, hungry and curious. His fingers tangled in my hair. My skin was on fire, and my insides scorched.

In all my life, I'd seen romance as a release. A way to momentarily escape. To seek pleasures that made life more bearable so that I could return to being a huntress with a secret.

My relationships were a way for me to hide. To keep myself locked away from others. Because if my partners never knew me, then there was no risk.

But this was different. Vince knew me to my core. The good and the bad. And still he loved me. As I pressed myself against him, longing for more of him, I felt a new kind of release. A sense of belonging. A sense of peace that my wounded mind craved.

This love, this feeling wasn't an escape. It was a haven. A fortress to ground me. Not a pit stop to tide me over until the next one, but a destination.

Our breaths mingled. His mouth was hot against mine. His hands slid up and down my back, and his tongue explored my mouth. Our kisses turned more urgent and frantic. I caught his lower lip between my teeth.

In other circumstances, I might have pushed him

farther. Maybe tried removing his clothes. The office had a door, after all. If I locked it, we wouldn't be disturbed.

But I didn't want this to be like all the other men I'd been with. And it wouldn't make our parting hurt any less.

So, reluctantly, painfully, I withdrew from him, my lips still clinging to the memory of him. His eyes were dark with need, and I almost pulled him back for more. With every ounce of restraint I possessed, I took a step away from him, still breathing heavily.

"Don't forget me, Vince." My voice cracked, betraying me. I closed my eyes, my face feeling hot.

"Never," he whispered. He squeezed my hand once.

And then he was gone.

CHAPTER 36

VINCE

I SAT ON MY PORCH STEPS, TRYING TO PUT OFF SAYING goodbye.

But the magic crackling in the air told me I was out of time. Dad sat next to me. We said nothing, our gazes fixed ahead at some unseen spot. Nephilim poured onto the street, heading toward the meetinghouse where the Ceremonial Rite would take place.

My body itched to join them. My magic was responding to the call.

But this time, things would be different. I wouldn't just be an observer. I would be a participant.

Once a year, every year, the officials in the clan combined their magic in a special ceremony. Everyone who had turned eighteen that year had the opportunity to pledge fealty to the clan.

And those who didn't were banished.

My birthday had come and gone. I didn't feel any different. But I knew the change wasn't necessarily from my birthday—it was from the ceremony.

My Nephilim powers would be stripped soon. Just like Mom's had been.

"Give her my love, will you?" Dad said in a strained voice. His eyes tightened, but other than that, he betrayed no emotion. When I'd told him about Mom, he'd locked himself in his room for two whole days. Occasionally, I heard him sobbing.

"I will."

Silence fell again. I breathed the crisp air, trying to memorize it. Would the air be different in the Underworld? I was certain it would.

I glanced at Dad. His expression was hollow. Broken. I couldn't bear it.

I had to be strong for him.

With a heavy sigh, I rose to my feet and extended a hand to help him up.

My fingers tightened around the lacrosse ball I still held in my hand. Earlier this morning, I'd Jumped back in time two months to the championship lacrosse game— when I'd first seen my Mimic across the parking lot.

That moment had started a sequence of events, all leading me to right here. Right now.

I felt it down to my bones that I needed to appear to

my former self. I had to preserve the timeline. To close that loop.

Bitterness filled my mouth. Now I was starting to sound like Luke.

Gritting my teeth, I set the lacrosse ball on the ground and shoved all thoughts of Luke out of my head. A breeze whispered against the trees, ruffling my hair. Energy crackled around me, swelling with power.

I closed my eyes and breathed deeply. "It's almost time."

Dad drew me into a tight embrace, clutching me as if he could keep me here by force.

A knot formed in my throat. My eyes felt hot. I breathed in the scent of my dad one last time, trying to memorize it too, before pulling away. His eyes glistened with tears, making the knot in my throat tighten. I tried swallowing, but I couldn't. All I could do was choke on my tears.

Dad squeezed my shoulder and offered a wobbly smile, which I returned.

We joined the other Nephilim on the street, following the crowd to the meetinghouse. With each step, the magic pulsing in the air intensified, reverberating off my bones in a powerful rhythm. It blared in my ears, drowning out the sound of footsteps and hushed voices.

It felt so familiar. And yet, so foreign. My magic

churned within me, a violent river of chaos. As if it *sensed* this time was different.

We entered the dining hall where our clan awaited. Almost everyone was already seated among the crowd. At the front of the room was the panel of clan officials, with Hector missing, of course.

It felt odd to carry on after everything he'd done. Like we were committing some grievous crime by not addressing Hector's betrayal and the despicable things he'd done.

My eyes fell on Peter Wilkes, Jocelyn's father. His eyes were cold as they fixed on me. The hatred rippling from him only confirmed my decision.

I couldn't stay here.

Dad looked at me, his eyes moist, and squeezed my shoulder. Then he vanished into the crowd.

Today, he was merely a bystander. A witness to the Ceremonial Rite.

Tomorrow, he would be an outcast. Just another mortal. The thought wrenched through me like the twist of a knife.

I knew where to go. I'd witnessed the Rite many times. But my feet remained frozen in place, refusing to move forward.

"Vince," said a voice behind me.

I turned and found Jocelyn standing there. Her eyes were grim, her lips spread into a thin line. She jerked her head toward the front of the room, where the officials waited.

I felt like a coward, but I was grateful to be able to walk alongside her. Even if we were making different choices today.

Jocelyn's gaze was steady, her jaw rigid with determination. Her arms were crossed as she walked next to me. The room seemed to stretch on and on. Each step pulled me farther and farther away, like I would be walking forever. Never reaching my destination.

Trying to steel my nerves, I glanced at Jocelyn. Her face was stony. Was she angry with me? I wouldn't blame her.

"I'm not pledging," she whispered suddenly.

I almost stopped walking, but my feet were on autopilot, just following her movements. "Why not?"

A solemn grimace tugged at her lips. "I can't be a part of what my dad's been doing." She sighed. "Ever since you told me Reapers aren't really executed, I couldn't go through with it."

I nodded, understanding completely. When I'd returned to the clan, I'd told everyone what had happened: my time travel, Hector's betrayal, and my mom's banishment. Many believed me—including Jocelyn. But most of the clan stood by her father.

Stood by Hector.

Together, Jocelyn and I had done some digging and

found the officials had left a paper trail so it would seem like the Reapers all died. It was easier to cover up the truth that there were dark Nephilim out there somewhere.

Jocelyn's eyes turned wistful and curious. "Don't you want to know more about them?"

I didn't need to ask who she was talking about. I nodded. "It'll be a relief not to do this alone."

Jocelyn smiled, but sorrow lingered in her eyes. I had to remember she'd lost her father. Not in a literal sense. But he wasn't the man she thought he was.

We finally reached the officials, who sat at their long table, spines straight and chins lifted. Power rippled from each one of them as they watched us stand before them.

My breathing turned ragged. I clenched my fingers into fists to keep from shaking.

Peter Wilkes rose to his feet, and my heart lurched in my chest. With Hector gone, Mr. Wilkes was now our clan leader.

The thought made me nauseous.

Mr. Wilkes stretched his arms and said in a booming voice, "Welcome to the Ceremonial Rite. We are here to acknowledge these two individuals as they embrace their true power and cross over to adulthood."

A faint thrumming quivered through my body, tickling my skin. I wiggled my fingers, searching for my familiar warlock magic. It was still there, but it mingled with something else.

Mr. Wilkes gestured to me first, his eyes hardening. "Vince Delgado." He spat my name like a filthy curse. "Do you pledge fealty to the Nephilim clan and embrace the highest order of light magic?"

The words had never seemed as condescending, as judgmental and supremacist, as they did right now.

Resolve hardened within me. I relaxed my hands, no longer shaking, and said in a firm voice, "I do not."

Murmurs echoed behind me. Was anyone really surprised? I had *never* been a true member of this clan. The thought used to fill me with bitterness. But today, it filled me with strength. A reminder that I was making the right choice.

Mr. Wilkes's nostrils flared, his mouth growing thin. "Very well." He turned to Jocelyn. "Do you pledge fealty to the Nephilim clan and embrace the highest order of light magic?" His voice had softened slightly, his eyes warming at the sight of his daughter.

Jocelyn took a deep breath. "I do not."

Gasps and loud protests sounded behind us. Mr. Wilkes stiffened, his face turning white. To her credit, Jocelyn didn't flinch. She didn't even blink. She only met her father's stare with venom and loathing.

"I—uh—Jocelyn," Mr. Wilkes sputtered, his voice cracking. "Are you certain?"

Jocelyn's eyes were fierce, her face unyielding. "It's my choice. And I choose not to pledge."

Stunned silence rang from her words. I held my breath, watching Mr. Wilkes. His lower lip quivered as if he would burst into tears.

He cleared his throat, recovering quickly. "I—I invoke the power of this clan, the highest order of light magic, and strip you both of your Nephilim powers. You are henceforth cast out of this clan and forbidden to return." His voice trembled at the last word.

Suddenly, a stab of pain sliced through me, and I cried out, hunching over. Jocelyn did the same. The agony was so consuming I couldn't hear or see anything.

A burst of blinding white light blazed in my vision. Something sliced through me like my chest was cracking open. A scream tore against my throat.

My Nephilim magic exploded. It broke through me, shooting out of me violently. My body shook and throbbed with the anguish of losing something that had been tethered to me for so long. I felt so raw, so wounded, that I was certain I was nothing but a bloody corpse now.

Slowly, the bright light faded and then vanished, leaving me blinking against a sudden darkness that surrounded me. Pain still pulsed through me, making every breath hurt, but I forced myself to stand upright and take in my surroundings.

All I saw was darkness. As my eyes adjusted, I made out the stony outline of a cavern wall. Water dripped, echoing nearby.

And a figure stood in front of me.

"Joss?" I croaked.

But I knew it wasn't her. The figure drew closer, her magnificent black wings stretched behind her. Her face looked the same as in New York, save for a few more wrinkles and scars. Her blond hair was tied up behind her, and her gray eyes gleamed with pride. "Hello, Vince," she whispered.

I sucked in a shaky breath, blinking tears out of my eyes. How many years had I envisioned this moment? All I could do was stare, taking in every detail from her black shirt and pants to the jagged scar above her eyebrow that hadn't been there before.

At long last, I found my voice, but it still trembled as I said, "Hi, Mom."

Find out what happens when Vince joins the Reapers in Book 2, The Angel's Vow!

ACKNOWLEDGMENTS

Thank you for reading! First and foremost, thank you, dear reader, for being a part of this journey. If it weren't for you, I wouldn't succeed. I am so grateful you chose my book!

A huge thank you to my beta readers: Kari, Melanie, Ben, Melissa, and Jenni. Without you, the story wouldn't be complete. Thank you for taking the time to read and critique and help me make this story the best it can be.

I'm so monumentally grateful for my ARC readers: Beba, Felicity, Joi, Tiffany, Christine, Marlen, Kenzie, Meg, Shivani, Faith, Ifeoluwa, Michelle, Deborah, Kristin, Chelsea, Christina, Erin, Savanna, Andi, Donna, Gilda, Tammy, and Pamela. Thank you for being so enthusiastic and supportive!

And lastly, Alex, Colin, and Ellie. My heart is yours. You are my rock.

ABOUT THE AUTHOR

R.L. Perez is an author, wife, mother, reader, writer, and teacher. She lives in Florida with her husband and two children. On a regular basis, she can usually be found napping, reading, feverishly writing, revising, or watching an abundance of Netflix. More than anything, she loves spending time with her family. Her greatest joys are her two kids, nature, literature, and chocolate.

Subscribe to her newsletter for new releases, promotions, giveaways, and book recommendations! Get a FREE eBook when you sign up at subscribe.rlperez.com.